H
YOUR BREATH

An absolutely gripping crime thriller full of twists

EMMY ELLIS

Detective Carol Wren Mysteries Book 2

JOFFE BOOKS

Revised edition 2023
Joffe Books, London
www.joffebooks.com

First published in Great Britain in 2022

This paperback edition was first published in
Great Britain in 2023

Cover art by Nebojša Zorić

ISBN: 978-1-80405-890-9

PROLOGUE

21 Larch Lane — Scudderton

Dad had spent the last ten minutes filling an old, plastic-lined wooden barrel in the night-black garden with water from the hose. Nine years old, a skinny, underfed Carol Wren watched him from her bedroom window, the moon observing along with her. Dad had sent her upstairs in one of his drunken rages and told her to wait quietly until he came for her.

She hated him and once again wished her mother hadn't left.

Where was she? Why didn't she ever phone or write a letter? Why had she run away? Dad had said she had. Mam running didn't make sense, especially when she'd said Carol was the best thing to have ever happened to her in this sorry-arsed world. Why would you leave the best thing behind?

The water had reached the top and Carol tensed. Dad stomped indoors and she waited, her breath held. His footsteps whacked on the stairs, and she turned from the window to stare out onto the landing. His head appeared through the balusters. It moved up to poke over the rail, then his chest followed. He stood at the top of the stairs and crooked a finger. He didn't have to say a word. She knew not to argue.

She left her room and followed him into the garden.

"It's bath time," he said, "so take your things off and use the stepladder to get in."

She shivered. It was winter and snow covered the grass. And she didn't understand. Was their bath broken? Did it have a hole in it or something?

He left her, and she waited for him to go inside and close the back door. Tears streamed, but she removed her clothes and shoes, indoctrinated as she was, the chill of the snow burning the soles of her feet. If she didn't do as he'd said, he'd hit her, and this must be the punishment he'd mentioned. All she'd done wrong was drop her cup when he'd come back in from the Lion — he'd been earlier than usual, and it had frightened her. Instead of walloping her, he'd gone to fill the barrel.

A bath in there must be better than a punch or a kick, mustn't it?

She climbed the stepladder and dipped a toe in the water. Cold, so very cold, even more so than the snow, and she yelped in alarm. Winter's arms wrapped around her, goosebumps sprouting on her skin, and she bent over to balance her hands either side of the barrel. Then she pushed, tucked her knees up to her chest and plunged in.

The water swaddled her, stealing the breath from her lungs, the freezing temperature seeping through her skin and deep into her bones. She cried out, the sound of an animal. Her feet hit the slippery bottom, and she stood straight, teeth chattering. The shock of it made her head muzzy.

She glanced at the back door. Dad stood watching, the light from the kitchen behind him. He flattened his hand and made a downwards movement then put his finger beneath his chin to indicate where the water should be.

Carol sobbed and lowered herself, the water turning into a rabid creature that bit her all over, chewing her insides.

"I want my mam."

It wasn't the first time she'd said that, and she was sure it wouldn't be the last. She brought her mother to mind, the woman with the pretty blonde hair after she'd had it dyed, the bright-blue eyes, the quiet laugh. It helped a little, to think of her, but the coldness of the water dug deeper, and her whole body trembled with violent shudders.

She must have only been in there for a short while, but it felt like hours. Dad came outside and gripped her hair and the top of one arm, hauling her out and dumping her on a mound of snow.

Everything hurt.

"Next time, you can stay in there until you die," he said and kicked her in the side. "Drowned like the little rat you are."

CHAPTER ONE

Scudderton — 10 p.m.

Mason Ingram loved riding his bicycle. It had belonged to his mother back in the day and had a handy wicker basket on the front to carry all of his tools inside an old-fashioned shopping bag, also hers. Flower-patterned. Cloth. Wooden rings for handles. He sped up, recalling the times when, as a kid, Mam had sent him up the shop for her fags and whatever else was on the note she'd written for the shopkeeper, so he knew it was okay to hand a young boy nicotine and alcohol along with a loaf of bread and a pot of jam. Sometimes, if she'd already been three sheets to the wind and therefore wouldn't notice, he'd opened the vodka and sipped, the burn going all the way down to his belly.

It dulled the pain.

A vicious wind whipped at his flowing hair, salt from the sea clinging to his lips. The weather wasn't too dandy at the moment. The long, hot summer had come and gone, autumn settling in, but there was a storm on the way, although he didn't need a person on the telly to tell him that. He sensed it in the air, could predict wind and rain a mile off, having been a fisherman up until Ortun Bevan had sacked him off.

Bastard.

There hadn't been any need for that, not when Mason was so good at his job. He prided himself on his work ethic. A hard grafter, he'd always given his everything on the boat, desperate for praise, to feel important. Needed. Someone. Ageist, that's what Ortun was, wanting his crew younger and fitter, which was a laugh, seeing as Ortun was seventy-something himself. Well, Mason wasn't young anymore either, but he was fit for his fifties, no doubt about that. No one could say he didn't watch what he ate, nor could they claim he was lazy. He worked out in the cellar, had a treadmill and all sorts. He could give Ortun a run for his money any day.

Being fifty-two didn't mean Mason was past it — it meant he tried harder to look after his body, to live long enough to see his dream come true. But in the two years since he'd been unemployed (no one else he'd asked would take him on), he'd convinced himself Ortun had engineered it so there were no seafaring jobs to be had. This was why Mason had come up with his idea. The thought of people gossiping about him hurt. He could hear it all:

"Don't be taking him on, he's a rum one."

"Why's that, then?"

"Didn't you hear what he did? He'll be after someone in your family next."

"Nah, not Mason. He's not the type."

"I saw it with my own eyes. I'm telling you, he's a baddun."

"Why are you still talking to him, then?"

"Keep your enemies closer, that's why my dad used to say."

That was the issue with some people around here. They took offence at the slightest thing then made you pay for it. Mason hadn't even done anything wrong, not in his eyes anyway. Men did *that* all that time, didn't they? How else were you supposed to let someone know you wanted them? And as for Ortun, who let everyone within earshot know his name meant "from the shore", as if that made him a *proper* fisherman, well, he had some cheek pulling Mason up.

It had just been an excuse to get rid of him.

"Folks in Scudderton have long memories," Mam had once slurred. "They don't let you forget nowt, the little fuckers. Take me, for example. They're always saying I used to be such a nice person and now I'm not, but what do they fucking know? They haven't lived the life I've lived. They're not *me*. None of them would understand how shit happens and changes you."

Mason didn't understand why she'd turned nasty — that was all he'd ever known, couldn't imagine her ever being nice — but he *did* understand shit happening and things changing. Nevertheless, how could a mother do what she'd done to him? How could his absent father have stood by and not done anything to help him? Mason had a long memory, and he wasn't the type to forgive and forget, not with her, and not with Ortun and the others either. All he'd done was feel that woman up in the corner of the pub, and that was that. Ortun had taken exception to it, the hypocritical bastard.

One rule for him, another for everyone else.

Mason had walked off that boat on the morning he'd been "let go" and vowed to have Ortun begging for mercy one day. It took planning, though, that kind of thing, and with Jobseeker's in his pocket plus the suitcase of cash under his bed, money he'd found after Mam's death, he was well away financially. Once she'd been buried, he'd had a good old root around the cottage and read her bank statements. The truth was there in black and white. She'd gone out every day for ages to withdraw the maximum amount allowed from the machine, which at the time meant there was over two hundred thousand he could play with. He'd asked himself: *How come she had so much? Why hadn't I seen any of it in my childhood?* He'd been slung up, not brought up — a ragamuffin, a lad people felt sorry for but gave a wide berth all the same so they didn't have to face what was happening to him.

So why did I hang around when I got older? Why didn't I take the chance and leave when I was sixteen and Ortun offered me that bedsit?

He knew why. Because despite everything, he'd loved Mam, and whether or not her bond to him was slim at best, his to her had been strong. She was his *mother*, for God's sake. That had to count for something.

The afternoon he'd browsed those bank statements had put his world in such a spin he'd become dizzy and needed to take a seat. One person paid her a lot of money each month, and he knew who it was. What he wasn't entirely sure of was why, but he aimed to find out.

He pulled his mind away from that and thought of better things. He missed being out on the sea, no question, but he had a little boat of his own, paid for with some of Mam's stash. It was tucked away in the marina at Scudderton Cove, one among many that bobbed and wobbled on the undulating water. It wasn't fancy, just an old seventeen-foot thing with a Yamaha outboard motor, white hull, red cabin, and it had enough *oomph* to take him far out into the water, past the safety buoys.

When he sailed in the middle of the night to get some peace in his soul, no one seemed to notice. Nor did they take any notice of the trailer he sometimes attached to the back of his bike on a metal contraption, humming along behind him on silent rubber tyres. Times past, he'd used it to cart cod around for Ortun, delivering it to the various pubs and hotels after they'd come ashore from a successful fishing trip.

The memory of happier times brought a lump to his throat and sent anger shooting through his veins.

Another spiteful gust of wind snatched at his long hair, tossing it around and slapping it onto his face.

Should have put it in a ponytail.

He peered between two greasy strands, smiling at the Ferris wheel on the pier, lit up and enticing, but no one would be getting another ride tonight. Old Clem shut it down at ten, and all the other people who manned the fair rides, stalls, shops and the café did the same. Soon, the pier would close for the winter, appearing as a skeleton with no flesh to its bones, no people to give it life, silent save for the creaking struts.

He shook his hair from his face and recalled days spent walking up and down that pier as a child, envying the kids who'd come here for their holidays. Clean kids. Happy kids. They had nice parents or nans and grandads with them, ice lollies, wide-brimmed hats to shield their sun-kissed faces, buckets and spades to use on the beach. They'd had *fun*, whereas he'd merely *survived*. Back then, if he hung around the ice cream van for long enough, Mr Samson handed him a cone, then sent him away saying he was bad for business, untidy and smelly as Mason had been.

Funny how he'd chosen a profession where he was even smellier as an adult. The scent of fish seeped into the skin, the hair, and remained underneath his nails if he didn't use the scrubbing brush on them.

Life had been brilliant during holiday season back then — if he didn't count his life at home in the cottage. He'd spent all day outside once school had shut up for six weeks, Mam locking him out when she left for work of a weekday morning on her bike, her with a worn handbag, him with a bottle of water from the tap — and no food. She'd told him he had to work for his grub like she had to. Mason had found money, fivers or tenners dropped in the packed crowds on the pier, his eager eye catching it falling from their hands to the decking. Skinny as he used to be, he'd dipped between the many bare legs and snatched it up, rushing to June's, the chippy at the end closest to the sea. He'd filled his belly to bursting with cod and chips, sitting on one of the benches and swinging his legs, happy for the amount of time it took to gulp down the meal. Seagulls had come to strut in front of him, waiting for scraps, but he'd never given them any. He'd needed food more than them.

"Those were the days," he muttered and rode past the pier.

He ignored everyone streaming off it in the dark, probably heading back to their caravans on the clifftop, wishing they hadn't come to the coast with the weather so inclement. Mind, a holiday was a holiday no matter whether it stormed, wasn't it? A change was as good as a rest, so the saying went.

Mason was about to create a change.

He continued towards the marina, using the Backstreet rather than the main thoroughfare. It was a cobbled effort, a jolt to his bones, so he swerved onto the wide path instead, his headlight painting a slice of white on the pavement. The Backstreet contained warehouses either side, their rears facing the road, only one set of high windows beneath their up-in-the-sky roofs. Dusty ones at that. He reckoned, when the workers were on their breaks and wanted to see outside, they'd be shit out of luck, and anyway, who'd want to stare into an empty street while munching on a cheese and pickle sandwich?

At the end, the sea came into view, an obsidian expanse that never failed to call out to him. It shouldn't, not with what had happened years ago — he should be afraid of water by rights. But no, it'd been a welcome reprieve from life with his mother. Sometimes, if the crew had gone to Scotland to fish for Atlantic Salmon, he'd be away from home for days and get to stay at a bed and breakfast, where he could fiddle with himself under the blankets without fear of Mam hearing him through the dividing wall.

At the end of the Backstreet, he came to a stop, switched his headlamp off and stared to the right at the marina. That rich prick who called himself Senor De León had arrived, his big yacht hogging space beside a smaller one. Coloured strobes flashed through the windows. He must be having one of his noisy parties. While that was good in one way, the music loud, it wasn't good in another.

Too many people.

Mason hadn't figured that into the equation. Also, Senor De León wasn't meant to be here until next week. Fucking hell. But if Mason hurried, he might not be seen, and by the time he came back this way, everyone would be so pissed up they'd probably ignore him if they were out on the deck. Unlikely in this weather, so that was okay. Otherwise he'd have to alter his plans and come here yet again, after he'd done what was already on the agenda. Wait until the party died down and people left the yacht.

It was going to be fine.

Letting go of the brake handles, he pedalled past the marina and down the alley towards the estate behind the Little Devil pub. The cul-de-sac, Fisherman's Rest, had five bungalows, all belonging to men who earned their money at sea. All of the lights were off. Stood to reason. They had to get up early to go to work, didn't they? But his mate who lived in number one had agreed to keep his bungalow dark for appearance's sake.

Mason switched his mind to his other "friend". Ortun lived in the middle bungalow at the top of the horseshoe, so Mason rode between that and the next and parked his bike and trailer around the back. He'd been here enough times to know the tall wooden gate was never locked, and he got off his bicycle and stretched his aching muscles. Pointed his hands to a sky full of clouds waiting to unleash the rain they held, thunder grumbling, threatening to shout so loud it scared the bejesus out of everyone. Half of the full moon peeped from behind one of them, and he shuddered.

He didn't like the moon.

He cast his gaze to the houses in another street to his left that backed onto the side of Fisherman's Rest, their rear windows mainly in darkness, but those with lights on had their curtains drawn. A quick swivel had him facing Ortun's place, and he moved closer to the fence to peep through a knothole. The bedrooms were at the back. Two of them. A circle of brightness told of a lamp being on in front of the curtains of one, and blue shone through the cheap material — he was watching telly, then.

Some things always remained the same. People had patterns, routines they followed, and Mason was one of them, although he was deviating at the minute. All worthwhile, though. At least he'd have peace of mind when this was over. In the morning, he'd be able to tell his mate it was done. This part anyway.

I wonder if he's excited about doing his side of the deal yet?

He collected a stubby-handled, metal-ended mallet from the shopping bag and weighed it in his hand. It should do the trick. He popped it in the deep pocket of his waterproof mariner's poncho and turned the iron handle on the gate, his leather gloves tightening on his fingers. His heart skipped a couple of beats as he stepped inside the garden and approached the bungalow. He tapped on the back door — uPVC with a rectangle of glass in the top, the kind with patterns in it. Ortun had chosen one that resembled waves. Cliché.

Mason waited.

The light clicked on, a bulb beneath a dusty blue shade, one he'd seen countless times, and he imagined it splashed on the Anaglypta wallpaper that had been painted a nasty shade of brown, illuminating the picture in an ugly yellow frame of Ortun holding up a sixty-pound cod years ago, the sea a backdrop, his smile revealing his missing tooth at the front. He'd tripped arse over tit around a decade past and banged his face on the side of his boat. Never did get it fixed. Reckoned the loss of a tooth gave him character.

Mason thought it gave him the air of being a vagrant, but whatever.

Ortun's slender shape ventured to the door, distorted by the glass waves, his arm extended towards the handle.

Mason could do this. Pretend for a bit more.

The door opened, and a tousle-haired Ortun stood in his Bermuda shorts, belly draping over the waistband, the only overweight part of him. Too much beer in the Little Devil. Hops were the culprit, so Mason had read. They bloated you.

Ortun's eyes bleary, his whiskers as unruly and as grey as the cotton wool mop on his head, he said, "What the hell are you doing here at this time of night? Nowt better to do?"

"Heard about another job for you," Mason whispered to give the effect he didn't want the other fishermen in the cul-de-sac to hear him. They could be in their gardens, listening, having a last ciggie before hitting the sack.

Ortun smiled. "Fuck me, that's good news. Come on in, then."

Mason trailed him down the shit-coloured hallway to the blue-walled living room at the front. It was a state, no other word could describe it. Two stacks of magazines about ocean fishing leaned against the right-hand wall, as drunken as the sailors of old, threatening to lose their sea legs and topple. The peach sofa had only one seat without anything on it, the middle one. Ortun had slung his salt-stained jacket and fish-gut-splashed green wellies on one end, while his rucksack and a transparent lunchbox, nothing but a tumbleweed of clingfilm inside, perched at the other. Of course the lunch had all been eaten; Ortun was a greedy bastard. Bundles of washing covered the two armchairs — could be clean, probably weren't — and the man himself poked a finger in the air towards the sofa.

"Park your arse, then. Tell me what you heard." Ortun threw clothes on the manky orange carpet littered with bits of paper, takeaway packaging and empty cans of Sprite, and sat on the chair closest to the door, a *whoomph* coming out of him and a creak coming out of the chair.

Mason sandwiched himself between the wellies and the backpack. "Skipper Kinnock has found a better reef for catching cod in Whitby. He's off there come six in the morning. He even caught a fucking ling there yesterday." He shuddered again. Ling reminded him of meaty eels.

"So that's why he came back so happy. Where's the reef?"

"He's making a killing. Sold a lot of it to June at the chippy, so he's poaching your bloody customers. And the reef's past the west pier. Got himself double the load, so he said. One cod was about sixty-five pounds in weight, so he's stripped you of your record."

"What a bastard! Cheers for letting me know. I appreciate it, I really do. I'll follow the bugger out there. Nowt he can do to stop me."

Mason smiled. He'd been pretending to like Ortun and had given him tips since he'd been sacked so the man still trusted him, wouldn't cotton on to what he was about to do. He always visited in person too, so this wasn't seen as suspicious at all, plus there were no records of him using the phone. "I could do with a cuppa before I head back. Want me to make you one?"

"Yeah, a hot chocolate would be nice." Ortun snatched up his pipe from the side table, the dusty surface packed with empty mugs. One had furry mould and a circular noodle stuck to the inside. Probably a Cup-a-Soup.

Mason swallowed bile and walked down the hallway to the kitchen. He sighed. What a fucking mess, just like his childhood home. Forensics were going to have a field day in this place. He pushed aside a load of things to make space in front of the kettle — half a loaf of bread, the top unsealed; an open can of beans, the juice dried on the rim; a packet of paracetamol, four tablets missing — then clicked it on. He found clean mugs (or as clean as Ortun could get them) on the draining board beneath the large saucepan Ortun cooked fish stew in. Mason rooted out the hot chocolate that balanced on top of a tub of beef Super Noodles in a larder stacked with nothing but convenience food.

Drink made for Ortun, nothing for himself, he held the cup in one hand and the mallet in the other, hiding the weapon down by his thigh in the folds of his poncho. He stopped in the hallway. Ortun was in his bedroom, thumbing a message on his phone. Who was he talking to?

Probably telling the crew about the earlier start.

Mason waited for Ortun to nip past him and sit in his chair. In the living room doorway, he stared at the back of Ortun's head.

And poured the steaming drink over it.

Ortun screamed and planted his hands on the burning skin. That was an inconvenience; Mason couldn't get a clear shot with the mallet now. Broken fingers weren't the order of the night. Ortun shot up, dancing around, blinking the hot chocolate from his eyelashes, rivulets of brown creeping down his face.

He looks as shitty as his hallway.

Mason held back laughter.

Ortun glared. "What the fuck, Mase?"

His red cheeks and slack mouth annoyed Mason, as did the shortening of his name, but he adopted a pained expression tinged with sympathy. "Jesus, I tripped. I'm so fucking sorry . . . Quick, get in the bathroom and put some cold water on your head."

He moved out of the way, and Ortun stumbled past, whimpering then grouching about Mason being a clumsy wanker and, "I'd better not get a ruddy great blister." Mason dropped the empty cup on the chair and followed him into the bathroom, waiting by the scummy basin that had more than a week's worth of whiskers in a circular line where Ortun had shaved with a sink full of water. Ortun grabbed the shower off the holder and got down on his knees, bent over the bath and sprayed cold water on his burgundy-coloured scalp.

Mason whacked the back of his former boss's head with the mallet. Ortun slumped, the showerhead clonking on the base of the bath, the water spurting upwards. The hose writhed, a metal snake, and the stream hit Ortun's temple.

Mason leaned over and turned the cold tap off. Admired the blood oozing from a gash in Ortun's skull.

He prodded the man in the back. "Are you okay, pal?"

No response.

Mason chuckled and slapped a crusty blue hand towel on the wound then took a carrier bag out of one pocket, placing the mallet in the other. He fitted the bag over Ortun's head, ensuring the hole he'd made in it was at the front so the unconscious drip could breathe. A quick tie of the handles at the nape of the neck and the towel was secure, soaking up the blood. Good. He wouldn't get his trailer dirty now. All he needed to do next was check Ortun's phone to make sure he hadn't mentioned Mason's name in a message (the twat didn't use a passcode), wait so there was less chance of someone seeing him, hope his victim remained sparko, then drag him out to the bike trailer. He'd load him up, hide him under the tarpaulin cover.

Everything had gone to plan.

* * *

Scudderton Cove was a creepy place when no one else was around. Mason reckoned he could hear the warbling of ghosts, people who'd once ridden the Ferris wheel, their shrieks and laughter carried on the wind. Except it was *just* the wind, nothing else.

He was imagining shit again.

No lights were on at the fair or the little souvenir shops, so everyone had gone home now, and it was only him and Ortun at the end of the pier behind June's Chippy.

The water was high here. If there wasn't a wooden rail and Mason sat on the boards, his feet would almost touch the surface. With Ortun still out cold in the trailer, Mason took the mallet out of his pocket and hit a baluster. It didn't take long, and a few more strikes later, the piece of wood gave way and fell into the sea. He removed four more, enough space to do what he wanted, then popped the mallet in the shopping bag in the bike basket and withdrew two lengths of rope from the trailer. He placed them on the decking, smiling to himself at how Ortun would feel once he realised what was going on.

A groan matched that of the wind, and Mason turned to look at the trailer. Ortun had pushed the tarpaulin down to his legs and sat up. He rubbed the back of his head, his expression one of *ow*. He wasn't supposed to have roused yet. Mason was meant to have done the next phase first.

I might have to hit him again.

"Ah, you're awake." Mason strutted over there. "You slipped in the bathroom and whacked your head. Scared me to death, it did." The lie wasn't difficult to tell. He'd practised it enough while riding here, over and over until he had it down pat.

"What the fuck are we doing *here*?" Ortun glanced down at the trailer. "Did you bloody well cart me in this?"

"Obviously. Come on, let's get you out."

"What are we here for, and why have I got a fucking *bag* on my head?"

"I thought the fresh air might help wake you up, and the bag was to stem the blood. I put a towel on the cut and needed something to keep it in place. You ask some weird questions."

"Weird? You could have just taken me into my back garden for air. Christ, my head hurts."

Mason took the bag off and kept the towel inside. As a present to the police, he dropped it into one of the wheelie bins that stank of fish and cooking oil. Back at the trailer, he helped him out and guided him towards the gap he'd made.

Ortun wobbled.

"Blimey, steady there, pal. Have a sit down," Mason urged.

Ortun sank to the decking, his eyes rolling.

"Lie down, for God's sake," Mason said. "You've got a concussion."

Ortun did as suggested. Closed his eyes. Appeared to drift back off to sleep. Fate on his side, Mason took the chance to tie one end of each piece of rope around his ex-boss's ankles and the other ends to the two balusters either side of the gap. There was enough length for Ortun to stand without noticing he'd been secured to the struts, no tautness to give the game away, and besides, the state he was in, he probably wouldn't notice anyway.

Mason tapped Ortun's cheek. "Oi, wake up."

Ortun opened his eyes. Blinked several times. Stared at the half-hiding moon. "Got a headache."

"I expect you have."

"I fell over, you say?"

"Yeah. After I tripped and burned your head with that drink."

"That's right . . ."

"Look, up you get. I've changed my mind. It's probably best to be on your feet." Mason helped Ortun to stand and guided him towards the handrail stretching above the gap. Shame he hadn't walloped it so it broke and created a bigger space. He'd have to make do with what he had.

"I feel sick," Ortun groused.

"Bugger. Get on your knees and put your head down."

"But you said to stand."

"I know. Just do as you're told." Anger whispered a promise that it'd blow if Mason didn't watch himself.

Ortun obeyed. "That's better. I don't feel like I want to throw up now."

Mason crouched behind him. "You know you sacked me . . ."

"Jesus, do we have to talk about that *now*?"

"Yes. Well, I took a bit of an exception to it. I hate you for taking the sea away from me." That was true, he did hate him, but Mason still had the sea, his little boat taking him out there. He loved the *Jar*. He'd named it after what his mother used to call him during her particularly nasty times. He squeezed his eyes shut to prevent himself from thinking about that. "Oh yes, you stopped me earning a wage. I'm on Jobseeker's, did you know that?"

Ortun groaned. "Pack it in, this isn't the time or the place."

"It's the *perfect* time and place."

Mason gave Ortun a shove, and the man shot forward, his top half sailing through the gap, his stomach landing hard on the edge of the decking. Mason grabbed Ortun's ankles and stood, planting his feet firmly as the weight of the body slid forward and down. A small splash, his hands hitting the water.

Ortun shouted, "What the fuck?"

Time to beg for mercy, pal.

"Say sorry," Mason shouted.

"Get me the fuck up!" Ortun raged back.

"Say. Sorry."

"Jesus Christ, what is *wrong* with you? I'm sorry, okay?"

"Doesn't sound like it."

"Please, just get me up. Please."

Mason smiled and let the ankles go. Smiled again at the point a louder splash signalled Ortun's whole body smacking through the surface. Mason knelt, tugged on the ropes so the soles of Ortun's feet appeared above the water. He strained with the effort of gripping as Ortun kicked, trying to swim. The rest of him appeared, floating face down, his arms powering to keep him afloat, so Mason sat and braced his boots against two struts, hanging on tight while Ortun attempted to breaststroke forward.

The bastard sank again, bobbing back up, then back down he went.

Mason laughed.

"Hold your breath."

CHAPTER TWO

Undisclosed Location

Butterfly could laugh and joke with the best of them, pushing their past transgressions aside for a time, but tonight wasn't one of the nights they felt they could do that. Something was in the air, it always was when the so-called Senor De León returned to town. That man brought on the jitters. He tended to look at Butterfly funny, as though he *knew*, and that made for unsettling times until he sailed off again in his cost-a-fortune yacht. If he *did* know, Butterfly almost wished he'd just come out and say it, get it over and done with, but that was the guilt talking. Senor De León didn't even know anything about that time when . . . well, the less thought about that the better. And anyway, hadn't De León managed well enough, crafting his new self and sticking to it? It didn't seem like he had any remorse, so why should Butterfly?

Because De León hasn't got a conscience and I have.

The past was murky but should stay where it was, far away where it couldn't hurt anyone. It had hurt *her*, though, ruined her, and if she were here today, God, Butterfly reckoned it would be about time to say sorry. But that meant exposure, admittance, and there was no need for that.

Thank God she was dead.

People milled around in what amounted to a ballroom but on a smaller scale. Fairy lights flashed annoyingly, strung up at the tops of every wall, and music blared from hidden speakers. Drinks flowed, food all but weighed down a table and De León scowled, seemingly annoyed at the company he was keeping. If he wasn't in the mood for a party, why the hell had he invited the usual crowd?

Butterfly looked around at everyone. Familiar people, some of them seen on a daily basis, folks who'd be shocked at what Butterfly kept stashed inside them. Disgusted. Noses turned up, eyes narrowing.

Why am I here? Why did I think it was a good idea to come?

Because Butterfly always attended these yacht parties. Maybe it was some perverse game, daring the secret to come out and spoil everything. Whatever it was, there was free food, free drink, and that wasn't to be sniffed at. Butterfly had tried so many different foods at De León's show-off bashes. He got a caterer in, and Butterfly had eaten all sorts of stuff with fancy names, but give them a good old-fashioned dinner from June's Chippy any day over this posh grub.

Butterfly sighed. It was time to go. De León brought back bad memories, and there were only so many reminders of those one could take.

CHAPTER THREE

Robottom Street — Mollengate

Ready for work in her usual trousers and blouse, a suit jacket on because it had turned decidedly nippy, Carol Wren observed a neighbour from one of the other flats downstairs. He hadn't lived here long, but she'd seen him around the village, especially in the Lord, giving his elbow some exercise. He drank lager and preferred peanuts over crisps, a scowl over laughter, and had the faint whiff of fish about him that time she'd squeezed past to use the loo.

He stood in the communal back garden, face to a sky which nursed bruises from the storm last night. He gripped his hair and appeared to be having a crisis. Was it personal, or did he need help? The copper in her prodded, telling her to see if he was okay, but the human side whispered to leave it be, she had enough on her plate without adding more.

The copper won.

She opened the balcony doors in her living room and stepped out, leaning on the railing. "Are you all right?"

He spun to stare up at her, lowering his hands. His dark hair was squashed on one side, and he had Marvel pyjamas on and a navy-blue dressing gown. His face, crumpled from sleep, scrunched farther into a scowl that said *back off.* "Do I look all right? Do I?"

Carol encountered many different people in her line of work, but this type, they got right on her nellies. "Well, no, that's why I asked. I tend to do that when someone's about to make themselves bald."

"What are you *on* about?"

"Ripping your hair out?"

"Argh!" He slapped his forehead several times. "Right, if you must know, some bastard broke into my flat during the night. While I was *asleep*. They nicked the work laptop. Christ, I'm in so much shit it isn't funny."

A break-in? Her guts churned. "So just to confirm, you were at home when it happened."

He gestured to his outfit. "Does it look like I wasn't? I don't generally gad about in my pyjamas, thanks."

"Did they take owt else?"

"I just *said* what they took, cloth ears."

She ignored his belligerent attitude, put it down to stress, although her cynical side whispered he was likely a prick all the time, going by how he'd butted into a conversation in the Lord last weekend, offering what he probably thought was sage advice but was, in her opinion, a load of bollocks.

"Have you phoned the police?"

Her neighbour let out a scathing laugh. "Fat lot of good *they're* going to do."

Used to people dissing the ones who tried their best to keep everyone safe, she said, "At the very least, you'll need a crime number for your insurance."

"What?"

"I said—"

"I *heard* what you said. Oh, just fuck off and mind your own business, you do-gooder."

She gawped at him. How sad to be like that, taking everything out on others. She'd been on the end of that sharp stick with her father, the drunken wanker, and she wasn't about to go through it again with this rude fuck. "Shame you've got that mindset, I could have helped you." She took a step back to leave him to it.

"How the hell can *you* help? Some middle-aged woman poking her nose in, that's all you are."

"I might be middle-aged, but I *am* the police, but not to worry, you want to go it alone, so have a nice day, won't you." She returned inside, locked the doors and, despite his offensiveness and the uncharitable thought of letting him cope with this by himself, phoned the station.

Joy Parsonage, the daytime desk sergeant, answered with a cheery, "Good morning, Scudderton police station, how may I help you?"

"It's Carol. Can you send uniform to my place, please? Well, not mine, the one next door to Dave. Robottom Street." She gave her the flat number. "A fella here's had a burglary while he slept. I tried to help, but he's not interested. I'm too middle-aged, apparently."

"Cheeky bugger. I was just about to phone you, actually. It's a good job you asked for assistance, because you can't deal with your neighbour right now. Something more important has come up, namely murder."

Carol's heart sank. It had been quiet on that front since the summer. "Shit. Where?"

"The end of Cove Pier."

"Okay, I'll get Dave up and we'll go straight there."

"Rib is en route, as is Todd."

Carol relaxed a bit. If the pathologist and lead SOCO were already on their way, she didn't have to worry about racing from her little village into Scudderton to give out the initial actions. "I take it uniform are down there already?"

"Yes, June called it in."

"The chippy lady?"

"That's the one. She discovered the body."

"Right. I'll be about half an hour. If you can get someone out to my neighbour, then—"

"Mulholland and Grebe have just walked in. I'll send them. What's the neighbour's name?"

"No idea. Hang on."

She walked back to the doors, unlocked them and peered over the balcony. The bloke sat on a bench smoking a cigarette, bobbing one leg up and down. A burglary was more than unsettling, it was a violation of privacy, and victims rarely felt safe in their home again. But this seemed more than that, as though he worried about something other than the break-in. His work laptop, most likely. It'd have things on there the public shouldn't be privy to, she'd bet, hence him saying he was in so much shit.

"What do you want *now*, woman?" he ground out, not bothering to look up at her.

"Listen, whatever beef you have with women, and it's clear you have one, don't take it out on me. I don't deserve this sort of crap. What's your name?"

"George Lamb."

"Right, George Lamb, stay home, because my colleagues will be arriving soon. They're young, so your aversion to middle-aged people won't be a problem, will it?"

"Whatever." He waved his hand to dismiss her.

There was no helping some people.

Carol retreated and locked the doors again. "Did you get that? George Lamb," she said to Joy.

"Okay, they'll be there shortly."

"Thanks. Get them to ask him if there's any reason someone would choose his place to rob. I think he's hiding something. Gut feeling, nowt more. Bye for now."

Carol slid her phone in her pocket, grabbed her keys and coat, and left her flat. She knocked on her work partner's door, half an hour earlier than their usual leaving time, smiling at the reception she'd get as Dave was likely still sleeping. He opened the door in his suit, surprising the hell out of her.

"Fuck me, did you shit the bed or something?" she asked.

"No, I got woken up by the prat who lives next door. Shouting and all sorts, he was. Thought I may as well get up."

"He's been burgled."

Dave frowned. "When?"

"Last night."

"I didn't hear owt."

"Me neither. The storm must have muffled any noises. Uniform are on the way. He didn't want my help and probably doesn't want theirs either, but that's not our concern. We have a murder scene to attend."

Dave sagged against the doorframe. "Shite."

"I know. We're such lucky ducks."

* * *

Cove Pier

In protective gear, Carol stood at the end of the pier, the scene thankfully hidden from the shoreline by June's Chippy, which wouldn't be opening for business today. Neither would any of the other attractions. Also thankfully, last night's storm had moved down the coast, so they didn't have to stand there getting soaked and competing with thunder so their voices could be heard.

PCs Kenner and Lloyd manned the other end of the pier with Sergeant Richard Prince, a cordon in place, Richard turning away workers who'd come to open up for the day, explaining why they couldn't and asking them where they'd been last night. They'd also had a quick word with the café owner, who hadn't seen anything odd this morning and had grumbled at them for being told to close and go home.

Another thing Carol was grateful for was that it wasn't summer. That would have been a nightmare. Too many people arguing the toss about not being able to venture onto the pier for work, fun and games, food and drinks, and to see if they could spot the dolphins farther out at sea, wanting to take pictures of them, *oohing* and *ahhing*. "Would you look at that, Harold, there's six of them. Our Beryl will be so jealous."

They'd be denied that today, perhaps tomorrow, too.

Such is life.

She cared more for the dead man and any family that would be wrecked by his passing. They were who mattered, not stroppy tourists.

She stared at where the dolphins usually surfaced to give observers a show. The storm had probably kept them beneath the water for now. She'd lived in this area all of her life and planned to finally give in and use the money her father had left her. She hadn't touched it, prepared to live on her wages, forever stuck in her flat, but something had clicked inside her recently. He *owed* her that money. He owed her a chance to live a better life than the one he'd given her. Pride had to take a back seat. It was silly to be so stubborn and leave the cash in the bank account she'd put it in so she wasn't tempted to dip into it. She'd maybe invest in a static caravan. She could let it out all year round and move out of her flat into one of the nice cottages in her village. Mind you, some new ones were being built on scrubland next year, so that was an option. Maybe she could persuade Dave to move in with her. They were with each other a lot anyway, not only for work but in their spare time, since his wife had cheated on him and told him to leave the family home.

A photographer clicked away, wrenching Carol out of her head, and Todd Butcher helped his three SOCO colleagues on the decking, each kneeling on evidence steps looking for clues. Another three came from around the side of the chippy carrying the makings of a tent.

Rib had already explained June had found the body in the water when she'd gone over to examine the broken railings. Photos had been taken of the floater, then the corpse had been hauled out — Rib had gathered by the state of the body that it hadn't been in the water for long, possibly going in last night.

The dead man was on plastic sheeting on the decking. Rope attached his knobbly ankles to some struts in the wooden railings, and while Joy had mentioned murder, it might not be the case. The old bloke could have tied himself up. Some of the balusters had been taken out, roughly by the looks of it, but where was the tool used to do that? It could be at the bottom of the sea, she supposed, or the struts had been missing previous to this. If he'd decided to end his life, he must have come back here at some other time to know there was a convenient, body-wide gap. But if that was the case, why would June have gone over to investigate the damage?

Carol's intuition screamed. Yes, this was murder.

Rib Shears, a nickname the pathologist preferred to go by other than his given one, crouched on an evidence step beside the body. He found it amusing to share a name with one of the tools of his trade. Carol hadn't got on with him until the last murder case, where he'd stopped winding her up as much, although he still called her Bird on account of her surname. It didn't bother her now they'd come to a truce of sorts, and since she'd got to know him better, she rather liked him. In the summer, if someone had told her she'd feel that way now, she'd have laughed them out of town.

"Definitely murder," Rib said, his shaved head covered by a hood, his droning voice a tad muffled from his mask.

"How so?" Dave asked beside Carol.

"Before you arrived, I turned him over. He's got a gash on the back of his head. Blunt force trauma. A wide-ended hammer of some kind."

That brought back memories of Sue Cuttersby, killed in her back garden, the claw end of a hammer doing the damage.

"Same kind as the summer murder?"

"No, more of a mallet. Do you want to see the corner shape in his skull?"

Dave groaned. "Do you have to say that sort of thing? I mean, we don't enjoy seeing that shit, unlike you. I'm sure I told you this before when we were in Sue's garden."

Rib chuckled. "You did. And I don't enjoy it in *that* sense — it fascinates me, that's all. The dead speak, you know. What's left on their bodies tells me a story. I'm sure *I've* told *you* that before, too." He paused. "So I'll take that as a no, then, shall I? Do you feel the same, Bird?"

She nodded. "I'll accept your word for it that there's a mark on his head, thanks. So if he was struck, that also means someone tied him to the rails and threw him in?"

"Or," Dave said, "he was walloped, left for dead, then he woke and fell in? The killer could have tied him to make sure he went over if he was drunk or whatever."

Carol shook her head. "Doesn't work for me — there's still a handrail over the gap. And this fella here could have untied the knots, pissed as a fart or not." She took a picture of them, planning to find out if they were a specific kind of knot made by a specific type of person. With so many fishermen around here, it would narrow down the suspects. "Saying that, they look pretty tight, so maybe he wouldn't have been able to free himself."

Rib glanced her way. "That's a lariat loop knot, and whoever did this to him had quite a grip."

Carol frowned. "What do you mean?"

Rib pointed to the man's ankles; the deceased only had a pair of gaudy Bermuda shorts on. "Bruises, look. Finger marks, thumbs. Someone held him tight. Made sure he stayed under the water?"

"Or they dragged him down the pier," Carol suggested. "Parked up at the other end, got him out of a vehicle."

"There's insufficient wounding to suggest that happened while he was alive," Rib said. "No scrapes, no bruising from being jolted along the slats."

"That's sick, holding him under." Dave shook his head. "Who the fuck *does* that?"

"Err, the killer?" Rib said.

"Very funny." Dave tutted. "It was a rhetorical question."

"I know." Rib's eyes crinkled where he was presumably grinning beneath his mask. "I was being a prick."

"Nowt unusual there," Carol muttered loudly enough for Rib to hear.

Rib stood. "And there was me thinking we were friends now."

"Sod off, I was giving you as good as you give everyone." She turned to check behind her. "No CCTV, then." She swivelled to face Rib again.

He took a wide pace backwards onto another step so the team could erect the tent, lowering his mask then scratching his nose with the back of his wrist. "Todd's checked, haven't you?" he called over.

Todd came to stand on the other side of Carol. "There's no CCTV on the whole of the ruddy pier."

"Fuck it," Dave mumbled.

Carol sighed. "I bet the killer knew that."

"Regardless," Todd said, "there *should* be cameras on here because of the amount of traffic. Look at all the pick-pocket calls we get in the summer. CCTV would solve that, or if it didn't stop them stealing, we'd at least have their faces on video so we could charge them."

"I doubt the council will stump up for it." Rib moved back another step. "And the shop owners and the fairground people won't want to splash the cash. Seasonal place, this is. They need to keep all their summer earnings to get them through the winter."

Normally, Carol would grumble to herself that he was stating the obvious, and his pointless information would have got right on her nerves, but these days it didn't. Rib was a complex character who went through life trying to get a rise out of people. She'd seen him in the Lord last month, and he'd explained a little. If he got a reaction out of people, even if it was negative, it meant they were alive, vital, breathing, whereas in the morgue, he dealt only with the dead, folks who couldn't react to his taunting.

Whatever gets him through the day . . .

"So they don't earn much, then?" she asked.

As a kid, she'd watched, fascinated, at how much money changed hands each time someone went on a ride or picked out stuff to take home to relatives. Sticks of rock, knick-knacks, miniature buildings of the pier, the cliffs, dolphins in snow globes, things like that. She'd always thought the pier workers made a killing.

"No, my mate runs the waltzers," Rib said. "Skint by December. Then again, he does like his beer, so maybe that's why he's boracic come Christmas."

"Right, so we have a reason for there being no CCTV," she said, "but us standing here nattering about that isn't getting things done. Got owt for me yet, Todd?"

He focused on the horizon. "Because of the storm, whatever might have been here has been washed away — no cigarette butts, no *red* blood. However . . ."

Carol rubbed her gloved hands. "I like the sound of *however*."

Todd laughed. "There *is* blood, I'm sure of it, but it's a dark-brown patch soaked into the decking, leaving more of a blot the size of a tea plate. Could have come from the back of the head. So either he was alive when he was laid out, blood still pumping, or if he was dead, the blood on the wound and in the hair was enough to dirty the wood. The rain got rid of the rest. We'll take swabs and see what's what — it could, of course, be fish blood. A fox or whatever getting into the bins."

Rib added, "Shame we can't tell if it's an old stain or not yet. The wood's damp so it's difficult to tell. I noticed that there isn't any smaller spotting either, which would have indicated he'd been hit here. Castoff and whatnot."

"Hmm. So there's a second crime scene," Todd said. "Or would that be the first and this one's the second? On another note, we've found a carrier bag in the wheelie bin, the handles tied, and there's a hole in it. Inside, a hand towel covered in blood. It's already been sent down to the lab."

Carol pondered that. Why were the handles tied if there was a hole in the bag? It wasn't like tying it would stop someone from seeing the contents. "Hopefully, it'll have the victim's blood on it. Do we have an ID?" She held her hand up when Rib opened his mouth. "I know, he's only got shorts on, but what I mean is, does anyone recognise him?"

Todd rolled his shoulders. "June confirmed what I thought. It's Ortun Bevan. Fisherman. She gets all of her cod off him. Or she did until Skipper Kinnock offered her a better deal on bigger fish yesterday."

Carol's mind ticked over. Was this a spat to do with the sale of fish? *For fuck's sake!* Had this Kinnock fella killed Ortun to cut out the competition? "Interesting. Give me two secs."

She walked closer to the chippy and took her phone out. Now she had a name, the two other members of her team could get cracking at the station. DCs Michael King and Katherine Anderson would be wondering where Carol and Dave were if Joy hadn't informed them when they'd arrived at work.

She dialled Michael.

"Morning, boss," he said.

"Morning to you, too. Have you heard?"

"Yep. Not a great start to the week. What needs doing?"

"We've got a name — Ortun Bevan."

"Bloody hell, he's a mate of my grandad. Well, they have a drink sometimes in the Little Devil. They're not mate-mates, if you know what I mean."

"Yep. I need a next of kin."

"That'll be Hattie Lamb, although she's an ex-wife now, reverted back to her maiden name, so maybe not his NOK."

A memory prodded Carol. "Has she got a son of around thirty, by any chance?"

"Yep, George, but he isn't Ortun's."

"Bloody hell . . ." she said, more through relief. This meant the break-in that morning wasn't anything to do with her. No one had come to get her and had chosen the wrong flat. But did the burglary have anything to do with Ortun Bevan's death? "You'll need to dig deeper, see if Ortun has any parents, siblings or children still alive. Failing that, Hattie'll have to do. Ask Katherine to get hold of uniform for information. George had a break-in during the night — don't know if you're aware, but he lives in the same flats as me and Dave. We didn't hear owt, and neither did George — I spoke to him this morning. Rude little twat, but he mentioned being in the shit because the work laptop was stolen. Do you know where he works?"

"No, but I'll add it to the list. I'll also put in a request for Ortun's phone records."

"Thanks." She returned to the others, slipping her phone away, and related what she'd found out.

"Sounds like things are coming together," Todd said.

Rib folded his arms. "George Lamb drinks in the Lord. Surprised you haven't seen him, Bird."

"Are you saying I'm a lush?" She raised her eyebrows.

"No, I'm saying you and Dave live in there out of work hours."

"Not all the time. We have our dinner at home on the odd occasion."

Laughter from them all brought some much-needed relief.

"And I *have* seen him in the pub," she went on. "So up yours."

"Charming." Rib rolled his eyes.

Carol sobered, her mind sifting through the family connection — Ortun, George the stepson. The common denominator, Hattie. Had *she* done this? "While Michael and Katherine are doing checks and trying to locate a NOK, we'll have a chat with June, then find this Skipper bloke."

"According to June, he'll be back at the marina around now," Todd said. "Boat's called the *Poisson Mort.* Translates roughly to 'Fish Death'."

"Weirdo," Dave said.

Todd shrugged. "Takes all sorts, and it makes sense. He does kill fish."

"Let's hope that's all he kills," Rib said.

Todd laughed. "If he's our man, case closed quickly. I can't see any of us objecting to that. Anyroad, June reckons he went out to a reef at Whitby at six this morning. Said he'd drop her fish off about twelve."

"He won't be doing that now, obviously, but that works for me — it'll give us time to see the NOK if Michael finds one." She pulled her mask down and smiled at Dave. "Come on. You never know, we could get lucky and June might make us a brew to warm us up. It's bloody nippy out here."

Rib perked up. "Ask her if she'll make us lot one as well, then."

"I might do." She winked and walked away, Dave following.

At the front corner of the chippy, they took off their protectives and placed them in a bag to be checked for trace evidence. Carol knocked on the door, and PC Alan Pitson, her favourite uniform, glanced away from June where they were sitting at one of the restaurant tables. He got up to let them in.

"Here we go," she said to Dave. "Tea and sympathy coming up."

CHAPTER FOUR

Kettlestone Rise

Mason sat with his mate, Steady, in the cottage Mam had left him when she'd died. That had surprised him. He'd expected her to bequeath it to someone else out of spite. For some reason, Mason had grown up thinking it was a council cottage, but no, she'd bought it many years ago, outright. Another thing he'd been unaware of when he'd made a prick of himself at the council office, asking if he could take it over as a legacy tenant. Until he'd discovered how she'd paid for it, he hadn't a clue how she'd managed it, but the money going into the bank had solved that riddle. Prior to that discovery, as far as he was aware, she'd been a cleaner at night and a cashier in Woolworth's during the day on the music counter until it had closed down, then she'd gone to Superdrug. He also didn't know how she managed to convince everyone she wasn't a pisshead. Then again, they said a functioning alcoholic could pull the wool over anyone's eyes.

Most days she'd drunk enough to "get her through", which he supposed meant the same as people who guzzled coffee like it was going out of fashion. She'd needed sips every hour or so, easily passed off as her leaving the till to go to the toilet. A weak bladder. During her evening job, no one else had been around apart from other cleaners, and seeing as they'd scrubbed loos, well, it was easy enough for his mother to nip into a cubicle, lock the door, and swig from the silver hip flask she'd always kept in her pocket. On Saturdays and Sundays and late nights in the week, she'd drunk more and showed signs of being blotto. Mason had hated those times the most. She'd become evil.

Steady eyed him funny. "You okay, pal?"

Mason laughed off the scrutiny. "Yeah. Was just thinking, that's all. So tell me what you did from start to finish."

He was excited Steady had done his part — or at least he *said* he had.

He could be lying.

Mason was an expert in spotting liars, he'd lived with one until Mam had snuffed it, then realised she'd been an even bigger liar than he'd thought with the cottage and everything, so he was content Steady was telling the truth. He'd yet to produce the goods, though, which was a bit concerning. What if he didn't have it? Mason's plan for ultimate revenge on Ortun would go right down the swanny. Killing was one thing, but that wasn't his main goal. He wanted to show them all he could handle a crew by himself, like he'd done whenever Ortun had been off sick.

I wonder if anyone's found him yet.

Steady smiled and leaned back, cradling his cuppa. "It went like clockwork, pal. Fucking clockwork."

* * *

Robottom Street

With Mason and Ortun long gone from Fisherman's Rest, Steady drove from Scudderton to Mollengate at the height of the storm, the wind bullying his little dark-blue van, sending it veering to the side with every mean gust. He had to grip the steering wheel tight to retain command of the vehicle, struggling against the incessant pushing. It was as though

God knew what he was doing and had sent the storm to prevent it from going ahead, the rain pouring onto the windscreen so his wipers had one hell of a job to keep them clear. Mind you, he didn't believe in God, so that was a stupid thought. He'd considered staying home, doing this another night, but Mason had insisted it had to be now. He needed something stolen, and as Steady was a bit of a criminal on the side, breaking and entering was his forte.

That and catching fish.

Steady parked around the back of the cottages down the way from the Co-op and the Lord, behind that a vacant space of scrubland that was due to have new cottages built on it sometime soon. Snooty Señor De León was a developer and travelled to places he planned to build on, getting there in his fancy yacht. What a pleb. Normal people used a car. He lived in a big house on the cliff when he wasn't gallivanting about, and it was rumoured he'd built a place for a famous footballer, although Steady would believe it when he saw it.

He crept down the road in his all-black gear, getting soaked despite having his hood up, his face covered by a balaclava, water seeping through the wool. He was eager to play his part in Mason's game. It was exhilarating to break the law. It got his blood pumping. He felt alive, truly alive, instead of eking out a sedentary life.

He'd gone along with Mason because he understood his friend's pain. Not only had Ortun sacked Mason, but he'd sacked Steady too, who'd been just shy of fifty at the time. Being let go by Ortun had knocked him sideways, destroying his plans for retirement. Mason was different, he had his mam's money so he wouldn't go short, and he could sell the cottage if he ran into bad times. Steady didn't have that luxury. A divorce and a mad ex-wife in the rear-view mirror, he was on his own. No family, no one to give a shit if he struggled to make ends meet.

What he hadn't told Mason was that he worked for Skipper Kinnock now — had done ever since Ortun had got rid of them — and his retirement fund was back on track. He was surprised Mason hadn't found out, what with the way he listened in on conversations in the Little Devil, plus he visited the marina a lot, spying from his boat, sitting there with his packed lunch and flask of tea like some creep. God, the number of times Steady had had to duck down on the Poisson Mort *and hide from him, even though he always put a snood over the lower half of his face. He didn't think Mason would take it too well, especially as Skipper had told Mason to sling his hook when he'd gone begging to him. Something about touching up women, and wasn't that rich! Ortun was fond of doing that himself, so how could he have sacked Mason for doing the same thing, then spread gossip about him? Skipper and his crew had agreed to keep it quiet that Steady went out with them three times a week, and it had been Steady who'd told Mason about the good catches at the Whitby reef. Skipper would go mental if he found out.*

Steady sidled down an alley beside the flats and entered the back garden. He held his breath in case a security light flashed on, but all remained in darkness. Thunder bellowed like an angry beast, and he fetched his lockpick from his pocket to open the communal door that led to the foyer.

He gained access easily.

Inside, a light did click on, a motion sensor effort, but he wasn't fussed. It was 3 a.m., and with the heavens making such a racket out there, he doubted anyone would hear him or get up to investigate.

He prowled by the front door to check the pigeonholes for post. Pulled out a few envelopes with the fingertips of his wet gloves, inspecting the names on the fronts. Best to check and be sure. Relying on hearsay wasn't the done thing in this situation. One wrong move, and you'd be in cuffs quicker than a hook snagged a fish. The man he wanted lived on the ground floor, like Mason had said, so he went to the correct door and inserted his pick again. It unlatched the lock, but a chain prevented him from going farther.

He sighed, pissed off at this hiccup, and closed the door, wincing at the click it created. He tromped back outside and, gathering the patio doors belonged to the flat in question, he did his thing, a bit trickier this time, and drew the heavy door open, thankful thunder roared once again to hide the sound. He stepped inside the living room and waited for more thunder. It came a minute later, so he dragged the door back across, leaving a small gap to ease his exit in case he got caught and needed to run.

He took his mini torch out of his pocket and switched it on. Panned the beam around. Briefly wondered if anyone was awake in the buildings opposite and saw the light. Decided he didn't care. He'd be gone by the time any police arrived. They'd have to come all the way from Scudderton, and he'd pass them on the way home.

The room had a minimalist approach — that or the resident didn't have much money, which could be the case. Steady knew him but not well enough to know the ins and outs of his life. He inspected the area. Nothing here said it was a cosy home. No pictures, cushions or even curtains, just closed Venetian blinds, a corner sofa, an armchair and a desk with a cheap plastic stool in front.

He spied the laptop on the desk and smirked. Steady could take it now, get out, go home, but that would be boring. A waste of a good opportunity. Breaking in wasn't a thrill unless he gave the occupants a visit, listened to them breathing while they slept on, oblivious to him being there, watching them in the dark, as much of a creep as Mason was spying in his boat.

Steady trod carefully, slowly, out of the room and into a narrow hallway. A quick splash of his light, and he spied the door he needed. The other two were open — a kitchen, with only a kettle on the work-top, and a bathroom, the shower curtain half hanging off the rod, some rings missing. He took a moment to stabilise his breathing, his excite-ment, then turned the handle down. Opened the door a crack. Spied through the gap, positioning his torch low so just enough light allowed him to see the person in bed, more of a shape than anything.

A snore. A pause. Another snore.

Steady pushed the door wider and walked up to the side of the single bed, the beam of his light pointed towards the concrete floor. Fucking hell, no carpet? Mind you, the bloke hadn't been living here long, a previous Scudderton tenant. Steady leaned over and stared at the sleeper's closed eyelids. Sucked in the man's exhalation, the breath hot on his chin. He poked his tongue out and licked the side of the fella's face from his jawline to his eye. A tickle of lashes on the tip had him withdrawing, retreating, his heart rate skyrocketing.

This lark was amazing.

He closed the door. Rolled his tongue around his mouth and tasted the sweat from the man's skin. This fella was going to bring trouble to Mason's doorstep if he found out what was going on. But that wasn't any of Steady's business. He was doing a mate a favour, wasn't he? Anything else that happened wasn't his problem.

He returned to the living room, picked up the laptop and secured it beneath his bomber jacket, the ribbed hem acting as a trap. Outside, he closed the patio door and left it unlocked to shit the sleeper up in the morning, and made his way down Robottom Street, shoved from behind by the wind, chuckling along with the thunder, laughing louder when a strike of lightning split the sky like a wonky arse crack.

Steady loved this, but he wouldn't be doing it again for Mason, no matter what he said. He preferred working for himself.

* * *

Kettlestone Rise

Mason roared with laughter as Steady handed over the laptop, placing it on the coffee table between them, relief that it was here flooding through him. He should never have doubted his friend. "Fuck me, imagine if he'd woken up. He'd have shit himself."

Mason reckoned Steady had balls of steel — the bloke could have seen him and phoned the police — but he wasn't sure Steady would keep his name out of it when push came to shove.

Steady shrugged. "It was like riding a bike."

Worry pinched Mason's conscience. "What about DNA?"

"Eh? What about it? One, mine isn't on record, only my fingerprints from the only time I got caught robbing, and two, he's likely to get up, go straight for the shower and wash it off, isn't he? If he doesn't and goes to make a coffee or whatever, why would he even think to tell the police he thought someone licked his fucking face? He doesn't even know it *happened*."

"I suppose." *Now I look like a dick who hasn't thought things through properly. Mam always said my mouth engaged before my brain had kicked in.*

"Now, if I'd killed him, *then* we'd have a problem. Post-mortem and all that. By the way, it would have been wiser, me doing him in. I've got a bad feeling about him. I could have dumped him in the sea after. Or buried him on the moors."

"He doesn't need to be dead. He hasn't done owt. He just happened to have what I wanted, that's all."

"And what if there's nowt on the laptop?"

Mason flinched at that. "We'll soon see."

Steady grunted. "You do realise it might need a password to open it, don't you?"

Mason shook his head. "Nah, his stepdad owns it, and you know what he's like. He can't remember his own phone number." He dragged the stolen laptop across the table and opened it. As he'd thought, no password nonsense to contend with, and he smiled smugly at being right. "See? What did I tell you?" He couldn't resist the *I told you so*.

Steady sighed, probably feeling a right old wally.

Mason homed in on a file on the desktop titled "Customers". He opened it. Clicked the Excel document inside. A long list of names, addresses and sale prices came up. "Here we are, look. So, listen, this is what I've got up my sleeve. Are you ready for this?"

Steady nodded, although he didn't seem too enthusiastic.

Mason went on anyway. "We can hire a big boat to start with because my smaller one won't handle the catch. We'll go out to that reef Skipper was on about. Catch the best fish, sell it."

"What do you mean, *we*? I agreed to nick the laptop, nowt else."

Mason didn't like the sound of that. Why wasn't Steady excited about starting a new business with him? It was always the same. No one wanted much to do with smelly Mason when it came down to it, excluding what Steady had done for him up until now.

As browbeaten as he'd been as a child, Mason forced himself to appear disgruntled about what Steady had said, not from the hurt dragged up from the past. "So you don't want a job with me, then? Don't you think I'm a good enough skipper?" He thought of a clincher. Wasn't pleased about it, but he needed Steady to agree to this so he could do one of the other things on his list. If Steady didn't get on the boat, Mason would have to adjust his plans. "I'm not greedy, I'll hand over half the profits. We'll be a fifty-fifty partnership."

"I'm not sure . . ."

"What, do you want to stay on Jobseeker's for the rest of your life?"

Steady looked a bit shifty. Why had the mention of Jobseeker's sent his face bright red?

Mason sensed bullshit. "What aren't you telling me?"

"Nowt." Steady stood. "Let me think about it. The boat thing."

"Don't think too long. I'm going out first thing next Monday morning." *And I need you on that boat with me.* Mason remembered what he'd done after he'd seen to Ortun during the night. Remembered who was down in his cellar. "It's time for you to go. I've still got shit to do. By the time I've built up my business, I'll have a better boat than Ortun *or* Skipper. Fuckers."

Steady held up a hand in a static wave. "See you when I see you, then."

"Yeah. Monday morning, don't forget. Five a.m."

With no response and Steady leaving the cottage, Mason got on with writing all the names down from the list on the laptop — he didn't have a printer. He'd be rich within six months, the king of the sea, and Skipper and the other fella who'd turned him away because of what Ortun had said about him could go and fuck themselves.

And hold their breath.

CHAPTER FIVE

June's Chippy

June had made coffee, and Pitson had taken a tray of Styrofoam cups to Rib and SOCO out the back. He was on his way in to collect the rest for the officers at the front end of the pier — more SOCO had arrived to do a fingertip search of the decking and check the shops and rides for any evidence. Thankfully, their job wasn't hampered by rubbish. The pier was kept clean and tidy, as required by the council. Still, it would be a big job. Once Pitson had come and gone again, then returned to stand inside by the door, Carol put an end to the general chitchat with June and got down to the nitty-gritty. They'd purposely sat so June didn't feel intimidated with two officers opposite her. Instead, Carol faced her and Dave sat to her left, his notebook out.

"Okay, love, firstly, I'm sorry you had to go through this today," Carol said. "How are you feeling?"

June, as old as the hills, her hair a snowy-white cloud, shuddered and rubbed her skinny bare arms. "It brought back memories, that's what it did."

"Of what?" Carol thought she knew, but as she couldn't be certain, she had to hear the woman out. Assuming could get her in the shit if her reports didn't have all the information.

June turned in her seat to grab a pink cardigan from the next table and put it on over her royal-blue cook's tabard. "My husband. He fell over that rail one night, didn't he, Alan?" She glanced over at Pitson, who nodded sagely. "Pissed, he was. Drowned. Alan will remember it well because he was part of that case." She sipped some coffee. "My old boy, he'd been doing a stocktake, brought beer along for company, and he didn't turn up for days. I thought he'd left me. Upped sticks and buggered off with whatever floozy tourist had caught his eye that week. He used to go up to the caravans, get up to all sorts, and he thought I didn't know. Well, I did. Anyroad, he ended up in Scarborough. On the beach. Dead. Bloated. A terrible time. I did think maybe a husband had found out what his wife was up to while on holiday and came to sort my fella out, but it seemed he'd just fallen over the railing. Probably got so drunk he thought it'd be a laugh to walk along it. Lost his balance, that kind of thing."

Carol recalled the incident from her younger days. A body washing up on a nearby beach had sent shockwaves through town. News had spread from Scarborough through Whitby to Scudderton, and folks had gossiped. "That must have been traumatic."

"And the rest." June sucked on her bottom lip. "Well, we move on, don't we? And to tell you the truth, it was a blessing in disguise. He used to knock me about, see. Many round here thought *I'd* done him in, what with all the bruises and excuses I made for them, but the police didn't. I was at home with my kids, and my sister had visited — we'd spent the evening baking for the fête that summer, had a bit of a tipple ourselves, and she ended up staying over."

Carol felt sorry for the woman. Having to explain herself all these years later for something she hadn't done . . . Carol knew what having suspicious eyes on you was like. She'd found her father dead in the bath. *He* used to knock *her* about, too — when he was drunk, when he was sober, it didn't matter. Some people had long memories around here and didn't forget such things easily. Deaths, possible murders, they tended to stay in the brain, didn't they?

Carol had to switch the conversation around to the present. While two men had gone into the water at the same spot, she didn't think they were linked, not so many years apart. "What time did you close the shop last night?"

"Ten, as per usual. Young Sammy was working, and I sent him home and cleaned up by myself. His wife's just had a baby, lovely little thing, and the mite was playing her up, poorly, so she needed a break. I left here about half past. Walked home with Old Clem."

"The Ferris wheel man?" Carol confirmed.

"Yes, that's him. We live next door to each other, have done for years. Spend time together when we're not working. Companionship, you know? His wife died, did you hear about that? In the summer it was. She was such a kind soul."

Carol hadn't heard. She'd been too busy catching a killer and their one-handed father. "Poor man."

"Hmm. Nice fella."

"So did you see owt when you walked down the pier, or even round the back?" Dave asked. "I presume you had to take the rubbish out."

June sipped again then put her cup down. "I did dump a bag, but no, I didn't see owt. Everything was as usual. If it wasn't, I'd have noticed. I'm on the committee to make sure the pier is kept tidy, so it's my business to check on my way down to the shore, pick up any rubbish."

"This morning, then. Give me your movements." While Carol didn't think for one minute June had killed Ortun, she'd go through the motions anyway. "Anyone hanging around who shouldn't be?"

"How would I even know if they shouldn't be here? We've still got tourists. There are a lot of strangers about."

"Fair point."

"I walked from home, down to the beach with Clem — we'd had a bit of breakfast at mine. *Not* what you're thinking."

She shook her head as if to admonish them for their dirty thoughts, or maybe her morals and the safe-keeping of her reputation had prompted her to be clear on the matter. "We're not into *that* at our age. So, what was I saying? Oh yes, everything was just the same as it always is. I left Clem at the café — he sits in there until he starts the wheel at eleven. I expect he'll have been sent home by your lot." Her eyes glazed over. "Anyroad, I did a bit of housekeeping and ended up with more rubbish, so I went out the back. Saw the railings had been broken. I put the bag in the wheelie bin and checked what the heck had happened. It looked like someone had broken them on purpose to me, not that a boat had come by and walloped it."

"Does that happen, then, vessels coming too close?" Carol drank some coffee now it wasn't so hot.

"Yep. People anchor, climb over onto the pier, go and get their jollies. Swines. I've been thinking of getting a sign put up about keeping back. I'll put it to the council at the next meeting." She closed her eyes for a few seconds then stared at the tabletop. "Then I saw him. Ortun. Except I didn't know it was him at first because he was floating facedown. I panicked and grabbed the ropes he was attached to, and he rolled over and . . . and I knew who it was then. I thought of Hattie."

Carol cocked her head. "In what way? They're divorced, aren't they?"

"That's what I mean. An angry ex, she is. Makes no bones about what she thought of him having it away with some tart down the Little Devil. I tell you, that was a scandal and a half. Hattie went there, all guns blazing, and thumped the woman. Louise Roberts, her name is. Always was a loose one, her. That night, Hattie moved out of Fisherman's Rest — that's where Ortun lives, see — and found herself a flat down by Sainsbury's. One of them new ones Senor De León put up a couple of years ago."

Carol thought about Ortun's place. They should go and check, see if it was the other crime scene they were looking for. Could Hattie have gone round there and whacked him, then taken him to the pier?

"So then what did you do?" Carol asked.

"Well, I phoned the police, naturally. How long will I be closed for?"

"You *could* get lucky and the officers may well be finished by the end of the day. With the weather as it was last night, the rain would have washed a lot away, and wind would have blown things into the sea, although, like you said, the pier was tidy when you left." She didn't add that they were searching for blood droplets where Ortun had possibly been carried along the decking, but now June had mentioned boats coming by, the investigation had taken on a new slant. Anyone could have sailed along, slung him on the pier, then climbed over. They'd have had the tools to break the struts, too, and knowledge of how to do knots.

June shrugged. "Ah well, can't be helped. I'm quite glad really. I could do with a day off. The season has been a long one, and this old girl needs to put her feet up."

Shame the police don't have seasons.

Carol grimaced. She wouldn't be getting a day off anytime soon.

* * *

Fisherman's Rest

The back door stood wide open, swaying, the handle whacking on the inside wall from the breeze that had stubbornly remained from last night. Irritating. Monotonous. A living room at the end of a brown hallway provided a slice of view to sniff at, as did the smell of the place. Despite fresh air probably blasting in there overnight, the stench of cooked fish, unclean crevices and general dirtiness lingered. Carol didn't want to imagine what it had been like before. Probably cloying.

The home had clearly gone to pot since Hattie had walked out, or maybe she'd been crap at keeping house, too. Like attracted like, or maybe it had been a case of opposites attract. The disorder was something she and Carol could have had in common once upon a time. Carol understood mess. She'd been a mucky pup once, hoarding not only her things — they'd given her a sense of comfort and safety — but her father's, the latter reminding her of what he'd done, bringing back awful memories each time she'd seen them. The time had come for her to let go, to accept it hadn't been *her* fault her mother had left them, it hadn't been *her* fault her father had taken it out on her, no matter what he'd said to the contrary. He was a liar, not accepting any responsibility, and she'd hated him for it. So she'd purged his and her things as well as her mind and was on the road to recovery.

Viewing a similar mess to her own brought on a sense of shame. How could she have lived in such filth?

Carol glanced at Dave and raised her eyebrows, jerking her head at the light that was still on. A blue shade. Dusty. Either Ortun had been abducted or had rushed out at some point last night. Carol preferred the former as a reason for the home being left unsecured, because the thought of him being lured outside on the pretext of some emergency or other was sadistic. Then again, abduction was, too. If lured, he'd have panicked, evidenced by him only having his Bermuda shorts on, and to go out in a storm like that spoke of someone being incredibly cruel in orchestrating him leaving his home. Messing with his head. Sending him into a spin so the killer had an easy job of hitting him with a weapon — a man not thinking straight might not have seen it coming.

Carol and Dave had put on protective booties and gloves. Carol led the way, a large photograph in a frame on the wall showing her what Ortun had looked like in life. She vaguely recognised him. He appeared much healthier than the dead version, obviously, although something she hadn't seen at the pier was the missing tooth, the black gap in his otherwise kindly smile.

How had he lost that? In a fight? Did he have an enemy?

A quick scoot around the messy bungalow showed he hoarded — lots of cardboard boxes in the spare room — and she had her answer regarding this being another crime scene. Blood in the bathroom, so it pointed to him being hit here and abducted. Spots of red in an arc, castoff from a wallop. Had he been killed here? Rib would find out. Water in the lungs would point to drowning; she hadn't noticed any signs of strangulation, a gunshot or a knife wound.

They moved back into the living room. A cup sat on one of the chairs, on its side, and even though the bungalow was a mess, it seemed out of place — all the other dirty mugs stood on a side table.

"What do you reckon this is, Dave?" She pointed at stains on the chair and the wall behind. Splashes and drips of liquid? Brown against the peach fabric and light-blue paint, too dark for tea or coffee.

"Spilled drink with the cup being like that?" he suggested.

"It doesn't look like he spilled it in the spilling sense, though, does it, unless he threw it over himself. There's a clean shape where he might have sat. Well, a cleaner shape than the other grubby stains anyroad. The furniture isn't exactly pristine."

"Forensics will study the spatter, give us an answer." Dave glanced around. "Fuck me, aren't you glad you don't live like this anymore? Clutter messes with my head."

She nodded. "I am, and it messes with mine now. Too much chaos. But I get why it's like this. Either he was too lazy or upset to clean after Hattie left or he was depressed. Been there. Sunny on the outside, dying on the inside. I'd best call this in. The blood in the bathroom . . ."

Three SOCO arrived, Todd on hand via the phone should the small team need to run anything by him before he could get there. He had a few things to do at the pier first. Carol called in for a uniform to attend and stand at the front by the cordon. She and Dave removed their booties and gloves, placing them in designated bag one of the SOCOs held out.

"There's a mobile in there," she told the officer. "On the bedside cabinet. Phone records have been requested, but it'll be quicker to access the actual device. Can you get that down to digi as soon as you can, please."

"Will do."

She recalled the telly still being on in the bedroom, and her heart hurt. The poor sod must have been watching it when whoever it was had arrived at his home. She imagined him snug in his bed, nothing more pressing than going out on the water in the morning, except he'd gone *into* the water instead.

"House-to-house enquiries for us, then," she said, glad of a chance to push her thoughts from her mind.

They went to the other four bungalows, starting at number one. Only a lady was in, number five, about sixty, in a trendy silver lounge suit and her hair a lovely shade of white-grey, a short back and sides with a longer, styled top brushed up and over, away from her forehead. She reminded Carol of the singer Pink.

"Sorry to trouble you." Carol held her ID up. "DI Carol Wren and DS Dave Waite. Can we have a word, Mrs . . . ?"

"Violet Kinnock."

Something to do with Skipper? Small world.

"Come away in," Violet said, her Irish accent pronounced but her tone soft. "I don't want to be standing here in the cold, and I don't imagine ye much like it either." She led them into an everything-white kitchen, so much cleaner than number three, all the worktops free of clutter and a bunch of red roses in a pink vase on the round pine table. "Do ye want a cuppa?"

"No, thank you," Carol said. "We've not long had one."

Violet gestured to the table. "Take a seat, the pair of ye. Ye're making it look untidy, standing around."

Carol smiled, Dave chuckled, and they sat in the same formation as they had with June. Dave took his notebook out and leaned back as though this was a tranquil interview, Violet just as relaxed — no bunched shoulders or darting eyes. No guilt. Carol sensed she wasn't the sort of woman to let her temper fly. Too gentle.

"So what I can do for ye?" Violet folded her hands on the table. A diamond ring glistened from the overhead light, butted up against a thick gold wedding band.

She obviously hasn't heard. "Ortun Bevan. What do you know of him?"

"Aww, he's a nice enough man, so he is. My Skipper doesn't think so for the most part, but ye know, that's the way it goes with the fishermen around here. They're not like back home. In Ireland, I lived in a little village, and every fisherman looked out for the others. Passed on tips and the like. Here? A different story altogether. They're rivals. Can't say I care for it, each man out for themselves. There's plenty of cod and plenty of places that want it. Enough for everyone. Skipper and Ortun, they're the worst — on the outside, at least. I remember when they had a big row, long time ago now, and Ortun took to Scotland to be getting the salmon. Probably thought he'd be better off out of the way for a bit, but he was soon back, after the cod."

"You say a big row. Is that how Ortun lost his tooth?"

Violet frowned. "No, the daft eejit slipped on the deck and banged his face. Despite what he says, Skipper wouldn't hit him. It's more a love–hate relationship. I can't even explain it. They cuss each other out but have a drink in the pub. And they have a thing going, seeing who catches the heaviest weight. I think Skipper was after saying he'd won this round with the cod he'd landed. Sixty-five pounds or something like that."

"Their row. What kind?"

Violet lifted her ring hand and waved it. "Aw now, it's nothing but a bit of manly animosity. Ye're aware of the type, I mean, aren't ye? They strut about, but deep down, if either were in trouble, they'd be there like a shot. It's a difficult relationship to get across to ye."

"I think I know what you're saying. So, his home. The mess. Do you know the reason for that?"

"Your man Ortun went downhill after Hattie left. She caught him with his trousers around his ankles. Not literally, he just had his zip undone, but word spreads, and she heard about him with that Louise Roberts. Hattie left him, so she did, and I don't blame her. A man who does that isn't a man worth having."

"What's Hattie like?"

"Nice enough if ye're on friendly terms, but she has a tongue like a whip and can take ye down a peg. Everyone in the Devil that night saw the rough side of her, I can tell ye, and I won't be crossing paths with that one anytime soon."

"The night she went in and confronted Ortun and Louise?"

"That's the one. It was a while ago now."

"Do you know whether Hattie is still holding a grudge?"

"I expect so."

"Back to Ortun. Apart from Hattie and your husband, do you know of anyone else who'd have a problem with Ortun?"

"I don't think so, but ye're better off asking Skipper about that." She glanced at the clock on the wall. "He'll be back from Whitby around now. He's old school and will be gutting the fish on deck. I've told him about health and safety these days, but ye know how these men are. Maybe ye could have a word with him, scare him into following the rules."

"I could slip it in somewhere, although his practices in that sense aren't something we're interested in at the moment. Now, for the reason we're here. Did you hear owt either in the evening or during the night? See owt in the street?"

"I didn't, no. I was tucked up under my blanket in front of the fire. With the storm and everything due, and Skipper needing to be up early, we went to bed at nine. What's this about?"

"I can't say at the minute." *Not without the next of kin being informed.* "Do you know the other residents well?"

"Well enough to know who'd stab me in the back and who'd hand over a cup of sugar. There's Edward Fields in number one, he works for Skipper, although he isn't on the boat today as he phoned in sick. I saw him going out a while ago, so maybe he's taken himself off to the doctor. Then there's Callum Roberts at number two, husband no more of Louise Roberts on account of her dabble with Ortun. He'll be with Skipper, part of the crew."

Carol perked up, and she caught Dave straightening. "Isn't Callum angry with Ortun about Louise?"

Violet laughed. "God bless ye and all, but Callum was glad to be rid of the wife. She was a harlot many times before Ortun, still is, and she was on her last warning. Ortun was drunk, so he claimed he didn't know who he'd been with, and Callum took it as fact so he could tell her to leave. The bungalow is his, left to him by his father."

"So there's no animosity *at all*?"

"None whatsoever. I'm telling ye, they drink in the pub together, him and Ortun." Violet smiled. "Men are a weird bunch — pardoning ye, of course," she said to Dave. "I'm sure ye're a fine fella. So then we have Ortun himself in number three, and next door at number four is a nice man — you'll want to be knowing him as William King. He's a retired fisherman. Got a grandson in the police. Wife died two years ago, God rest her soul. He'll be down at the town hall today. Dominoes. Gets back around three. He always brings me a bun from the bakery along the way there, and we have a natter together until he goes home at five with a dinner I'll cook for him later."

That must be Michael's grandad. "Thank you, you've been really helpful." Carol stood and waited for Dave to do the same. "I'm sure you'll hear what's happened soon enough, and you'll no doubt be aware of other police presence bar ourselves, but for now, we'll be off."

Violet saw them to the front door and peered across at Ortun's. PC Helen May had arrived while they'd been talking and stood on the doorstep.

"Something's happened, hasn't it?" Violet hugged herself.

"It has." Carol smiled. "But don't worry yourself, and try to have a nice day."

They walked off towards their car, Carol waving at Helen.

Carol's phone rang, and she answered it.

"Got owt for me, Michael?" She leaned her backside on the car door and stared at the sky, blistered with purple-bottomed clouds. Seemed like more rain on the way.

"No NOK for Ortun. Parents and sister deceased. Hattie isn't picking up her phone. Her son is at home — he usually works on Ortun's boat but hasn't gone in this morning because of the break-in."

Carol sighed. "With Hattie in the wind, it isn't looking good. Any record of where she works?"

"She's with a company called Constant Cleaning. They don't know which house she's in at the moment. She apparently has five of them to do today, although they're also not sure exactly which clients she's got on her roster. A bit lax to not have it written down, but what do I know? One house is a 'deep', whatever that is."

"Probably one of those cleans where they gut the place. Maybe she switched her phone off so she could just get on." *I'd love to do that sometimes.* She told him what Violet had said. "So poke into all the residents in Fisherman's Rest, even your grandad, plus Hattie and a woman called Louise Rogers." She explained why. "It's a bed of gossip at Mrs Kinnock's."

"Bloody sounds like it. Rather you than me."

"Shift some of the jobs to Katherine, she's good at social media digging. Can you also ask your grandad what he knows about Ortun, although Violet said he'll be down the town hall playing dominoes. Obviously don't tell him the man's dead. I'd rather see Hattie first."

"On it."

She got in the car, Dave following. It was time to go to the marina and see Skipper. Violet may well think the rivalry between her husband and Ortun wasn't anything to write home about, but Carol would be the judge of that. People killed for many reasons, and getting Ortun out of the way so Skipper could be the main seller in Scudderton wasn't an airy-fairy notion.

In some minds, it was reason enough for murder.

CHAPTER SIX

Undisclosed Location

Butterfly had secrets. Didn't everyone? Except Butterfly's still might come back to bite them one day. That was the thing, you lived your life in the hope they didn't tumble out of your carefully constructed closet, praying they remained locked in the box you'd placed them in, tucked away in a deep, dark corner. In Butterfly's case, no one else but the women knew what had happened, but then again, that was a grey area when talking of a specific incident. *That* woman knew, yet she didn't know everything. It was difficult to explain. Butterfly hoped they wouldn't have to explain it to anyone, ever.

Butterfly had a family. A good, loving band of people who'd be devastated if they learned the truth — that once upon a time until recently, Butterfly had done things so awful, something they'd struggled with every day since they'd stopped doing it, and it would put them in a terrible light. It had started with one moment of madness, and life had changed forever.

Youth, it shouted at you to do things you normally wouldn't, a devil on your shoulder, and in the thick of it, the consequences were far from the mind. All Butterfly had seen was an opportunity — a wicked one, but an opportunity, nonetheless.

Maturity, it shouted at you just the same as Youth: "What the hell were you thinking? Why did you even imagine it was a good idea? Now look, you beat yourself up every day, and when you see *him*, you're reminded of what you did."

Thank God Butterfly's soulmate was no longer here. One less person to hurt. One less heart broken if the truth came out. Sometimes, Butterfly contemplated ending it. They weren't much use around here anyway, and their passing would fade in memories eventually, the family moving on. If Butterfly died before it all came out, at least they wouldn't have to go through the pain, the shame, the explanations.

At least they wouldn't see the disgust in their nearest and dearest's eyes.

The revulsion.

CHAPTER SEVEN

The Marina

Mason stood in the darkness beyond the row of streetlights and stared at the fancy yacht, the rain soaking his jeans, but the rest of him, apart from his face, was dry enough. Waterproof boots, gloves and ponchos were made for this kind of thing. The wind pushed against his side, a wall of pressure, and he wondered how his mate was getting on, driving in these conditions. Steady would be on the way to Mollengate by now — if he'd kept his promise.

He better had. Mason needed what Steady could get him. Without it, he'd have to do a lot of guesswork. He cursed himself for not following Ortun's delivery driver this past week, but then again, his bicycle couldn't keep up with a vehicle. No, this was the only way to get the information.

Mason braced himself; a particularly violent gust had him side-stepping a few paces from the force. The wind had a nasty bite to it, too, and he reckoned by next week, autumn would be more like winter. Some would say he was mad for standing there in this weather, but it was perfect and couldn't have come at a better time. No one else would venture anywhere in it, but some might poke their faces to the boat windows to look out, the frenetic bobbing of their vessels ensuring they couldn't sleep. A few people lived aboard the boats, and obviously there were the two yachts, but because of the way they were all moored, only the first few people in vessels to the right would be able to spot him. The yacht on the left, Señor De León's, was too big and ostentatious to see around.

He had easily found the man's mobile phone number and had sent a message on a burner, and now, he waited for either a response or for the fella to appear. The big yacht swayed, only one light on behind a porthole in the middle. Maybe the fella was asleep, all of his guests having departed a while ago. How long should Mason give it before leaving? The target might not have heard his message bleeping.

The sea rose and fell, the swell of it birthing a yearning inside Mason to be out there, storm and all, battling the elements, goading them to toss him into the sea and do their worst. He grasped the mallet handle in his pocket to stop himself from boarding his little boat and going out there. His soul was wounded, riddled with incidents from the past, things he needed explanations for. Had he not looked at those bank statements, he wouldn't be standing here. He wouldn't know his mother had purposely kept them poor and wanting, her son's belly empty more often than not.

He'd parked his bicycle and trailer in the darkness a few feet away and itched to place the man beneath the tarpaulin. He had a lot of questions, a lot of anger to expend, and keeping him locked in the cellar would go some way to ensuring he felt better. Mason's cottage was just outside Scudderton, the first one on the road out to Runswick Bay, so it wasn't too far to ride, although he'd struggle in this weather. The wind might have it in mind to toss him from pillar to post, but he'd give it a good go. He had to.

The deck light came on, and Mason jolted. What if it woke whoever was in the smaller yacht beside it and they came out to investigate? He quelled the momentary panic; no, the owners were away.

Someone in a raincoat and woolly hat came up from below deck on De León's yacht, shielding their face with their crooked arm. Rain slanted at them sideways, and a crack of thunder added to the excitement of the scene. It was like watching telly.

Mason stepped into the light of a streetlamp, and the person on the deck looked his way. Mason wanted to shout, "Over here!" but didn't. While his voice might be snatched away by the gale, he couldn't risk it, so he walked forward, egged on by a kick to the backside from a blast of wind. He stopped on the wooden walkway, the slice that was the top of an upside-down T. The lengthy jetty in the middle poked out into the sea, the end around two hundred metres ahead, the vessels lined up and tethered to posts. Waves sloshed onto the boards.

He waved for shits and giggles.

The older man on the yacht didn't return it. He slipped and slid his way along the deck to the stern, where he climbed down a long ladder to the planks of the jetty. He held his coat closed at the neck and approached in dress shoes, staggering, either still drunk from the party or from the wind buffeting him. Once he made it to the light, it was clear from his expression he wasn't happy about being called outside in this shitty weather.

Mason took the mallet from his pocket, and in one perfect arc, he struck Señor De León on his temple. The man went down, his groan lost to the howling wind, and landed on his side, unmoving. Mason tucked his mallet away and idly hoped he hadn't killed him, not when he needed so many answers. He gripped his ankles and dragged him towards his bike, not giving one shiny shite De León's face scraped against the pavement.

That'd be sore come the morning.

CHAPTER EIGHT

Kettlestone Rise

He was cold. So cold. Where *was* he? The darkness hid his location, the blackness absolute, and with his head so muffled, he couldn't think straight. Strains of what had come before his moment of waking loitered at the edges of his mind, but he couldn't grasp them, couldn't hold them there so he could make sense of them. His heart knocked about, fear of the unknown suffocating him, and he took a deep breath in an attempt to stop himself panicking.

He tried to move his hands to lift them and rub his gritty eyes, but they wouldn't budge, held down by his sides. Metal bit into his wrists. Cuffs? Had he been arrested? He placed his palms flat — concrete? His backside ached, not just from the chill but the hardness. Was he in a garage?

From the softness of his clothing, he had his favourite pyjamas on, and the collar of his raincoat rested against his cheeks; he recognised the feel of the material.

He racked his brain.

Come on, think. What was I doing before . . . this?

Eventually, his mind cleared, and he recalled sailing to Scudderton Cove from Devon, a week earlier than expected.

He'd sealed a renovation deal, a mansion belonging to someone loosely affiliated with royalty. Their meeting had been shorter than anticipated. He'd braced himself for it to go on over several days, him persuading, showing how his company was the best, but the fella hadn't needed his arm twisting. They'd signed on the dotted line within an hour. His southern employees had started work the next day, the same day he'd sailed home to Scudderton.

He'd celebrated his good fortune with a party on the yacht, inviting his old friends from school, people who'd once thought he didn't have it in him to make anything of himself. He'd shown them, he'd proved he had the brains to go far. They'd turned up in their best clothes — ones he'd consider his worst, the stuff of jumble sales — and partied, drank his drink, ate his food and danced to the music he'd provided. They'd *taken* from him as though it had been their right and he owed them, guzzling, scoffing, cavorting, and it had incensed him so much he'd called time at around 2 a.m.

Thank God *she* was dead. But Fiona wouldn't have turned up even if she were alive. She'd have shunned his party, like she'd shunned him all those years. He'd kept a close eye on her, and it was clear she hadn't used any of his money except to buy that hovel of a cottage just outside town. She'd cycled the mile or so into work, and that child of hers had had to walk to get to school.

He felt no guilt. When news had come that she'd died, he'd stopped the payments and dusted his hands of that sorry mess, the same as he'd done that time as a thirteen-year-old.

So, the party. Everyone had left. He'd showered and gone to bed, couldn't be bothered with going to his house on the cliff at that time, although he'd wished he had. The storm had hit, and he'd had trouble sleeping. Then he'd received a text message from Fiona's child, a man now, but he'd always be a kid to him. A pest. A reminder of a bad decision.

He recalled leaving the yacht, stumbling against the wind, hating the fact he'd gone out to see what the little bastard wanted. The message had been too ominous to ignore: *It's her child. Come outside or I'll tell everyone what you did.*

Of course, a threat like that couldn't be ignored, and he'd contemplated punching the wretch and throwing him into the violent sea to drown. It would have looked like he'd slipped in the storm, and everything would have been okay then, like it had been before when he'd . . .

With Fiona's kid dead, he could have put things to bed and moved on. And he'd known then that the child had found out about the payments, had possibly put two and two together and was after some payments of his own. Money to ensure silence. Money to keep reputations intact.

"God . . ." he groaned, the memory of what had happened after he'd left the yacht smacking into him. "He hit me . . ."

"I did."

The reply from the depths of the darkness startled him, and he let out a grunt. "What do you *want*?"

"You seem to have lost your Spanish accent. Mind you, you only lived there for five years, so why you'd come back talking like you're a native is beyond me. Mam said you'd done that. We'll start the ball rolling with some questions, shall we?"

"Let me go."

"Or what?"

It grieved him to know there *wasn't* a "what". Not this time. There was nothing he could do, cuffed as he was. This wasn't his everyday life where he could use his wiles to get what he wanted. His fists. His hands.

"Ask them, then." He winced at a pain shooting through the side of his head. It felt funny around his temple, tight, as though the skin had stretched. Did he have a lump there? Or was it dried blood? And his cheek. God, it stung. A deep graze?

The memory of another lump, of different blood, filtered into his mind.

Mason harrumphed. "Number one. Why did you pay my mother so much money?"

Ah, either he didn't know or he was confirming the reason. Toying with him. Should he tell the truth? Was there any point in lying? Yes, there was. He didn't want this child knowing the truth, any of it, but what if he was tortured, forced to reveal it?

"To shut her up." That was all he was prepared to say for now.

"Why?"

"Piss off."

"You don't get to tell me what to do, Senor De León, or should that be Mr Eamon Perks? I mean, that's who you were before your mam married the Spaniard and took you abroad. Do you think people don't realise what you did there? That you wanted to reinvent yourself? What, was it so people forgot who you really were? They laugh at you, you know. Behind your back. The ponce who left town and returned a different person, like *that* could erase everything."

He knows. He's got to . . .

"People knew you as Eamon, they thought you were a little dickhead, yet you came back a man with your stepdad's money behind you and made a name for yourself. People don't forget who you were before."

Christ Almighty, did the child know more than what had happened years after the first incident? Did he know about the thing young Eamon Perks had done? The thing from that day on the moors? Only *she* knew about that, so she must have told her boy. On her deathbed? Had she confessed her part in it all?

I'm too old for this. I shouldn't be God knows where in my seventies.

"I'm not prepared to discuss it," Eamon barked.

"I didn't think you would, but you will. I took the liberty of getting a swab from your smarmy gob while you were out cold. Sent it off to a DNA place this morning along with mine. They won't give a shit about the signature I forged for you. We'll soon see what's what, won't we?"

Oh God, she told him he's mine. He's going to tell everyone. But what about the other thing?

"I'll leave you to have a think," the child said. "A bit of solitary confinement will work wonders."

It wouldn't, it never did. All that would happen was he'd think too much, remember, and he'd strived all his life since that day to forget.

But some things could never be forgotten.

CHAPTER NINE

The Moors

Fiona Whitley had dreams of becoming someone, the same as Eamon. They'd often talked about starting again, leaving Scudderton and all its small-town boredom behind. Going to London or something, earning a fortune then returning to show everyone they'd made it. Fiona couldn't see it happening, though. Mam wouldn't let her go, even when she got to sixteen. There were another three years until she reached that age, and the prospect of living here all that time with nothing to do but go to school and read books at home every evening took the shine off her plans.

Eamon's mam and dad had divorced, something people looked down on. You were meant to marry for life, stick it out, not throw it away when someone else caught your eye. A Spanish man had swept into town last year, here to do a business deal, and Eamon's mam, Cheryl, had taken a fancy to him. Fiona's mam said that had been the beginning of the end, and now they'd shacked up "in sin", poor Eamon having to put up with the stigma.

Fiona would never play away when she was married to Eamon. They'd promised each other they'd marry as soon as they were eighteen.

"They're going to the registry office tomorrow," he said.

Fiona stared out at the moors, the summer sun hot on the back of her head and neck. "They don't even know each other that well. They had a fling for a couple of weeks, then he went to Spain. He's only been at yours for two months since he came back."

"She says she loves him and he loves her, and that it's enough."

"God, can you imagine it?" Fiona felt all romantic then, thinking of being swept off her feet by a foreign man who was so dishy that she went funny down below whenever she looked at him. She didn't understand what that meant, those strange feelings there, but they happened every time. They happened when Eamon kissed her, too.

Eamon tsked. "Oh God, what is she *doing here?"*

Fiona glanced in the direction Eamon stared. "She" was Nerys Bevan. Fiona didn't like her. She was a little cow and always picked on her. Eamon didn't like her much either, saying Nerys thought she was a cut above because her father had the best haul every day. That was true. Dad worked on another boat and said they didn't bring in half as much as Vic Bevan. Still, that wasn't any reason to prance about as if you were royalty, was it? Funny, because Nerys's twin brother, Ortun, wasn't anything like her. He hung around with them sometimes and was a right good laugh. One day, he'd boasted, he'd own his dad's boat and catch all the biggest fish, be the smartest skipper around.

Fiona smiled at him having dreams, too. Did everyone?

Nerys approached in her pink shorts and top and stood in front of them, the sun in her face. She shielded her eyes, the shadow created by her hand giving Fiona an unsavoury view of her spiteful blue eyes.

"Get lost, Nerys." Eamon glared up at her.

"Having another little kissing session, are we?" Nerys said, the sun burnishing her blonde hair. "Did he feel your tits this time, Fiona?"

"Go away." Fiona blushed at the mention of tits. Nerys could be so crude sometimes. "You're just a nasty cat, you are."

Nerys laughed and shifted her gaze to Eamon. "I hear your mam's a loose one, letting that fella live with you, and them not even married. It's disgusting, my mam says."

"I don't care what your mam says," Eamon snapped. "Mine's happy, and Joaquín's a nice man, so leave off."

"Ooh, Joaquín, is it? Very lah-di-dah." Nerys twirled in a circle then peered down at Eamon again. "You do know she'll be damned to Hell, don't you?"

"I don't believe in that rubbish, and like I said, leave off." He stood, fists down by his sides. "Because if you don't stop talking, I'll—"

"What will you do? Hit me like your dad used to hit your mam? They say the apple doesn't fall far from the tree, so it wouldn't surprise me if—"

Eamon's punch sent Nerys falling in reverse, and she landed on her backside in a patch of dried grass. Her eyes watered, and she held a hand to her cheekbone where he'd struck her.

"You're going to regret that when I tell my dad." Her voice wobbled, and she blinked to stop tears falling. Nerys never cried, even that time she'd fallen over and grazed her knees, so she must be hurting. "He'll tell the police, and you'll be in so much trouble." She scrabbled to her feet, her eye swelling into a lump alarmingly quickly, the red skin changing to purple.

Fiona got up and stood between them. "Make up with her. Say sorry, Eamon."

"Fuck off will I." He looked at Fiona. "She asked for that. She's been goading me for ages. She got all of her school friends to follow me on the playing field and chant at me. That my mam was dirty and all that."

"Still no reason to hit her," Fiona said. "That was bad, and you said your dad shouldn't have done it to your mam, so why did you *do it?" She couldn't understand it. Eamon had never done anything like this before.*

"Like I said." Nerys smirked, even though she must have been in pain and could barely see out of her closing eye. "The apple doesn't fall far from—"

Eamon punched her again, and the momentum sent him down on the ground with her. They wrestled, having a scrap, and Fiona didn't know what to do. Boys shouldn't hurt girls, and Eamon was hitting her over and over on the head, the face. He pinned her beneath him, and she kicked at the ground with her heels, one of her pretty white sandals flying off. Fiona picked it up and, her heart hammering, stepped over to them and whacked Eamon on the back with it.

"Stop! Please, stop it!" Why wasn't he listening?

"No, I hate her." Eamon continued thumping.

"Help me . . . Fiona, please . . ." Nerys gripped Eamon's top and tried to pull herself upright, then she slapped at his cheeks.

Fiona attempted to get him off Nerys, but he was too strong, too angry for her to haul him away. Fiona picked up a rock and lobbed it at Eamon, but as it sailed through the air, he moved to the side, and a jagged edge struck Nerys in the temple. Nerys screamed then went limp, falling onto her back again. Blood spurted and, horrified, Fiona went down on her knees to push her palm on the gash. She must have broken an artery or something, there was that much red. Why wouldn't it stop bleeding? Why was Nerys asleep?

Eamon got up on his feet and stared down while Fiona stared up. "She had it coming, she did. She asked for it. You can see that, can't you?"

"What are we going to do?" Fiona asked. "We'll be in trouble and everything." She pressed harder and took in Nerys's ruined face. It was one big bruise now, different shades of red and purple. The first bruise had been bad enough, but this? "Oh God, the police will take us to one of them homes for bad kids, and I'll never see my mam and dad again. Nerys is going to tell on us and everything."

"No she won't. Move out of the bloody way."

Eamon pushed Fiona, and she fell backwards, her bloodied hand moving from the wound. Desperate to put her palm on there, to help, she lunged forward, but Eamon had straddled Nerys and fitted his hands around her neck.

He let out a long breath. "She can't tell on us if she's dead, can she?"

Dead? What?

He squeezed and, frightened out of her mind, Fiona tugged at his arm, trying to get him to stop, but the blood kept spurting, and scary gurgling sounds came out of Nerys's mouth. She was waking up. Her good eye bulged, veins of blood popping up in the whites, and time seemed to stand still. Eamon squeezed on, Fiona kept tugging, but his arm was rigid and wouldn't bend. She chopped at the inside of his elbows, but it was useless. She wanted to run. To go home and tell Mam what had happened. To beg the police not to lock her up forever.

"This is our secret," he said. "We don't tell anyone, you got that?"

The blood stopped squirting.

"I can't keep this a secret!"

"You have to." Eamon relaxed his hands. "She'd have told on us, and we'd have been put in prison not a home."

Was that true? Could children go to prison? She wasn't so sure about that, but Eamon knew lots of things, so maybe he was telling the truth. Fiona sagged back, scooting away on her bum, wanting to put space between her and Eamon. He was different, nothing like the boy he'd been before. Was it like Mam had said, some men had two sides to them? One good, one bad, and woe betide you if you set off the bad.

Panting from fear, Fiona stared at Eamon getting up as if he hadn't just strangled Nerys Bevan. His knuckles had red marks on them, and blood had got on his hands. Nerys lay silent, her one open eye pointed to the cloudless blue sky. Was she in Heaven now? Was she watching them from up there?

"Come on." Eamon at least looked a bit worried now. His eyebrows met in the middle, and he stared at his hands as if he couldn't believe what he'd just allowed them to do. "We need to wash the blood off us."

"What about Nerys, though?" Fiona stood, unsteady on her feet, and teetered like she'd done before when she hadn't had much food and nearly fainted that time. "We have to tell her mam and dad she's here. They'll be worried if she doesn't go home."

"So you want *to go to prison, then, is that what you're saying? If you hadn't thrown that rock, she wouldn't have been bleeding and I wouldn't have had to kill her to stop her blabbing. This is all your fault. Listen, no one knows we're here. You said you'd told your mam you were going to the park."*

"What did you tell your *mam?"*

He shrugged. "I didn't. She's gone to Scarborough with Joaquín. She won't know where I've been, and as long as we stick to the same story, no one will think we were here."

Fiona worried her bottom lip, pinching it between finger and thumb. She tasted Nerys's blood and wanted to be sick. "We've . . . we've got blood on our clothes."

Eamon shrugged again as if it wasn't anything to fret about. "Then we'll wash them in the stream and wait for them to dry."

"Wait? But what if someone comes for a picnic?"

"Shut up. We'll take her *with us. You hold her hands, I'll hold her feet."*

It took ages to get to the stream walking behind the tree line, or it felt like it did anyway. Nerys was heavy. Eamon reckoned they'd be safe as no cars had gone by on the main road. By the time they arrived, Fiona's mouth had gone so dry she couldn't swallow without it hurting. She dropped Nerys's hands and stepped into the water, sitting in it and washing her hands, scrubbing her fist against the splashes of blood on her top and skirt. They turned pink, which was better than the red, but Mam would still see it. Fiona scrubbed harder. She could say Eamon had bought her a strawberry ice lolly off the pier and it had melted and dripped, couldn't she?

How had the day turned into this nightmare? How had Eamon thought it was okay to kill someone? Oh God.

A big splash had her jumping to her feet and squealing. Eamon had thrown Nerys into the stream, and she floated along then lodged against some rocks sticking out much farther down the bank. He got into the water, too, and lay in it, swimming, going beneath the surface.

She wished he'd never come back up.

He did and swam towards her, sitting at her feet and washing his hands, his short-sleeved shirt. A glance up at her, and he smiled. "It'll be all right, Fi, you'll see. If we just keep it quiet, no one will know. We'll sit on the bank until we dry out a bit, then walk to the park. We'll be properly dry by then."

The park was ages away. More than two miles.

"We should go now. *I can't stay here. She's staring at me, look." A shudder brought on goosebumps. Fiona trudged up the bank, her T-bar shoes and white socks squelching with each step, and she broke into a run, desperate to put distance between herself and the dead girl.*

And Eamon.

"Wait," he called. "There's something I haven't told you."

Fiona didn't wait, but she did slow to a walk.

He came abreast of her. "I'm moving to Spain on Tuesday."

She stopped and stared at him. How could he do *this? Leave her to face things by herself? "Oh, that's great, that is. You can go and forget all this, but what about me?"*

"You just keep your mouth shut like I will, and everything will work out. I promise."

Fiona didn't believe him. Nothing could work out after this. Nothing.

She continued on for a while, determined not to speak to him. When they came to where they'd been sitting before, she spied the discarded sandal. A clue for the police. She'd touched it. They could find her fingerprints.

She sprinted over there and snatched it up, pulling the elasticated waist of her skirt out and placing the sandal in the front of her knickers.

"What are you doing?" Eamon asked.

"Making sure the police don't know I was here."

It was all the control she had in this situation.

Eamon had the rest.

CHAPTER TEN

The Marina

The weather threatened to call the storm back to terrorise the town, keeping people inside. The sky had darkened, and it gave the impression it was late afternoon, not mid-morning, sending Carol's sense of time skewwhiff. The clouds chugged by slowly, sluggish, as if reluctant to move on, loitering, Scudderton their chosen spot to dump their load. The breeze from earlier had picked up to a stout wind that pushed into them every minute or so. The chilled air held moisture, same as it did with fog, and Carol's hair had dampened, her face covered in a sheen of vapour. Good job she wasn't fussed about it. She never had been one to care much about things like that. Hair. Makeup. No, thanks. At least she'd had the foresight to pop her coat on. A soggy suit throughout the day would be a discomfort she didn't need.

She and Dave stood at the marina, at the part of the wooden jetty where the *Poisson Mort* was docked. It wasn't as big as she'd thought it would be, about twenty metres in length, seven wide if she was any judge, a blue hull with a white cabin. She stood on tiptoes to get a better look. Men did indeed gut fish on the deck, and she'd done a Google check prior to leaving the car to see what was actually on a boat like this so she could understand why the gutting was being done out in the open.

She *didn't* understand it and would be having words about it.

She held back a heave. She'd seen carnage in her career, but watching them butcher the fish churned her stomach. Blood and guts spread out, coating the men's wellies, their yellow waterproof overalls, and nefarious-looking *bits* had been scattered, probably flying off their knives with each slice. Innards sat in a pile.

One of the fellas glanced over, a massive fish held in one hand, a knife in the other. The hem of a black woolly hat covered his eyebrows, tufts of dirty-blond hair threaded with grey poking out by his temples. He was around fifty, although his element-ravaged skin could put him at seventy in a bad light. She knew his face. She'd likely spotted him around Scudderton, someone she knew by sight but not by name, the way of towns and cities all over. Familiar faces seen from week to week, no verbal interaction.

"Oi, what are you two gawping at?" he shouted. "You'll get them poncy suits dirty if you hang around here for much longer."

Poncy suits. Nice.

The devil inside Carol urged her to mention health and safety to put the wind up him, to change his scowl into an expression of alarm, but her good side overruled for now. She smiled and held up her ID. "We need a word with Skipper Kinnock."

"What do the likes of you want with him?"

"That's for us to discuss with Skipper, not you."

An older man, white hair sticking out every which way, held his knife up and stormed over to the stern. He leaned on the metal railing and scowled. "I'm Skipper. Who's asking?"

Carol lowered the heels of her flat shoes, no longer needing to be on tiptoes. "DI Carol Wren and DS Dave Waite. Can you come down here, please?"

"What's this about?" No Irish accent like his wife. He was clearly from around here.

She wondered how they'd met. Violet had mentioned Irish fishermen, so had she been a part of that community and met Skipper on one of his trips? Or had she visited here for a holiday and ended up staying?

"If you come down, you'll find out, won't you?" she called.

She engaged in a battle of wills, him trying to stare her out from his lofty position, not realising she could crane her neck to look up at him all day if he had a mind to keep this going. He must have sensed her stubborn streak, as his shoulders slumped and he walked off, handing his knife to someone else and whispering. He returned, climbed down the steel ladder, and jumped onto the decking. He walked over, blood dirtying his overalls.

"I'm busy, got a good catch to gut and deliver, so be choppy about it," he snapped.

Carol studied him. White coarse curls that the wind had multiplied by sifting through it, spreading them out. Red cheeks, a few thready veins, maybe from a glass of whiskey of a night. Large nose, a hook on the end, the ultimate depiction of a baddie. And beady eyes, dark, the pupils almost lost in the irises.

They reminded Carol of her father, and she endured a shudder.

"It'll take as long as it takes, gutting and deliveries or not," she said. "Why don't you use the processing room on board?"

"Fucking hell, has someone got hold of health and safety?"

"Not that I'm aware, but I *will* be doing that once I go back to the station if you don't follow the guidelines. You *do* have a processing room, yes?"

"Well, yeah, but it isn't big enough. Only space for two people. Out on deck, I've got the whole crew gutting, getting it done quicker. My fish is known for leaving the sea and reaching the customer faster than anyone else's."

"You won't be getting owt done if you don't heed the rules."

He chuffed out a breath. “Fine. I’ll sort it. If that’s all, I’ll be off now.”

“Um, no. We haven’t finished. What were you doing last night?”

He glanced at Dave. Must have clocked the size of him and decided he’d play ball. “Went to the pub till half eight, then I was at home with the wife. A bit of telly, bed at nine. Why?”

“Which pub?”

He pointed behind her. “The Little Devil.”

“Did you hear owt in your street at any time?”

“Nope. Was I supposed to?”

“See owt?”

“Nope.”

“Tell me about your relationship with Ortun Bevan.”

“What about it?”

Carol sighed. “Look, maybe you like being awkward, but it really isn’t the time to be doing that. Just answer my questions, and we’ll leave you to it.”

Skipper shook his head, perhaps annoyed at being called out and told off by someone younger than him. “You’re Harry Wren’s kid.”

Carol bristled. “That has nowt to do with this investigation. Tell me about Ortun Bevan.”

He grunted. “He’s a prat. Wants to hog all the fish for himself. Doesn’t like sharing.”

“How do you get along with him?” Present tense. Saved him twigging something had happened to the man — or maybe he’d killed him and already knew.

“I tolerate him. Can’t stand the way he goes about when it comes to cod, though. He even got rid of good fishermen and replaced his crew with young’uns so he could ‘beat’ me by getting the best and biggest haul. I’m tired of it; I’m getting on and can’t be doing with games. He’s just as old, so why he wants to mess around with me, I don’t know. So I moved on to Whitby reef to get away from him. He can have the rest of the water. I’m finished fucking about with him.”

“So there’s rivalry.”

"There was until yesterday. Ortun still thinks there is, but that's his lookout." He leaned close and said quietly, "Between you and me, I found out two days ago I've got a dicky heart and I'm meant to be lowering the stress, so I've been cutting out the people who bring it on. Ortun does. I've only got to see him down here and I want to punch his lights out."

"And have you?"

He tsked. "No. It's best we stay away from one another at sea and on this jetty, maybe everywhere else, too, although he isn't too bad in the pub."

"Which boat is his?"

Skipper pointed behind them. "That one there, opposite mine. Used to be called the *Red Dragon*. He's from Welsh stock, although he's never stepped foot there as far as I know. His father used to own it. Passed it over to him before he died. Worst thing he could have done. It went to Ortun's head. He lost his roots, got above himself."

"You say it used to be called the *Red Dragon*. What is it now?"

"It's the *Nerys Angel*."

"I heard it's unlucky to change the name of a boat. Any reason for that?"

"Old Bevan, the father, he renamed it after his daughter. She got murdered, see."

Carol jolted at that. "When?"

"Oh, bloody years ago now. She was thirteen, and someone battered the shit out of her, throttled her, and dumped her in Scud Stream up on the moors. Nasty business. She was Ortun's twin. He took it hard."

And now he's dead, too . . . "How many years ago?"

"Got to be about forty, give or take."

She didn't allow her shoulders to sink. Didn't want this man knowing what she'd thought was a link wasn't. But *was* it too much of a gap to be connected? Or had someone been biding their time like the last set of murders she'd had to deal with? Waiting. Holding a grudge. No, it felt too convenient, too easy — she'd go with it being a big coincidence. For now, until proof told her otherwise.

"We'll take a look at that case." She realised too late she'd said that out loud instead of keeping it in her head.

Skipper frowned. "Why? It's done and gone."

Bugger, she'd have to brazen it out. "Did the police find who'd killed her?"

"Well, no, but—"

"Then it isn't done and gone, is it? Okay, moving on. When did you last see Ortun?"

He choked out a laugh of exasperation. "What's with the questions about him?"

She folded her arms. "Did you not *hear* what I said earlier? Get on the wrong side of me, and I'm telling you, health and safety will get a call. And I'll be sending someone to check every day that you're not gutting out in the open." She wouldn't, she'd nip by herself from time to time, let him see her watching, but it wouldn't hurt to scare him. "Plus, you said you're a busy man. We're also busy, and if you want to get back to work, don't answer me with questions of your own. People who deflect not only get my back up but make me think they've got something to hide. *Have* you?"

"No!"

"So *when* did you last see *Ortun*?" The last word went up an octave in irritation.

He rubbed his bristly chin. "Yesterday, after he brought the *Nerys Angel* in. He shouted at me from his deck."

"Saying what?"

"That I was a prick."

"Is that usually the way you speak to one another?"

"It was, but like I told you, I can't be doing with it, so I ignored him." Skipper seemed proud of that, puffing his chest up.

"What do you know about Hattie Lamb?"

He laughed, maybe to cover his surprise at her quick switch to another subject. "She's a feisty one, she is. Left him. He was playing around on her."

"We know."

He eyed her, assessing, clearly trying to work out *why* they knew. "This is all sounding a bit iffy. What's *she* got to do with owt?"

"Do you think she'd hurt Ortun?"

"Look, what's going on here?"

He's asking me bloody questions again. She glared at him. Raised her eyebrows. She was cold and pissed off and he was adding to it . . . *This must be how he felt dealing with Ortun, getting riled just by talking to him.*

"Well?" she said.

"Yeah, she'd hurt him, but only by kicking him in the bollocks."

Dave chuckled.

Carol could have brained him. "She still has a problem with what he did, then?"

"Yeah, gives him filthy looks when she's in the pub."

Dave poised his pen over his notebook. "The Little Devil?"

"Yeah."

"Why go there when she lives over by Sainsbury's now?" Dave asked. "Why not go to the Castle instead?"

Skipper's mouth dropped open, the man obviously thinking that was a daft question. "Why should she? The Devil was her local when she was with Ortun, and she made a lot of friends. Why would she be expected to move boozers because he can't keep it in his Y-fronts? She wasn't the one in the wrong."

"Do *you* have a reason to hurt Ortun?" Carol asked.

Skipper's face clouded, and he bunched his fists. "Now hang on just a minute . . ."

Dave took half a step forward. "Answer the question, sir."

Skipper released his fingers and flexed them. "We go way back. I've known him a long time. We got by fine until he took over the *Nerys Angel.* Then he changed. Got on his high horse. We argued, we had rivalry, but no, I wouldn't hurt him. I hate him and I like him. We bicker and we get on. It's complicated."

Carol sniffed. "So your wife said."

Skipper's eyes widened. "You've spoken to my Violet? She never phoned and said."

"Maybe she didn't feel she needed to. We were doing door-to-door enquiries at Fisherman's Rest."

"How come you're doing that, then?"

Carol ignored yet another question. "Did Ortun's crew turn up as usual this morning, d'you know?"

"No idea, we went out earlier than normal. When we got back and his boat was here, I assumed he'd been fishing locally and they'd finished for the day."

"Which employee is Callum Roberts?" She gestured to the *Poisson Mort*.

Skipper turned around. "That fella there, the one who shouted at you."

"We'll need a word with him now."

Skipper opened his mouth, probably to ask her why, but she held up a hand.

"Thanks for your time." She smiled to end the conversation.

Skipper huffed and climbed aboard his boat. He approached the gobby fella in the woolly hat who turned to look at them, his expression one of fear. She could well imagine what was being said: *"They're asking about Ortun and whether anyone would hurt him . . . They want to speak to you. Watch it."*

Carol turned to Dave. "Do me a favour and call Todd. Ask him if he can get a small team down here. We need the *Nerys Angel* going over."

He walked away, farther towards the other end of the marina, phone to his ear.

Carol faced the *Poisson Mort* again and waited for Callum to descend the long ladder.

He stepped over to her and held both hands up, his troubled expression turning to irritation bordering on anger. "Now look here, my missus may have done the dirty on me with Ortun, but I couldn't give a shit. He did me a solid. I've got no truck with her, and as for him, we get along fine." He dropped his hands to his sides.

"If you could just wait a second . . ." She didn't like his attitude and wanted to wait for Dave to come back. While she wasn't afraid, she might need a witness to any altercation; it seemed Callum was after being a knob.

She faced Dave's way and waved him towards her. He finished his phone call and returned to her side, cocking his head at Callum and narrowing his eyes. So her partner had this bloke's measure, too, even though he hadn't heard him speak. Good. It wasn't Carol's imagination that Callum was a confrontational arsehole.

"Right," she said. "Where were you last night?"

Callum's eyes darkened. "Are you having a laugh?"

"Afraid not."

"I was at the Devil if you must know, you can ask anyone."

"We will. What time did you leave?"

He looked to the sky, either thinking back or working out a lie. "About eleven. I'd normally be in bed, what with the earlier rise to go fishing, but darts was on, so I stayed."

Glad Dave was taking notes, Carol planted 11 p.m. in her mind. She wouldn't find out the approximate time of death until Rib had done the post-mortem, but still. "What did you do then, after eleven?"

Callum's cheeks reddened. "Do I have to answer that? I'm not under arrest so . . ."

"It's in your best interests to answer, and no, you're not under arrest, but why *wouldn't* you want to answer if you have nowt to hide?"

"Because I do."

Carol's guts tightened. "And what are you hiding?"

He glanced around, seemed happy there were no eavesdroppers, then said, "I visited a lady friend after leaving the pub, all right?"

An affair with a married woman? Is that why he didn't want to say? "And she is . . . ?"

"What do you need to know for?"

What the fucking hell was it with these fishermen? Carol felt she had to enunciate every word to indicate she didn't want to fuck about. "And. She. Is . . . ?"

"Jesus Christ. Hattie Lamb, okay?"

Oh, bugger me. Had the pair of them conspired to kill Ortun? "So you went to her flat, did you?"

"Yep."

"And she'll confirm that?"

"She might not. She doesn't want anyone knowing what we get up to yet. Difficult situation, see?"

"Why's that?" She had a feeling she already knew.

"Ortun dabbled with my ex, and Hattie's *Ortun's* ex. You can see how it looks."

"I've got a good imagination. How did you end up with Hattie?"

Callum shrugged. "We talked. About what had happened. Got close. That's about it really."

"How do you feel about her?"

The fisherman frowned. "What d'you mean?"

"Well, is she likely to become permanent, or is this just you two scratching your itches, licking your wounds together, before you part ways?"

"It was ages ago Louise did what she did, and I didn't start seeing Hattie until around six months afterwards when the divorces were well underway, and I've been with her ever since, so work it out for yourself."

"You're more than a fling."

"Right. It's just people around here . . ."

"I know. They talk. They don't forget. So are you going to hide your relationship with her forever?"

"We haven't got around to discussing that."

She had a moment of weakness where she felt sorry for him. The fishing community sounded like it was everyone knowing everyone else's business, and folks judged. "You've got *one* life, do you understand what I'm saying? If you allow other people's thoughts and actions to dictate what you do, then you're not living your life as you want to."

God, don't I know it? "You're Harry Wren's kid . . ."

She'd lived under her father's shadow for too long and was now living *her* life how *she* wanted to. "It's been a while since it happened. Move on. If you've both found love or whatever out of a bad situation, run with it. Publicly. Scurrying around hiding is no life." *Unless the secret gives them a thrill.*

He considered what she'd said. "Aww, I don't know . . ."

"Think about it. Nowt is promised for tomorrow. Things can change in an instant, you'll find that out soon enough."

His demeanour changed back to when he'd originally approached her. "Is that a threat?"

"*What?* Of course it isn't. There's been an . . . incident. You'll know exactly what I'm saying when you hear about it. Thanks for speaking to us." She went to walk off then stopped. "Oh, one more thing. If you're with Hattie in that sense, do you know which house she'd be cleaning at the minute?"

"Nope."

"We know she has five to do but not which one she's in. She's not answering her phone."

"She won't, not when she's working. Why do you need to speak to her?"

"Like I said, you'll find out soon enough."

"Is she in trouble?"

"I have no idea." She smiled. "We'll be off now."

She strutted towards the street end of the jetty, Dave by her side. The sky let out a low grumble, and she shivered from a gust of wind sneaking beneath her coat collar. They could do without the storm returning, considering SOCO needed to check the *Nerys Angel.*

At the car, she leaned on it and folded her arms, a gust blowing her hair back from her face. Her eyes watered, so she blinked them clear. A small red boat reversed about halfway down the jetty and bobbed in place. She looked at Dave. "What did you make of all that, then?"

"I'd say neither of them are involved."

"I thought the same thing, but consider this: what about Hattie getting Callum to kill Ortun?"

"Owt's possible, but I didn't get any sense Skipper or Callum are guilty of owt except gutting fish where they shouldn't."

"We really need to speak to her — Hattie." She sighed. "We'll wait for SOCO, then go back to the station and catch up with Michael and Katherine. Things might become clearer once we've had a chat together. Four heads are better than two. Actually, we'll nip back to the pier first, see if owt's turned up there."

Dave bobbed his head. "They're here, the techs."

Carol pushed off the car and peered down the road. A van parked, and three officers got out. One approached her. Ben Asher.

Carol nodded to him. "It's the *Nerys Angel* you need. On the right."

"Cheers."

She left them to it and got in the car, drawing her seat belt across. The red boat had gone, so she assumed it had sailed out to sea.

Dave joined her, and they stared ahead.

Carol leaned her head back. "Can you phone Joy on the front desk and ask her to get an officer or two down here to speak to all the boat owners — if they're even on board. I also need a couple to speak to the landlord and staff at the Little Devil to confirm Callum was there. I just need to close my eyes and think for a minute."

While Dave got on with the call, Carol thought about Skipper mentioning who her dad had been, like it was *her* fault he'd been such a bastard to everyone. No one had liked him much since her mother had gone, him turning to booze, getting so drunk he'd incited fights then came home and took it out on Carol if he lost. That time with the barrel had scarred her for years.

She wished her mother hadn't left her behind. There had been no word from her, no birthday cards. Carol had suspected her father had thrown them away if they'd come in the post; they hadn't been in his house when she'd cleared it after his death. She'd run a search on the police database — not allowed for personal issues, but she'd done it anyway — trying to find her. Nothing.

"All done," Dave said, drawing her out of her head.

That wasn't a bad thing.

"Thanks." She rubbed her eyes.

"I'm bloody hungry," he said.

"It's too early for lunch."

"My stomach doesn't care, and there's always that thing called brunch."

Carol smiled. "We may as well go to the bakery before the pier, then."

"Not Greggs?"

"Nah, I fancy something from Buns 'n' Bread."

"Their thick-cut sausage sandwiches with brown sauce . . ."

"You read my mind."

Dave slipped his seat belt on. "On you go, then, driver."

She rolled her eyes and laughed. "Fuck off, pal, seriously."

CHAPTER ELEVEN

The Marina

Whipped by the wind, the *Jar* bobbed on the water. Mason, a blanket wrapped around him, a cap pulled low over his forehead, sat in his little cabin. He'd been observing. The police had been, or he assumed the man and woman were police anyway. He hadn't been able to see their faces clearly. When they'd left the jetty, he'd reversed to check on them. Spotted them talking by a car, then a van had turned up, and he'd shot forward into his mooring space again. Then they'd driven off, leaving the van men behind.

He waited for ten minutes then placed his blanket on a bench seat, locked the cabin and left his boat. He strode from the mid-point of the jetty where it was tethered and headed towards the *Poisson Mort*, smiling to himself about the upcoming conversations he'd instigate. Three men in white suits climbed aboard the *Nerys Angel*, one of them handing a toolbox of some kind to one of the others, and he sniggered at the fact they must have found Ortun and had to check his boat.

They'd find nothing there, it'd be a waste of their time, but it wasn't like he could tell them that, was it? Christ, he'd have questions coming at him from all sides, wouldn't he? And that wasn't in his plan.

At Skipper's boat, he whistled with four fingers in his mouth.

Callum came to the railing, gripping the top of it in his bloodied hands. At least Ortun hadn't allowed that. Gutting without gloves on. He'd done it right, using the processing room and the proper outfit for the job. Mason had missed a trick there. He could have dobbed Skipper in to health and safety and hung around to watch him having an inspection, then possibly getting closed down and paying a big fine.

Nah, this plan was better.

Callum's nose scrunched. "Aww, what do *you* fucking well want?"

"I came to see Ortun. Wanted to try again to get my job back, but there's men on his boat. What's going on there, then?"

Callum glanced across at the *Nerys Angel*. "Fucking Nora. Come up here."

Mason climbed aboard, the excitement of old seeping into his bones. God, he loved big boats, missed being on one. He followed Callum to the railings by the steps that led below and frowned at other fishermen sitting around on deck, two others cleaning it up with squeegee brooms, creating a pile of fish mess on the boards. "Where's Skipper and Joe?"

"Sorting the fish below."

Mason widened his eyes at that. "How come?"

"He's had a warning. Look, the police were here, asking questions about Ortun. Have you heard owt?"

"No, why would I?"

"You hang around here often enough, earwigging."

Mason hadn't thought he'd stood out while watching. Shit. Would Callum turn out to be a problem? "I can sit on my boat if I want. No law against it."

"I suppose."

Mason stepped closer. "I wonder why they were asking about him?"

"Something's happened, but the coppers didn't say what, just said I'd find out soon enough."

"That doesn't sound good. On your part, I mean. Like *you'd* specifically find out. Seems like they've got their eye on you." He stopped himself from letting out a mad giggle. "What would they be doing on his boat in those white outfits?"

"Shit, I didn't think of that." Callum stared at Ortun's boat again. "They must be police. What if something's happened to him?"

Mason shrugged. "What like?"

"I don't bloody know, do I! Fucking hell, you ask some stupid questions, you do."

"How can it be stupid if the police in suits have been and there's them fellas on the *Nerys*? Shit must have happened for them to be here."

Callum squinted at something on the deck. A scuttling spider. "They knew about Louise and Ortun."

Blimey, they'd got to work quickly, but that little dalliance was nothing to do with this. Well, apart from Ortun being a hypocrite regarding women and spreading rumours. Mason could only hope they never found out who'd killed him. He didn't plan on being caught. He'd do what he had to, then fish for the rest of his life. Why hadn't he thought of hiring a boat until recently? Maybe his mind had been addled by getting the sack and it had taken him a couple of years to come to terms with it. Who bloody knew.

"So what if they know?" he said. "Louise and Ortun happened yonks ago."

"I know, but I'm curious as to what's going on."

"Then phone Louise and see if she knows owt."

"I don't want to talk to her. She's scum. I should never have bloody married the bitch."

Mason shrugged. "Then you'll just have to wonder, won't you, until the police come and tell you what's happened."

"D'you think they will?"

"Probably. Anyroad, would you mind going and getting Skipper for me. I need a word, like."

"I wouldn't advise it. He's got a cob on. The copper visit has put him behind, and having to gut down below now, well, that's taking more time with only two people doing it. Plus we're a man down because he called in sick."

Mason studied the crew. Everyone appeared to be here, so what Callum had said didn't make sense. Hold up . . . His blood boiled. Had someone else been taken on when *he* was a seasoned fisherman and could have had the job? He forced himself to act casual, a bit of a feat if he was being honest. "Who's that, then, a new recruit?"

Callum flushed. "Listen, I'll only be a minute." He went to walk down the steps then stopped. "Sodding hell. Just go down there yourself. It's a tight squeeze, mind."

He walked off and helped the men scoop the mess into buckets ready to be tipped overboard, another of Skipper's naughty habits. The council didn't want fish guts in the marina or close to the beaches. It had to be incinerated on land or at least taken far out to sea.

Mason sniffed the air. More rain was on the way, plus the remnants of Callum's bullshit lingered in the air, him evading the question about a new recruit. Mason headed downstairs, wondering who the hell had been working on the *Poisson Mort* without him knowing. Hadn't he been watching properly? Yes, he got distracted by his thoughts, but surely he'd have seen someone new around.

That bloke who wears the snood over his face. Where is he?

He found the processing room and stood in the doorway. It reminded him of working on the *Nerys Angel.* He'd liked doing this part, taking all the guts and bones out, chopping the heads off. For some reason it had calmed him; he'd imagined the fish were Mam and he was disembowelling and decapitating her. The thought of it was still thrilling.

Skipper slid a prepared cod into a crate of ice at the end of the steel work surface. Joe glanced over his shoulder at Mason and nudged his boss.

Skipper turned. "Fuck's sake. What do *you* want?"

Why did people keep *saying* that to him?

Skipper griped, "I've told you, I'm not taking you on, so bugger off."

"Can we have a chat later?"

"We've got nowt to chat about, pervert."

"I didn't do owt wrong with that woman. I touched her arse, that's all. Fucking hell. Ortun didn't have any right to pull me up on it, what with him doing what he did with Louise in the corridor down by the loos in the pub. Can't you just drop it? I'm *not* a pervert."

"Well, that's your opinion. Now get off my boat." Skipper turned back to the steel worktop and hefted up another cod. He continued working with Joe as though Mason wasn't even there.

Mason shrugged. He'd tried. He'd given him one last chance, and he couldn't do more than that, could he?

He went up on deck. Approached one of the young lads sitting around. "Who called in sick today? The man with the snood?"

The kid shrugged. "Don't know his name."

The black-haired fella sitting next to him laughed. "You do. This is fucking stupid."

"What is?" Mason asked.

"Look, we've all been keeping it a secret, because the bloke didn't want you to know, but it's Steady who called in sick and wears the snood, okay? God, it's just a job, nowt personal."

Mason's head spun. What? Steady worked for *Skipper*? Steady had blushed earlier when he'd mentioned being on the dole. Now he had another reason for drowning him.

"How long's he been working here for?" he ground out.

"Skipper took him on after Ortun sacked you both."

Two years. *Two years?* Mason lurched around and staggered to the stern, Steady's betrayal burning his cheeks. He jerked his way down the ladder, so angry and hurt he could scream. What about last night's robbery? Steady could blab about it to his crewmates. Tell them Mason had killed Ortun. Fuck, why had he trusted him?

Mason calmed himself by muttering that Steady had been on his list anyway, he was a loose end, but now he'd discovered what had really been going on, it'd make his death even more tolerable.

He walked down to the trawler beside the *Jar*. It was a couple of metres smaller than Skipper's, but the *Black Pearl*, captained by Fred Collerton, was a tidy vessel, one Mason wouldn't mind owning one day. He wouldn't unless Fred's son sold it to him after his father's death, and even then Mason doubted he could afford it. He had a lot with Mam's money, yes, but he didn't want to use it all on a big boat, not until he'd earned some savings himself.

From where he stood, no one appeared to be on deck, so he climbed the ladder and went in search of Fred, who lived in quarters below. At the bottom of the stairs, he came face to face with the man himself appearing from around the corner. Mason jumped in surprise.

"What the devil are you doing on my boat?" Fred gritted out, the image of Captain Birdseye.

What a grizzly old bastard. "I just . . . please, will you reconsider and give me a job?"

Fred gnashed his dentures. "Not this load of old bollocks. I've told you time and time again, fuck off out of it. I don't want the likes of you on my boat. How long has it been? Two years or so? Yet here you are, week after week, pissing me off with your begging."

"I didn't do owt bad to her," he said. "Ortun's lying."

"So you keep saying, but I'm not listening, pal." Fred gave Mason a shove in the chest. "Get off here. Now. And if you come back, I'm calling the police. You're trespassing."

"You just missed them." Mason backed up onto a step.

Fred frowned. "What did they want?"

"Ah, so you want to know me now, do you? Well, sod off and find out for yourself."

Mason turned and stomped up the stairs. Another one he'd given a last chance to, and he'd been rebuffed, like with Skipper. Still, it was best to make sure, wasn't it?

Double-check whether you should kill someone or not. Those two twats had signed their own death warrants.

He left the *Black Pearl* and checked the *Nerys Angel*. One of the men pottered about on deck. Mason trudged off to the street end of the jetty and collected his bicycle, minus the trailer, which he'd left at home. He climbed on and rode towards Fisherman's Rest, thinking about what he was going to do there tonight, changing his plans yet again. He'd done that once already with De León. He'd planned to kill Steady next Monday when they went out on the hired trawler, but he hated him now, so things had to change. He'd enjoy killing Steady. Before Mason had been given the bad news regarding his friend's deception, he'd have felt a tad guilty holding his head beneath the water, but not now.

Steady was as bad as the rest of them.

* * *

Fisherman's Rest

Mason rode his bicycle to the turning and put the brakes on at the sight of a copper in a hi-vis yellow jacket standing at the entrance on the inside of a police cordon. His heart skipped a beat, but what had he expected? The police were on the *Nerys Angel*, so it was obvious they'd be here, too. They'd be checking everything to do with Ortun, going from bungalow to bungalow, asking their nosy-arsed questions.

Shit, now I won't be able to kill Steady tonight.

"Can I have your name, sir?" Plod walked towards the pavement, notebook out. He was young but had that self-assured air only a few people could carry off without appearing arrogant. Maybe when he put the uniform on he transformed into someone else and was a wuss at home. "Sir? Your name?"

"Oh. Sorry, miles away there. Mason Ingram."

Plod scribbled that down. "What are you doing here?"

Mason pointed to his bike basket. A bag of cakes he'd bought earlier from Buns 'n' Bread filled a white paper bag.

He'd planned to eat them all in front of Senor De León, sod his healthy eating regime, but they came in handy for something else now. "Dropping these round to my friend."

"And that would be?"

"Edward Fields, number one."

"Okay." The copper scribbled some more then lifted the cordon. "Go on through."

He watched Mason ride away.

Mason leaned his bike against the front of Steady's bungalow and knocked on the door. Two blind slats parted in the living room window, and Steady's eyes appeared in the gap. The blinds closed, then a few seconds later the door opened.

"Get in, quick." Steady peered over at the copper.

Mason entered and went into the living room. He twisted the rod to open the blinds a little so he could see the whole cul-de-sac, eager to know what was going on.

"What the fuck are *you* doing here?" Steady asked behind him.

Mason stiffened. So Steady had turned out just like *them*, had he, talking to him like that? Mam had always said that to him, too, like he didn't belong in her cottage. "I needed to talk to you."

"But we agreed to stay apart until all this shit is over. I got you the laptop, did my part of the deal, so that's the end of it."

"It's not, though, is it?"

"What are you on about?" Steady said.

Mason sighed. "Shut up a minute and let me see what's happening out there."

Plod at the cordon wrote in his notebook and kept glancing at Steady's place. It unnerved Mason. Why would the copper be doing that if Mason was just delivering cakes to Steady?

Shit. The cakes. He'd left them in the bloody bike basket.

Mason rushed out of the room and to the front door. Outside, he grabbed the bag and went back indoors, hoping that put the pig's suspicions to rest. "Here, these are for you." He thrust the bag into Steady's hands.

Steady stood there, staring down at it. "What's this, some kind of bribe on top of the money you owe me for the robbery?"

"What? You ought to be glad I bought them for you after what I've heard. Now be quiet." Mason returned to the window.

Plod had put his back to the cul-de-sac and stared ahead towards the woodland across the main road. It must have been the cake thing bothering him, then. Mason swerved his gaze across to Ortun's. A woman PC stood on the doorstep, and more police tape cut the bungalow and garden off from the rest of the street. A van had parked in front, the same as the one down by the marina, so people in white suits must be inside, working.

What did they think of the mess, the smell? The stench of fish permeated Ortun's home, and nothing had a place to be put away. Had they spotted the hot chocolate spill yet? The blood? Of course they would have.

Mason smiled. "What did the bloke copper say to you when you came back from mine earlier?"

"He wasn't there, it was just the woman at the door. She came over and checked my ID. Asked where I'd come from. I said I'd been to a visit a pal."

"Did she ask who that was?"

"Yep."

"Did you tell her?"

"Yep."

"And you didn't think to tell me so our stories matched?" *Was that so if they questioned me, I'd fuck up and they'd suspect me because of lying?* "What else did she ask?"

"She wanted to know what I was doing last night. I said I was at home watching telly, then went to bed, and after that she wanted to know if I'd heard or seen owt. I said no, and she went back to Ortun's door. It was fine, she didn't seem suspicious."

"Did you make sure you went to Mollengate avoiding any cameras?"

"Yes." Steady sounded weary. "We've been through all this. Stop panicking."

"When did the bloke copper come, then?"

"About half an hour after I got home from yours."

"What if he talks to the woman one. He asked me my name. She asked you who you'd been to visit. Why would I be dropping cakes round if I only just saw you earlier?"

"There wouldn't be a problem if you'd stuck to the plan and stayed away from here."

There wouldn't be a problem if I hadn't heard you work for Skipper. I wouldn't have needed to see you then.

Mason thought for a moment. Decided he wouldn't confront Steady now. He couldn't be doing with him getting funny, them coming to blows. If he left the place with a black eye, that policeman would notice. "Right. I'm going to go, but I'll be seeing you soon to discuss stuff."

"Mason, we said—"

"I know what we *said*." He swung round to face the man he'd once thought of as a friend. "But shit changed, people talked, and we need to have a little chat. Not with the police here, though."

"What about?"

"The *Poisson Mort*."

"What, you're going to kill Skipper on *there*?"

Mason wasn't about to let him know he'd got the wrong end of the stick. "I'll see you later."

He stormed out, switched his expression from angry to happy, and left number one. He rode his bicycle towards the cordon copper and belatedly realised he hadn't done the one thing most people would have — asked what was going on at Ortun's. He pulled the brakes and stopped in front of the cordon. It fluttered against the basket in the wind.

"What's happened?"

"Not something I can discuss, sir."

"Oh. Right. Is Ortun okay? Only, I went to the marina just before I came here to ask for a job, but he wasn't there."

"Know him well, do you?" The notebook came back out.

Shit. Why hadn't he just ridden away? "I used to work for him. Nice fella. A good mate of mine."

"When did you last see him?"

"Couple of nights ago down the Little Devil."

"Do you know of anyone who's got a grudge against him?"

"Blimey, no. Everyone likes him."

"Okay, thank you." Plod lifted the cordon with one hand and took his phone out with the other.

Mason rode beneath and parked on the pavement corner, doing up his coat to stall for time. The copper spoke to someone, telling them what Mason had said. Probably his boss.

". . . no, he seemed okay to me, nowt odd."

Mason smiled. Some people were so stupid.

CHAPTER TWELVE

Undisclosed Location

Butterfly wasn't enjoying today, which was a shame, because this, what they were doing now, was usually one of the highlights of the week. Scudderton had its fair share of gossipers, and some of them were at it now, their gums flapping, people discussing the new events so quickly, words tumbled out in jumbles from several mouths. Butterfly had seen the police at the pier, and a sense of doom had descended. Things weren't right, it was in the air, and their conscience had been pricked. Why, though? The police presence in the summer hadn't affected Butterfly, so why was it any different this time?

Because De León hadn't been here then. He'd docked in Spain for three months.

Things always seemed ominous when his yacht sat in the marina, the hulking white mass of it a constant reminder he was back. Butterfly hated seeing it gliding through the waves on its return journey, an ostentatious man aboard, standing at the prow as though he was that fella from *Titanic*, except there was no woman in front of him with her arms out wide, no jewel to be lost in the sea along with all those lives.

Butterfly wished De León would come a cropper like Jack in the film, sinking beneath the waves, never to be seen again. Butterfly associated De León with the night things had taken a turn for the worse, the one that had mapped out the rest of Butterfly's life. The days spent worrying until their guts twisted and vomit poured out, mainly at the beginning.

Over the years, the memory had faded for the most part, not so vivid, so in-your-face, although it *did* still visit every day, triggered not only by seeing certain people in town but small things: the smell of alcohol, the sound of heavy breathing or whimpers, the thud of the pavement beneath pounding feet, the thrill of the chase, the fear of being *seen* but doing it anyway.

They said life was sent to try us. Butterfly had sent themselves to trial in an imaginary court of law often, the guilty verdict ringing out every time, the gavel banging, sentencing them to a life in prison.

A prison of their own making.

CHAPTER THIRTEEN

The Pier

After a coffee and a visit to the loo in Buns 'n' Bread, then eating their sausage doorsteps in the car to get away from the chatty owner who'd wanted to know why the pier had closed, Carol and Dave stood on the path in front of the pier with Sergeant Richard Prince, who was in charge of the uniforms. Spots of rain fell, and Carol did her coat up, shivering from the wicked chill. Richard had a hi-vis on, his flat cap keeping his head dry. He was a lovely man, and Carol got on well with him.

"Got owt?" she asked.

"Nowt at all so far. It's the storm, see."

"I didn't think we'd be that lucky." She sighed. "Heard owt about what's going on at the top end?"

"June's gone home — Pitson took her. Rib went off with the body."

"Already? Todd usually likes to keep it in situ for longer."

"Todd reckons because of the weather fucking things up, plus Ortun being found in the water, there's nowt they can do on site. Leaving the body there serves no purpose. It's not like it is when we've got undergrowth and whatnot to sift through. The sea will have washed any evidence off the body. They've done all the swabbing and photos up there, so Todd's gone to Ortun's place, leaving SOCO to finish up here, but with it raining now . . . Lost cause, if you ask me."

"Suppose it makes sense. Do you know owt about Ortun and a Louise Roberts?"

Richard smiled. "If you're talking about the night Hattie went to the Little Devil, then yes, I know a thing or two. I was in there when it kicked off."

"Bloody hell. What did she do?"

"Punched Ortun in the face, spat on him and tried to kick seven bells out of Louise. People held her back. She was arrested, but Ortun and Louise refused to press charges. CPS didn't think it was worth processing. Hattie isn't exactly a danger to society, it was classed as a one-off domestic, and she hasn't been in trouble since, so the powers that be were right in a way. Would have been a waste of time and resources."

"Do you know Hattie well? We heard that pub's her preferred drinking spot even though she's moved."

"She's all right. She has a go if she fancies it, mind, a bit of the old verbal, but if you're on her good side, she's harmless."

"So you don't think she's in the frame for Ortun, then?"

Richard laughed. "I'd say it was highly unlikely, but you just don't know, do you?"

Carol brushed rain off her coat. "Bloody weather."

Richard rubbed his gloved hands. "Yep. The thunder kept me awake last night."

That reminded Carol. "I slept through it. A burglar nicked George Lamb's laptop from our block of flats, and neither of us heard a thing, did we, Dave?"

"Nope, although I heard him effing and jeffing well enough this morning." Dave stuffed his hands in his pockets and hunched his shoulders.

"Ah, the break-in Mulholland and Grebe went to." Richard paused. "That's interesting. Ortun's dead, his stepson got burgled . . ."

"The work laptop stolen," Carol added. "I assume that's something to do with Ortun's business."

Richard pondered that, his finger across his chin. "So the offender went to Ortun's to find it, couldn't, killed him, then went to George's to get it?"

"Possibly. So are we looking at Skipper and whoever else for this? I know you said you didn't think it was him or Callum, Dave, but who else would want Ortun's laptop?"

"Did you speak to Fred Collerton?" Richard asked. "Not that I'm saying it's him. He's the other major fisherman around here, although he sells his cod to the chippies in the Sandsend area, likely so he doesn't step on Skipper's and Ortun's toes."

"Just Skipper's toes now," Dave said.

"Shame," Richard said. "I liked Ortun. Fred doesn't bring in as much these days, not like he used to, but it keeps the wolf from the door and the chippies happy. He sails alone, doesn't bother with a crew anymore."

"No, we didn't speak to him. It didn't look like anyone else was aboard any of the boats other than Skipper's. No cabin lights or whatever."

Richard wiped rain off his face and turned his back to the sideways patter. "Fred lives on his, so he might have been below deck."

"So there's only the three of them we need to concentrate on, then," Carol mused. "Ortun, Skipper and this Fred?"

Richard nodded. "Everyone else, they don't bring in enough to be classed as competition, one of the big boys. Let me just get hold of the uniforms I sent to the marina and see if they've had a word with him yet."

He walked away to a bus shelter and stood beneath it, phone to his ear.

Carol stamped her feet, wishing she'd thought of going there to have this chat. "We should have checked who was on the other boats."

Dave shrugged. "It's not like they have a fucking doorbell, is it?"

"Fair point, and at least I got coppers down there."

"What's the problem? Are you worried about the DCI getting on your back?"

"Bugger. I ought to check in there. Give me a sec." She got in the car, passed on the details of the case, got told to get on with it, then returned to Dave's side. "He's a bundle of laughs today. Bit snappy."

"Oh dear."

Richard came back. "Fred didn't have a problem with Ortun, and nowt seems amiss with him. It doesn't surprise me. He's too old to be getting into spats with people. He just wants to fish and mind his own business."

"Skipper and Ortun are getting on a bit, though, and it didn't stop them bickering. Were any other people on their boats?"

"No, all shut up, except Senor De León's. It was left open, the deck light on. He wasn't on board. Had a party on his yacht last night, according to Fred. Maybe he forgot to lock it, although his wallet was in his bedroom, no phone, so I've got uniform looking into that."

"Bit odd, to leave your wallet behind when the door's unlocked," Dave said.

Richard frowned. "Hmm. We'll see what comes of it."

"Okay," Carol said. "We're heading back to have a catch-up with Michael and Katherine now, seeing as no one knows where Hattie is or which houses she's actually cleaning today. We'll go to her place later on our way home, then pop in on George."

Richard nodded. "See you when I see you, then."

Carol waved and walked to the car with Dave. She looked forward to a coffee, a wee and ignoring the paperwork on her desk.

Plus trying to work out who the hell had killed Ortun Bevan.

* * *

8 Slinghook Way

Hattie Lamb danced to the music blasting out of her AirPods, her phone in her pink tabard pocket. Alicia Keys sang about "no one", and Hattie competed with her in the best voice stakes. She swiped her orange microfibre cloth over the high-polished walnut sideboard and wished she lived in a big house like this instead of her poky home. She shouldn't complain, not really. Hers was still classed as a new-build, only two years old, and apart from some weird things going on with the walls when she'd first moved in, the plaster sweating or something, she had a nice place. Better than Ortun's shithole bungalow anyway.

She grimaced and switched to the curio cabinet, the job she hated most while here. Too many knick-knacks with deep crevices. She had to use a yellow duster and that cream for silver to get them shiny. Mrs Bamford-Fox insisted on it being done, even though Hattie's boss didn't consider it part of the job. A deep clean didn't mean touching personal possessions, it meant doing the skirting boards, the doorframes, all that sort of thing.

Her grimace didn't fade as she picked up a silver mountain goat that had lines carved into it to give the impression of a shaggy coat. Sighing, she took a cotton bud out of her tabard pocket and dipped it in the cream, getting to work on the ornament.

The real reason for her scrunching up her face was thinking about Ortun's place, which in turn had her thinking about the man himself. What a loser. She'd been nice to him during their marriage, had thought he was a good man, seeing as he'd taken George on. Not many men would do that, and even though George had been fifteen at the time, Ortun had still treated him as his. But he'd turned out like George's dad in the end, poking his chipolata in another woman, that bloody Louise Roberts, Hattie the last one to know. What had she done wrong for men to treat her that way? She put out enough, she *liked* sex, for God's sake, and she'd cooked and cleaned for them, so what was it? Even Callum was being cagey about seeing her. She didn't want people knowing about them yet, but still.

She joined in on the next song, Gloria Estefan unable to stay away from whoever "you" was. Well, that didn't apply to Hattie. She could stay away from Ortun Bevan no problem, the shitty bastard. She'd even changed her name back to match George's after the divorce. Some had said it was weird, taking on her first husband's name again, but they could think what they liked. What did she care?

She was about to place the goat back in the cabinet when a hard prod on her back had her spinning round, the goat going flying. It landed on the sofa, bounced, then came to rest, hoofs up. The cotton bud sailed to the floor. Hattie stared at Mrs Bamford-Fox, whose face was bright red, her mouth stitched up in a pout.

"Oh God, you frightened me to death!" Hattie must have said that too loudly, going by Mrs Bamford-Fox's wince, so she removed her AirPods and stuffed them in her pocket, taking her phone out to turn off Spotify. "What are you doing back? I thought you were staying out until I'd finished." She slipped her phone away.

"I bet you did." Mrs Bamford-Fox's eyes turned cold. "I returned early because I want a word with you about something that's gone missing."

Hattie *hated* this part of the job. Whenever a client misplaced something, the cleaner always got the blame. This was why she'd taken out extra insurance as well as being covered by Constant Cleaning. "What have you lost?"

"Lost?" the woman spluttered. "It was *stolen*."

That got Hattie's back right up. She was no thief. "*Excuse* me?"

"My diamond necklace. I left you in charge of cleaning my jewellery last week, and now it's gone."

Hattie wasn't supposed to clean jewellery either, but if a client asked her and offered to pay a few bob extra on top, off the books, she agreed. Now she wished she hadn't. The jewellery box had a padlock on it, so there was no way she could steal anything from it unless Mrs Bamford-Fox had unlocked it.

Hattie stood to her full height, pride inflating her. She wouldn't allow this baggage to put a dent in it. "It was there when I left, you checked every piece with me before I went home."

Mrs Bamford-Fox's face fell. "Well, you must have taken it when I went to answer the door. I recall I didn't lock the box until after that dreadful man had gone. I left you in the bedroom with it."

"Err, I followed you out and went to the door with you."

"So you say . . . I don't remember that, so you must be lying. That necklace was left to me by my grandmother, a one-of-a-kind piece, and I'm devastated. I want it back."

"But I don't *have* it."

Mrs Bamford-Fox gasped in the way only snobs could. "You've sold it on already?"

"No! I didn't have it in the first fucking place."

That gasp again, sharper this time. "*Don't* you swear at me. Apologise."

Hattie wasn't prepared to say sorry. She'd never stolen a thing in her life, and to be accused of theft stung. "I'm going to leave now and let my boss know what you've said. I won't be coming back. You can clear up your own mess."

"No, you must stay and let the police know what you've done with my necklace."

Hattie folded her arms. Tapped her bare foot. "Fine by me."

"Oh, the brazenness of you. I suspect you're going to lie to them and flutter your eyelashes, get them to let you off. Well, it won't do. I want you investigated."

Anger pierced the hurt. "D'you know what, fuck off, lady. I'm not sticking around. If the police want me, you know my address."

Hattie grabbed hold of her cleaning trolley handle and pushed it out into the large hallway, the floor gleaming at the sides from where she'd polished it but ruined down the middle where Mrs Bamford-Fox had just come in with wet shoes on, not bothering to take them off like she expected guests and Hattie to. Hattie hoped the woman had got her cream carpet dirty in the living room and had to get down on her hands and knees to scrub it off herself. She was *never* coming back here.

She stabbed her feet into her shoes, flung the front door open and grabbed the steel poles of her trolley to lift it over the doorstep.

Mrs Bamford-Fox came scurrying along, flapping her hands, shouting, "I want to check that *and* all your pockets before you disappear on me. God knows what else you've pilfered."

Hattie ignored her and shoved her trolley across the red-bricked driveway towards her car. She'd been planning to tell the woman she'd spotted a broken window in her "mudroom" as Bamford-Fox liked to call it, but she could go and fuck herself now. Let someone reach in and unlock the door, batter the old bag in her bed, Hattie didn't care. Someone else must have got in that way, taken the necklace. Could have had a pick for the padlock on the jewellery box.

She hefted her trolley into the back seat and put the safety belt around it. She straightened and shut the door, about to get in the driver's side, when her stomach rolled over.

A police car crawled onto the driveway, blocking her exit.

"Oh, this is just fucking *wonderful* . . ."

* * *

The Incident Room

Carol had asked Joy on the front desk to be a dear and keep trying Hattie's number so Michael or Katherine could get on with other things. Now in the incident room, half an hour after arriving (she'd nipped to the loo then her office and done minimal paperwork in the end), she sat at the spare desk and stared up at the whiteboard. Michael had written a few things down, and she'd filled in what she and Dave had found out.

She told them about their morning interviews and that Nerys Bevan had been murdered as a child. "Am I mad thinking it could be connected to her brother's death?"

"Not mad, no," Katherine said. "If her killer hasn't been found — and they're likely local if they know about Scud Stream — then what's to say Ortun found out who it was and went to confront the killer? Some families keep searching, don't they, even when the case goes cold, and they often come up with answers the police couldn't get."

Carol felt better about it now someone else was on the same page. "But why was the laptop taken? What would be on there that someone would want?"

"Fishing spots and the like?" Michael offered.

Dave shook his head. "They all know where each other goes, I bet. They nag down the Little Devil of an evening. People listen, pass the info on. We'll ask George later."

"Can you try to find out as much as you can about Nerys's murder for me, Katherine," Carol asked. "I know it was years ago, but you never know, something might crop up."

"Will do."

Carol got up and read the board again. "So, we have all these names, and many of them might not even be relevant. Louise Roberts, Hattie Lamb . . . are they cluttering up the case, sending us down the wrong track? The affair business, if you can even call a quick bunk-up an affair, may not be related to this case at all. We could be barking up the wrong bloody tree and wasting time."

"I'd say it's more along the lines of the fishing, the cod," Dave said, "but I just can't see Skipper doing it. With his dicky heart and wanting to step back from any altercations . . ."

"Unless he's just saying that," Carol said. "We don't know if he even *has* a dicky heart, he could have bullshitted us to throw us off the scent."

"True." Dave leaned back and swivelled. "So until we talk to Hattie and see what's really what with the . . . dalliance, shall we say, we've nowt much to go on. Then there's Louise to speak to, if you want to go down that route."

"We should really. Tie up owt outstanding." Carol added a few bits and bobs to the board. "Right, let's recap what we know. Ortun Bevan was likely struck at his home in the bathroom. Blood at the scene, a castoff arc from the weapon. He was taken to the pier — we assume he wasn't carted anywhere else before that. No one in Fisherman's Rest heard or saw a thing." She paused. "Michael, I'll come back to your grandad in a minute. So, because of the storm washing evidence away, we have no clue whether Ortun was dragged up the pier, although he has bruising on his ankles which suggests heavy manhandling. Rib says it's unlikely he was dragged because of the absence of bruises, scrapes and whatever. There's no CCTV, so we're out of luck there. I see from the board a uniform checked footage in the high street — not one vehicle or person spotted from half nine onwards, which sounds unbelievable, but we all know what happens when it storms here like it did last night, and it's not weather to be out in. We suppose everyone stayed at home, yes?"

She paced in front of the board. "So, whoever it was avoided the cameras, either knowing where they are or they got lucky — not that we have much CCTV here anyroad. They tied Ortun up then put him in the sea. Walked away. But did they go home? They could have gone on to Mollengate and stolen the laptop." A creepy feeling tickled her spine. "D'you know, Dave, I actually feel sick now I think about it. We were asleep, clueless, and as for George being at home when it happened . . ."

Michael, a fan of devil's advocate, said, "But what if he *wasn't* home."

Carol stopped pacing. "It's plausible. Although he told me he was, and his face looked like he'd been asleep, but he could have come home early doors, put his pyjamas on, had a screeching fit and woke Dave up, then went out the back to smoke while he worked out what to do next."

Michael nodded. "He could have got rid of the laptop himself so we wouldn't suspect he'd killed Ortun."

Carol smiled at Dave. "See why I said coming here and chatting is always a good idea? Okay, Michael, what else stands out for you?"

"It doesn't fit. None of it. I checked with uniform. No sign of forced entry at George's, and the patio door was left unlocked, so . . . either he *did* stage a burglary or whoever it was used a pick and happened to leave the door unsecure when they left."

"I'm getting sick of those picks being freely available," Carol said. "I saw one on my feed the other day, advertised as a tool 'in case you get locked out of your home'. Give me a fucking break. Criminals all over will be buying them." She took a deep breath, refusing to get on her soapbox. "Let's say George killed Ortun." She tapped the board. "You've discovered George owns a car. Any sightings of it, or am I asking too much?"

"Nowt so far," Michael said. "The uniform is still on it."

"Okay, let me think for a second."

"Before you think too hard," Michael said, "I checked with the uniforms who went to the Little Devil, and Callum was there and left about eleven. The landlord offered that information, he didn't need to be asked."

"Okay, so we can scrub Callum off the list if Ortun was killed before eleven."

Katherine's desk phone rang and she picked it up. Everyone remained silent while she spoke, and Carol pondered whether to go out to George now or wait until she'd spoken to Hattie. She supposed, what with the divorce, that it didn't matter now which one of the Lambs she informed first about the death. Both had been Ortun's family, and by the sound of it, Hattie didn't want to know her ex, but Ortun had still cared enough for George to keep him on at work on the *Nerys Angel.* Would the young man be the best bet, the closest person to Ortun these days? She'd have to ask George later if he had a grudge against the deceased. Some people wouldn't take too kindly to finding out their mother had been cheated on. Plus, if Hattie was volatile, it would be an easier route for Carol if he passed the news on to his mother.

And another thing. George hadn't gone to work because of the break-in. Had he bothered phoning anyone to let them know? And where were the other crew members of the *Nerys Angel*? Had they turned up for work and just gone home? Maybe Ortun's call log would reveal messages from his employees.

She wrote a note on the board and circled it: *Find out who Ortun's employees are.*

Katherine placed the phone in its dock. "Um, that was Joy. She said there's been a callout to a Mrs Bamford-Fox, Slinghook Way. Accusation of theft. Hattie Lamb is there."

Carol nodded. "That's made the decision for me, then, because I was just wondering what to do regarding her. Michael, I'll catch up with you about what your grandad said later, but get this done." She prodded her finger at what she'd just written. "I know I've given you a shitload of work to do already, but find and speak to these people."

"Will do."

She smiled. "Dave, let's go."

CHAPTER FOURTEEN

The Cellar

In the dark, Mason sat in the corner on Mam's yellow wing-back chair, rubbing his hands over the velvet arms, listening to Eamon breathing. It was laboured, a stuttering of rapid inhalations and exhalations, the sound of a man taken down a peg or two. A man who'd likely thought he was untouchable. The prat knew Mason had come down here — Mason had made enough noise on purpose, although he hadn't spoken to him yet, but Eamon had released a grunt of acknowledgement.

Baby steps.

A while had passed. The silence on Mason's part would be unsettling now, stretching Eamon's nerves. Was he frightened yet? In the old man's shoes, Mason would have been shitting bricks hours ago, at the point he'd been whacked on the head at the marina, but *this* Eamon wasn't quite back to being old Eamon yet, he still held the air of Senor De León about him, the bold, brash entrepreneur, someone who shouldn't be trifled with, the type who said stuff like: *Don't you know who I am!* God, Mason hated him for that, his well-to-do superiority. Eamon had had sixty years to perfect his image, going away a thirteen-year-old northern boy and coming back an exotic young man, someone completely different, so it might take a while to break him down again.

Mason would soon knock it out of him, that arrogance. He'd eventually see the real man beneath the carefully crafted veneer, layer upon layer that hid who Eamon really was at his core. Everyone had a breaking point, didn't they, and he'd find Eamon's. It was only a matter of time.

After he'd left Steady's earlier, he'd headed to the pier on his bike. Police were still hanging around, one fella in particular standing out. He'd been at the cordon in his hi-vis jacket, stamping his feet to keep warm, slapping his gloved palms together. Mason had been tempted to stop and ask questions, playing the nosy resident, but in the end had ridden past, just some fifty-two-year-old on an ancient bike, no one to take any notice of. He'd veered off then went down the Backstreet, turning right into town and making his way to Buns 'n' Bread to buy more cakes, the owner querying if he was a greedy guts today because he'd already been in for a Chelsea bun, a lemon slice and a couple of chocolate éclairs. He hadn't liked that, her noticing, commenting on it, *remembering* his order, for fuck's sake, staring at him with her beady little starling eyes. He'd had the urge to tell her to mind her own fucking business, but that would have brought more attention. Instead, he'd laughed and brushed it off by saying yeah, he was greedy, and her cakes were so nice his belly wanted more.

He hoped she didn't become an issue.

He sighed and stared to his right where his gym equipment stood, black shapes in the darkness. He should have a run on the treadmill really, but no, exercise could be put on the back burner today. He preferred to remain silent, Eamon wondering what he was about to do. Waiting. Anticipating.

Mason chuckled.

This prick could be his *father*. Mason was sure he was. The DNA website boasted the results were sent within *three business days or less!!!!!*, five exclamation marks at the end as if that meant their claim was genuine and amazing. He didn't mind keeping Eamon cuffed down here for that length of time. It was nice having someone else in the cottage anyway, another presence, no matter that he'd always had an aversion to the pretend-Spanish wally. Any companion, whether Mason disliked them or not, was better than being alone.

Eamon coughed, and Mason supposed the bloke was thirsty, going by the sound of the dryness. He'd better let him have some water if he wanted him lucid enough to talk. Couldn't have him going delirious without it, could he? Food could come later, maybe one of those instant pots of porridge you just added water to. A couple of days' worth of starvation wouldn't hurt, though. With enough hunger pangs, Eamon might well be inclined to talk. Mason reckoned Eamon must have been dreaming of filet mignon and all the other posh food people like him ate, the hunger pains getting worse.

Well funny.

Mason got up and switched his big torch on. Pointed the beam at the plastic-wrapped package of water bottles he kept down here for when he exercised. He dug his thumb into the casing, the *pop* loud, and ripped, taking one out, the plastic creaking with his tug. He snatched up the bakery bag. A quick walk down an aisle he'd created between the boxes of his mother's things stacked high in the other half of the cellar, and he came out at the bit of space Eamon occupied at the back. He flashed the torch low in the man's direction. Wet trousers. So he'd pissed himself. Mason had wondered this morning how long the dickhead could hold his bladder. Eamon lounged on the concrete as though his bones had melted, and he squinted at the brightness, his wrinkly face scrunching.

Mason sniffed. *He stinks.* "I've been nice and brought you a drink."

He placed the torch on a low box so it lit up the area, the bag beside it, Buns 'n' Bread in swirly red font with a hand-drawn picture of the bakery beneath. Eamon looked that way and licked his cracked lips. Did he think he was getting a fucking cake? Bloody cheek.

Mason chortled, opened the bottle and stared at Eamon. "If you kick out at me, I'll hurt you. Might chop your knackers off, I don't know yet. But whatever I decide to do, you'll be screaming."

"I haven't got it in me to kick you," Eamon said, voice croaky.

Mason let out a full-on belly laugh. "What, you're not the sort of person to strike out? That's not what my mam said. She reckoned you hit people."

Eamon sucked in a sharp breath.

Did I touch a nerve?

"No answer to that?" Mason shook his head. "You hit *her*, too. *If* you're my father, that is. I asked once, who he was, see? She was drunk — like, *really* drunk. It was the only time I could get stuff out of her, although she never told me his name. She said the man who didn't want to know me was frightening, he scared her, and she'd gone to live at the cottage when I was about three to keep out of the way. Weird, because working in a shop was hardly keeping out of the fucking way, was it? She never did make sense. So if you're him, you *are* the sort to strike out. Rephrase your answer."

"Fine. I haven't got any energy to argue or kick you, okay?" Eamon sighed as though Mason bored him, and he stared at the cake bag again.

Mason took a cinnamon bun out and bit a large chunk. He chewed. Cocked his head. Swallowed then ate some more. He studied the old boy and couldn't see any resemblance between them, but then again, the texture of Eamon's skin now had an affinity with raisins, and Mason didn't look like *that*. He didn't look like Mam either. Maybe his features were from someone else down the family line.

He wouldn't know, he'd never met any of them.

He finished the bun — Eamon had bent his head so he couldn't see what he wasn't allowed to have, and that was a bit annoying. Mason licked the icing off his finger and thumb and took a step forward. He put the bottle to Eamon's lips and tipped it. Could he smell the icing? The man drank greedily, and Mason smiled. *He* had the power here, not this wrinkly potato. For once in his life, he was the sole person in control. Not Mam, not Ortun, not anyone.

Eamon drank three quarters of the bottle straight down, and Mason stepped back, taking it away.

"That'll do for now. Can't be too generous, can I?" Lid screwed on, Mason set the bottle on the box beside the torch. "Do you fancy talking yet? Saying that, the DNA test is going to do all the talking for you. How will you feel when your dirty little secret gets out? Because I *will* be letting everyone know who you are to me. I don't care about who you *think* you are, who *they* think you are, they'll be finding out you're someone entirely different by the time I've finished with you. Loads of the codgers around here are aware of your old self anyroad, they just don't say so because they want to go to your yacht parties. They use you."

Eamon flinched. "It was a long time ago. We don't need to dredge up the past."

"*You* might not need to, but I do. It's not all about Senor De León anymore, pal. How do you think it feels, growing up not knowing who your father is? She never told me a name, so she was protecting you. Why?"

"I asked her to keep things to herself."

"Asked or demanded?"

"That's none of your business."

"What did it need to be kept quiet for?"

"I was getting ready to marry someone else when—" Eamon closed his eyes. Snapped his lips shut.

"Ah, just like I thought. You gave my mam a stuffing on the side. One last fling before married life. I'm a wrong-side-of-the-blanket kid, a baby to be hushed up because, back then, unmarried mothers were frowned on. God, the shit she must have been through. No wonder she turned to drink."

Mason was surprised at himself. He hadn't thought of things from Mam's perspective before. She'd have been an outcast, people ignoring her. Maybe that was why she'd bought the cottage, somewhere away from others so she didn't have to endure the filthy looks. That said, she'd gone to work, and she'd have had to speak to people and pretend they weren't thinking bad things about her. Mason had previously thought she'd put up with that because she'd needed the money, but things had changed with those bank statements. She needn't have gone to work *at all*. Why put herself through that?

She'd also told a story about her parents. Her mother, upon being told her daughter was pregnant, had a heart attack from shock and died. Her father had blamed Mam for it, casting her aside. Mam had said it wasn't so bad as she'd already moved into a flat before her announcement, but it had hurt being banned from the funeral. She'd gone anyway, standing at the back, then disappeared after the service. Where was Eamon during this time? Off on his fucking yacht?

"You're a bastard," Mason spat.

"Think what you like, child."

"Oh, I will, thanks. When I saw the bank statements . . . Do you know, she kept them all, going back years, except the older ones were little books, and she'd also written in a ledger. All your payments are there. I can show you, and you'll see how they went up with inflation, how the excessive amounts just . . . aren't . . . normal. You were giving her money long before I was born — you paid her from sixty-seven. Now then, I've had a lot of time to work this out, and when the payments went up in nineteen seventy, well, that was extra because I'd been born. So why did you stump up cash *before* that? What *else* did she have to keep quiet about?"

"You may as well stop wasting your breath, because I'll never tell you."

You will. "I mean, that was a lot of money. I can see how you afforded it. Look at your business, how much you make. Even back then you were loaded, but it seems a bit too *much* money, know what I mean? *Silence* money."

"You can do whatever you like to me, I won't talk about the time before I came back from Spain."

"The wife. Did she know about me?"

"Why would I tell her about some smelly child of no significance?"

That hurt. "Let me tell you something. Mam's friend in the care home — I've been doing a bit of private eye work, see — she said that's when my mother started drinking heavily, when you came back. She drank while she was pregnant, too. What the fuck could be so awful to drive a woman to not only risk her unborn baby's health by chugging on vodka, to then go on and drink throughout that kid's childhood, his adulthood, and treat him like shit? And you were always there, on the sidelines, doing fuck all about it except flinging cash at her. She was cruel to me, and you could have saved me from a life of hell. She said she'd called me Mason for a reason, called me 'the Jar' for a reason, and I want to know what it is."

Eamon cringed.

"You know something about that, don't you?" Mason asked.

"Go away."

Mason smiled. "Oh, I'll go away all right, because the sight of you, the *stench* of you, is making me sick — who's smelly now, eh? You, not me. But I *will* be back."

He took another bun out of the bag and wafted it beneath Eamon's nose.

"Smell good, does it?"

He grabbed the torch, the water, the bag, and strode off down the aisle, leaving Eamon to stew in the darkness.

CHAPTER FIFTEEN

5 Herald Way

Fiona stared at the policeman who stood in the living room on Mam's rag rug. It was Sunday, the day after Nerys's murder, and Fiona hadn't slept much, tossing and turning, seeing that blood in her dreams, the bruises, that horrible swollen eye, Eamon's hands around Nerys's throat, then Nerys in the stream. She'd seen it all in her head while she was awake, too, this morning at breakfast. Her guts constantly churned, her heart rate too fast each time she remembered. She was petrified the policeman had come to take her away. What would he do, tell her to pack a bag, say goodbye to Mam, then cart her off? Earlier, as Fiona had picked at her oats, Mam had asked if she was all right, and Fiona had said yes, but she wasn't. How could *she be after what had happened?*

What if he asked to see what Fiona had been wearing yesterday? The story about the ice lolly dripping had worked on Mam, but a policeman, he'd know the difference between strawberry lolly dribbles and blood, wouldn't he? And what if he searched the house?

He'd find the sandal.

"We're talking to everyone who's in Nerys's class, plus any other friends she has," the officer said. "Were you out yesterday?" He peered at her with all-seeing eyes.

Fiona, sitting on the armchair, nodded. "Me and Eamon went to the park."

He addressed his notebook. "Ah yes, he did say. We've spoken to him already, plus others who were there, and they said you arrived at the park at lunchtime, is that right?"

"No! They're lying because we were there in the morning. All day!"

"What time did you get there?"

"I don't remember, but it wasn't long after Eamon called for me. Early, it was."

"I wonder why they thought you weren't there until later, then," Mam said.

Fiona wished she'd shut up. She couldn't think straight. A lie landed in her head, but what if it didn't match what Eamon had said? "We went into the spinney behind the park for a bit. It was getting too hot, and we sat under one of the trees for shade. Maybe those people thought we'd only just arrived when we came out."

"That makes sense," the policeman said, "because they themselves got there at one o'clock. That's settled that, then. Did you happen to see Nerys at all?"

Oh God, what if Eamon had said they'd bumped into her or something? Why hadn't they got their stories straighter? She wasn't quite sure what to say so went with: "I don't remember seeing her." That would be okay, wouldn't it? It covered her if Eamon had said they'd seen Nerys. The police couldn't arrest her for not recalling it, could they?

Mr Copper hmmed. "That's what Eamon told me."

Fiona slumped in relief, and Mam gave her a funny look. God, did she suspect something?

"When was the last time you saw her?" he asked.

Fiona shrugged. "At school probably. Friday?"

"Are you good friends with her?"

Fiona shrugged again. "No. We don't go round together or owt. Her best friend is Ivy Stark."

Another nose at the notebook. "She's next on my list. So if you're not really friendly with Nerys, would you even know where she's likely to have gone?"

"No. She wouldn't tell me owt like that. What's happened?"

Mr Copper stared at her, grave as anything. "She's gone missing."

Missing. They didn't know she was dead.

"Okay, thanks very much for your help, duck." He smiled and put his notebook away.

"Is there owt I can do to help?" Mam said. "Her parents must be going out of their minds."

"Just keep an eye out."

"What do you know so far?" Mam wrung her hands.

"Vic Bevan called in last night, ten o'clock, when Nerys hadn't come home. A neighbour had seen her leave the house mid-morning, and just so you know, should you see anyone of this description, she had on pink shorts, a T-shirt and white sandals. She walked in the direction of the parade of shops at the end of her street — the one with the sweet shop around the corner here. According to the shopkeeper, she bought a mix-up bag of sweets, and when she left, someone else watched her go down a nearby alley, heading towards the main road. After that, no sightings so far."

"The main road?" Mam parroted. "Do you think she was hitchhiking?"

"We're looking into that."

Fiona wanted to be sick. She got up, calm outside, scared to death inside, and walked upstairs. On her knees, she pulled an old scratched school satchel from under her bed and fumbled with the buckle, her fingers turning into sausages. She opened the flap. Stared at the white sandal inside. She should get rid of it somewhere, but how could she when the police were looking for Nerys and someone might see Fiona put it in a public bin? And she'd have to wipe it first to get rid of her fingerprints. She shoved the satchel back into its hiding place and sat on her bed, waiting for the sound of the front door closing. She shot to the window, standing behind the curtain. The policeman strutted to the end of the street where Ivy lived and knocked on the door. Mrs Stark answered, and they talked for a moment, then he went inside.

Fiona's worry heightened. What if Ivy knew Nerys was going to the moors? What if someone had seen Fiona and Eamon going there?

Tears burning, her stomach rolling again, she rushed downstairs, tripping on the last step. She slipped her feet into her shoes — they were still damp from the stream — and wrenched open the front door.

"Going out to play, Mam!"

She left, walking slowly past Ivy's in case that copper watched through a window. If she ran like she wanted to, it'd look bad, like she was going to see her accomplice to talk about their secret. At the end of the street, she turned the corner and raced to Eamon's, banging on his door, sweating, breath short, her fear levels rising even more. He appeared from around the side of the house, and she jumped, screeching in shock.

"Bloody hell," she whispered. "You scared me."

"Act odd and people will wonder why, so stop it." He beckoned for her to follow him, walking down the alley as though nothing bothered him.

In the back garden, they sat on a tyre swing each, and Fiona rested her nose on the rope and stared through the kitchen window at his mam. She stood at the sink peeling spuds for Sunday dinner, Joaquín chopping them on the draining board beside her. Fiona had a clear view through the patio doors into the dining room. Packing boxes.

"The police came," she whispered.

"What did you say?"

"That I was with you at the park and I don't really know Nerys. Wouldn't know where she'd have gone. They just think she's missing."

"Hmm."

"What will happen when days go by and she isn't back?"

He shrugged. "They'll probably have a good look around, see if they can find her."

"They might be doing that already. Mam went and mentioned hitchhiking on the main road, and the copper said they're looking into it. They could go there, decide to check the moors, find her at the stream."

"So? They'll think some bloke did it. They're not going to suspect kids, are they? Anyroad, we were at the park, and that's the story we'll stick to."

Her eyes crossed from staring so hard at the knife in Joaquín's hand. Sunlight glinted off the blade. "You only have to stick to it for a bit longer. You're off to Spain on Tuesday. I'll be left here with it all."

"I can't help that. It's not like I can stay, is it?"

She swallowed the lump in her throat. "I don't like this — someone said we didn't go to the park until lunchtime. Who could that have been?"

"I know they did. The copper said it was Butterfly."

"Might have known, the little tattler."

"Listen, I don't like this either, but we just have to get on with it. As for Butterfly, don't fret about it. I said it was a mistake. What about you?"

Tears threatened again. "I said we went into the spinney for a bit." She thought about the places they'd walked that day. "What if someone saw us?"

"What, in the spinney? So what if they did?" He laughed.

"No, when we . . ."

"I doubt it. No cars went past when we carried her, remember."

Frustration bubbled inside her. "I mean before that, when we were on our way to the moors, and afterwards."

"Did you *see anyone out there?"*

"No."

"Well then, they wouldn't have seen you either."

"They could have, through their windows when we walked past."

"Stop it now. You're worrying over nowt."

On Tuesday, she didn't go and stand in Eamon's street with everyone else to wave and say goodbye to him. She couldn't bear to see his face anymore, to hear him talk as if what they'd done didn't matter. It did matter, it was all she could think about, and when he flew out of her life, she was relieved. Now she only had her own story to worry about, not his.

A week after that, the body was discovered.

CHAPTER SIXTEEN

8 Slinghook Way

It wasn't going well, and Carol had the urge to scream. While she was glad they'd found Hattie Lamb, she didn't need the shit coming from the woman's mouth. Mrs Bamford-Fox wasn't behaving much better, although she'd finished screeching after Dave had suggested she hold her horses and calm down. The uniforms in attendance stood by Hattie's car, their bemused expressions showing they were glad Carol was dealing with Mrs Bamford-Fox instead of them. What they weren't aware of was that she was only willing to listen to this drivel for a while longer, then she was leaving with Hattie, and they *would* be left to deal with the insufferable old woman.

"And she said I fucking *stole* it!" Blonde Hattie, small and skinny, stalked back and forth in front of Mrs Bamford-Fox's open door, which revealed a foyer that was bigger than Carol's living room.

How the other half lived.

"Do you have proof?" Carol asked the Fox woman.

"I don't need it. She was the only one here when I last opened the jewellery box, and I didn't open it again until three days later when I was off out to a charity bash. I've written the dates down." She held out a piece of posh, blush-pink notepaper.

Dave took it and gave it the once-over. "So, Hattie, you were here this time last week, and that's when you were asked to clean the jewellery."

"Yes. I'd just finished when someone rang the doorbell, and I went with *her* to see who it was. I didn't want to be left with the jewels because of this exact reason. There was a bloke selling dishcloths and whatever, said he'd just got out of prison, and *she* was nasty to him, told him to get off her property like he was scum. His badge had Barney on it and the name of a company. Better Way Forward or something like that, so you can trace him, ask him if I was with her when she opened the door."

Carol glanced at the uniforms. "Can you call in about that, please?"

One of them walked off towards the end of the driveway, his phone out.

"Well, it slipped my mind," Mrs Bamford-Fox said, "when we went back inside."

"What did?" Carol asked, confused by the woman's train of thought.

"That I forgot to lock the box, so whether she came to the door or not, she still could have pinched my necklace." She pointed at Hattie. "*You* went to the toilet upstairs, so you *said*, but I know better. *That's* when you stole it."

They'd been through this bit already, so Carol butted in, tired of the snarky back-and-forth rubbish. "When you went to lock the box after Hattie left, did you check inside it beforehand to ensure everything was present?"

Mrs Bamford-Fox bristled, and her cheeks took on a red stain, enhancing her orange blusher. "So what if I didn't? Who else could have taken the necklace? I didn't have anyone here last week other than Hattie, and I wouldn't pilfer my own things."

Not even to get an insurance payout?

Hattie snorted. "Let's consider this, then, shall we? The window in her mudroom has been smashed. I saw it earlier when I walked past the open door, or do you want to blame me for that an' all, Foxy?"

"Good grief, do *not* shorten my surname, you horrible little woman."

"Oh, d'you know what, just fuck off." Hattie turned her back and folded her arms.

Carol sighed and spoke to the other uniform. "Can you go and have a look, please?"

He went to go inside, but Mrs Bamford-Fox flapped a hand.

"Don't go through the house, it's a *crime* scene," Bamford-Fox said. "Go around the side there. The window is beside a door." She waited for him to disappear. "You'll see, she'll have smashed it to cover her thieving tracks."

Hattie laughed, her shoulders jumping, and she turned to face them. "If this is what having money turns you into, I'm fucking glad I'm just about getting by. It's disgusting the way she talks to people. She thinks she's a cut above, but she *married* into money, she wasn't born to it. Christ, she comes from one of the rough estates. Airs and graces, they do my head in."

The officer came back. "The pattern of broken glass indicates it was smashed from the outside."

Carol couldn't see Hattie traipsing down there to smash the window from outside, giving herself an alibi, especially with CCTV cameras in strategic places on the house. It was clear the woman hadn't taken the bloody necklace, and she wasn't stupid enough to do it with an electronic eye watching her. "Okay, Mrs Bamford-Fox, if you could go inside now, and PC Fisher will have a chat with you to see if you can recall hearing any glass breaking. He'll log this meeting and see what can be done. If you don't mind, he could have a look in your bedroom and elsewhere. The necklace could have fallen behind furniture perhaps. Also, show him your camera footage."

"Fallen? What a load of tosh. And she's the type to put on a disguise, so the CCTV won't be any good. What about *her*?" Mrs Bamford-Fox jerked a thumb at Hattie.

"Oh, we'll take care of Ms Lamb, don't you worry."

Fisher followed the older woman inside, closing the door. Carol let out a long breath, Hattie shook her head, and Dave chuckled.

"What an old bat." Hattie twirled her car keys around her finger. "Can I go now? I've got other cleaning jobs to get to."

Carol rubbed her temple. "I'd like to say yes, but we've been looking for you anyroad. Not about this, it's something else. Would you mind if we go to yours and have a chat?"

"Shit, what's wrong?" Hattie paled.

"Best if we speak in private. We'll follow you there, okay? You're not in any trouble." *Not that I know of.*

Hattie eyed them funny.

Carol went to the officer at the end of the drive. "Can you move your vehicle, please? Thanks."

He nodded. "Joy's looking into Better Way Forward and Barney."

"Brilliant."

She tapped her foot while he reversed, then she walked out with Dave onto the pavement, and they got into her car.

"Let's hope she goes straight home," Dave said as Hattie drove out and headed up the street.

"Why, don't you fancy screeching after her with the blues and twos on?"

"No, I've had enough excitement for one day. That Bamford-Fox woman almost finished me off."

Carol hid her smile.

* * *

12 Royal Gardens

"What?" Tears streamed down Hattie's flushed face. "*Dead?*"

"I can see it's a bit of a shock," Carol said. "Would you like me to make you a drink?"

Hattie nodded. "Tea, please. God, this is awful . . . I can't believe I won't see his ugly mug again."

Carol got up from the white kitchen table, filled the kettle and sorted the cups and whatnot. "How long were you married to him?"

"Years. He was okay for the most part but drove me mad with his hoarding. I kept tidying up, but more stuff appeared. It was like he couldn't let anything go, especially Nerys's things."

Carol understood that. She'd grown to detest her father, yet taking his possessions to the dump had scored a dent in her heart. He hadn't been the man she'd wanted or needed, the same went for him regarding her, and she'd had to accept him for who he was and convince herself it hadn't been her fault — his moods, his drinking, everything bad about him. Although it *was* her fault in a way. Innocent at the time, she hadn't realised what her words would have done, the ones she'd whispered to Mam, turning Carol into what he'd called a rat. Keeping his items had brought nothing but pain, although she got why Ortun hadn't thrown his sister's things out. His was a different story to hers, and the pain was for another reason.

"Are they in those boxes in the spare room at his place?" she asked.

Hattie nodded. "Old-fashioned clothes, even the ones she was killed in, which is gross. I mean, his dad persuaded the copper in charge at the time to hand them over once the case went cold. I thought they had to stay in an evidence locker or whatever, but what do I know? Maybe things were different back then. We're talking nineteen sixty-odd here."

"Some officers can have their arms twisted, unfortunately," Dave said.

"Well, whatever, it's grim to keep bloodstained clothing. When I lived there, he had a box in our *bedroom*. He used to get the things out and look at them, just sitting there on the end of the bed and crying. One sandal was missing, and that blood, it was brown. I know it must have been hard to get over it, they were twins, and they say it's like losing one half of yourself, but I told him it wasn't good for George to see him blubbing away like that, not to mention strange having that stuff so close to hand. A suitcase in the wardrobe, yeah,

I could have dealt with that, but a manky old cardboard box? I used to cover the top with a doily."

Although Katherine was checking into Nerys's murder, it didn't hurt to ask in the meantime.

"Do you know much about that incident?" Carol added sugar to the cups.

"Only that Nerys went out one day and didn't come back, then they found her in Scud Stream. I didn't live here at the time. I grew up in Robin Hood's Bay, moved here at the start of the eighties with my first husband, fat lot of good that did me. I remember it being in the newspapers, though. Ortun said he'd never stop looking for who did it."

Carol glanced at Dave: *Did the killer realise Ortun was getting too close to finding out the truth?*

Dave shrugged.

"So was he actively searching?" Carol said.

"More like bringing it up in the pub every chance he got and listening to what people had to say." Hattie tucked a strand of hair behind her ear. "He was waiting for someone to slip up. Now he'll never know who did it . . ."

Carol reckoned it was time to switch gears. "We heard about the Louise Roberts thing."

Hattie scoffed. "What, you don't think *she* killed Ortun, do you?"

"No, I'm just letting you know we're aware of the bad blood between you and him."

"Oh, so it's me, then, is it? Fuck me, what a day this is turning into. A thief and a killer all in the space of an hour. Owt else you want to lay on me? Maybe I did the graffiti on the pier yesterday an' all."

"Graffiti?" Dave asked.

"Yeah, someone wrote *Fucks Equal Death* on the side of the café."

Dave wrote that down.

No one else had mentioned that. Carol frowned, looking in the drawers for a teaspoon. "Was it cleaned off, then, because we didn't see it this morning?"

"Yeah, Militant June paid some kids to paint over it with rollers on poles."

"Militant June?" Dave chortled.

"Well, she prowls that pier like she owns it." Hattie sniffed. "You can't even eat an ice cream on there without her watching for the drips. She spouts on about keeping it clean, but come on, she's ridiculous."

I bet having a dead body on it didn't go down too well, but June didn't seem angry about it.

Carol poured boiled water over the teabags. "So graffiti and June aside, what are your thoughts on Ortun taking his own life?"

"No bloody way. He'd never do that."

"What about enemies? Did he have any?"

"Only me, but even though he did what he did, it doesn't warrant murder, does it? Okay, I've said a few times I could kill him, but I didn't *mean* it."

Carol squeezed the teabags and dumped them in the bin, enough time to create a stretch of silence so Dave could study Hattie's expression. "No, I understand why you'd have said it, and we've all muttered that phrase at some point. Can you tell me about your son, George?" She turned with two cups in her hands.

Hattie slapped a palm on the table. "Now don't you go saying it's him."

"Sorry, that wasn't what I meant." Carol placed the tea in front of Hattie then Dave. She stared at Dave for his take on things so far, and he shook his head: *I don't think it's her.* "I should have been clear. What I meant was, why would he have Ortun's laptop?"

"How do you know about that?"

Carol chose not to answer for now. "I understand he works on the *Nerys Angel*, but he'd be a fisherman, wouldn't he?" She collected her cup.

"He is, and he sorts the deliveries, which is why he had the lappy. He rang me last night and said about it. Wanted some advice. He was nosing through the list of customers to see where Ortun could expand. Skipper's muscling in more than ever these days, and poor old Fred's taken to selling up Sandsend. Ortun asked George to work out where else they could sell the fish."

"So George didn't usually have the laptop?" Carol asked.

"No, that was the first time he'd taken it home."

So whoever took it must have known he'd have it last night.

Had they listened to a conversation? Was it another member of the crew on the *Nerys Angel*? Carol glanced at the clock. Either Michael or Katherine would be speaking to them by now.

"What's your take on Callum Roberts?" Carol waited for the denial that Hattie had anything to do with him.

"The man I'm seeing, you mean? I expect you've heard about that on your travels. He's a nice enough bloke. Treats me better than either of the exes did, and no, I don't think he's capable of murder. He wasn't bothered by what Ortun did with Louise." She sighed. "And he was here last night, just gone eleven."

"Have you seen or spoken to George at all today?" Carol asked.

Hattie's eyebrows met in the middle, two vertical lines appearing between the overplucked hairs. "No, why?"

"He had a break-in during the night."

"What?" Hattie's face paled. "Why on earth didn't he say?"

My thoughts exactly. If Carol had a mother, she'd be the first person she'd phone. "They only stole Ortun's laptop, yet there must be other things they could have taken. A telly, for example."

"Fucking hell, is he all right?" She stood. "Where's my phone? I need to ring him. Jesus Christ."

Dave tapped the woman's wrist. "Sit. We're going to his next, and we'll take you with us. You can see for yourself he's fine. For the moment, calm down and drink your tea. He's okay, just . . . grumpy."

Hattie lowered into her seat. "He usually is."

Carol sipped some tea. Leaned back. "Any reason for that?"

Hattie shrugged and wrapped her hands around her cup. "Just his personality. You get sunny people, optimists, and arsey people, pessimists. That's George, always seeing the downside to everything. But he's a good lad."

So maybe his attitude towards me this morning is normal for him.

"You'll need to phone your boss," Carol said. "There's no way you can carry on working today — you've had three shocks in a row. If you need me to speak to them, I'll explain things. Let's drink our brews then go over to George's. Dave lives next door to him, and I'm in the flat above. Neither of us heard owt last night because of the storm. George slept though the burglary."

Hattie shuddered. "How effing creepy is *that*?"

Carol couldn't agree more.

* * *

Robottom Street — Mollengate

The uniformed officers had come and gone. Dust sat proudly on George's desk, and Carol had the urge to polish it off now she'd moved from skanky cow to clean freak. Instead, she remained standing in her spot in the Spartan living room, Dave to her left, Hattie and George on the corner sofa. Carol had already asked the basic questions about George's alibi, his feelings about Ortun, and any grudges he might have harboured regarding the dabble with Louise, but despite the man's short, sharp, sarcastic answers, she didn't think he'd kill anyone.

She was still on the fence about the so-called burglary.

He'd taken the news of Ortun's death badly, showing he had a soft side in there somewhere. Tears had come, and his bottom lip had trembled.

"He was like a dad to me," he said now. "Better than my own, anyroad. There's no way I'd have hurt him."

Could it be his father who went after Ortun? "Where is your dad?"

"Dead. Cancer got him. What did they . . . do to Ortun?"

Carol weighed up whether she should tell them anything. What if they spoke about it in public? She didn't want the killer knowing her thoughts. "Um, if you can promise to keep this to yourselves. We don't want news getting out just yet, although our boss will likely want to do a press conference if things don't get moving soon."

"*I'll* not be saying owt," Hattie said, indignant.

George swallowed. "Me neither. It'd seem wrong chatting shit about him, like we didn't care, when we do."

Carol moved to the window, the blinds open, affording her a view of the comings and goings. Liz, the manager of the Co-op, stood outside the shop chatting to a villager. Life went on no matter what.

"He was struck on the back of the head at his bungalow." She turned to face them. "We're not sure yet of the actual movements, but he ended up on the pier behind June's Chippy. He only had shorts on, we presume for bed."

"Not those bloody ugly Bermuda things?" Hattie said.

"That's right." Carol smiled sadly. Poor man. "He'd been tied with rope around his ankles, and the other ends were secured onto the struts of the railings. Some of those struts had been removed to create a gap." She took her phone out and selected the image of the knot she'd taken on the pier and held it out to them, thankfully without Ortun's foot on show, only the skin of the ankle. "Do either of you recognise this type of knot?"

George nodded. "We all use them."

"So it's something a fisherman would do," she queried.

"Yeah." George leaned back, fingers linked at the back of his neck. "So the hit on the head killed him?"

Carol put her mobile away. "We haven't established that yet either. We'll have to wait for the post-mortem results. He was found in the sea, facedown, still tethered to the struts."

Hattie yelped. "Oh my God, that's awful. So why tie him to the pier?"

George sighed. "Think about it, Mam. If they'd dumped him in the water alive, a knock on the head or not, you know Ortun, he'd have swum away, the stubborn bugger. Sounds to me like they wanted him close by, maybe so he'd be found. If he was drowned without the ropes, he'd have floated off, might not have washed up for days, and even then it might be farther down the coast."

Carol agreed with his assumption — or was it his true knowledge? *Was* George involved? Did he know exactly what had happened? Carol hated the way she did this, dismissing people as suspects one minute, putting them back in the frame the next, but that kind of talk was bound to prickle her.

"I take it that's conjecture on your part," she said to him.

He shot forward. "Of course it fucking is. Christ!"

"Moving on . . ." Dave said gruffly, sending George one of his glares.

Carol glanced outside again, giving the tension a chance to fizzle out. Liz had gone, replaced with Stanley, who usually worked the till at weekends. He puffed on a cigarette and blew the smoke upwards.

Maybe Liz has taken him on full-time instead of just weekends.

She swivelled around again. "We haven't got the results back yet from looking at Ortun's phone, but did you ring him this morning to tell him you wouldn't be going to work? I saw you in the garden around sevenish, and you'd surely have to be on the boat at, what, six?"

George flopped back again. "I got up about five. Didn't notice the laptop was missing until about half past, after I'd had my coffee. He'd sent me a message a bit after ten last night to say I needed to be at work an hour earlier than usual. I didn't reply, but yeah, I texted Ortun this morning and said I was ill. He didn't respond, obviously, but that's nothing unusual, so I didn't think owt of it. As far as I was concerned, he'd have already been out at sea."

"What were you doing between half five and when I saw you, then?" she asked.

"Stewing, worrying about the laptop being gone. Ortun didn't want anyone else to know what he was up to — you know, scouting for new places to sell — and last night I'd phoned around and spoken to a few chip shops and restaurants farther afield. They'd agreed to buy from him. One's well inland, and it'd mean me driving miles to deliver, but it was a good deal, and I wouldn't have minded. I was shitting myself in case whoever had stolen the laptop was another fisherman. Ortun would have brained me for that new information getting into the wrong hands."

Hattie picked at a fingernail. "God, what if that's true and Skipper or someone like that nicked it? Could someone have overheard you talking about it?"

Carol was glad she'd asked that question. It had been her next one.

George shook his head. "Nah, old Skipper's not desperate for sales — he bagged June as a customer, snatching her off Ortun. He's sorted in Scudderton now with the amount of fish she sells. Fred's cod goes to Sandsend. I can't see one of the smaller crews doing this, but then again, who knows?"

He didn't answer her about someone overhearing. "So you didn't discuss what you were doing in front of anyone?"

"Nope, not that I'm aware of."

It was a lot to think about — and a lot of people to talk to. Thankfully, uniform were dealing with the smaller crews.

"So let's go backwards a second," Carol said. "If you had to be at work an hour earlier, why weren't you up at four a.m. instead?"

George blushed. "I forgot to change my alarm, didn't I?"

This was about as far as they could go with George, but Carol planned to nip over to the Co-op. Liz was a nosy mare. Maybe she'd been awake last night and saw something, not to mention the landlord of the pub.

Who'd have thought it, sorting shit on her own doorstep? She shouldn't be surprised. She'd done it enough growing up with her father, dealing with irate people at the front door.

Some things never changed.

CHAPTER SEVENTEEN

The Little Devil

DC Michael King had phoned one of the men who worked on the *Nerys Angel*, and the bloke had told him they were all in the Little Devil for bevvies and a meal. Michael had left Katherine in the incident room flitting between Nerys Bevan's murder and looking into everyone living in Fisherman's Rest. He wished they had one more person on the team for big, busy cases like this, but the budget didn't allow it. Still, uniforms pitched in when they had to.

Michael sat at a table with three crew members: Ian Yates, Quentin Usher and Charlene Simms, all in their twenties.

"So, you have the day off, then," Michael said to see what they made of that.

Black-haired Ian nodded. He had a mole above his bottom lip some might consider a beauty mark. "Yep, Ortun got hold of us last night to say we needed to be an hour earlier at the marina and we were heading farther along the coast for a better catch, then he didn't bloody show up. The *Nerys Angel* was still docked, so he hadn't gone without us. We all rang him, but he didn't answer, then I tried George, that's his stepson — or ex-stepson, whatever. Anyroad, *he* didn't answer either."

Quentin, the blond younger brother of a woman Michael used to go to school with, rubbed his forehead. "Can't say I mind. It's nice having a day off. Even better with a pint in my hand."

The crew laughed and Michael smiled, although he didn't share their sentiments. He didn't enjoy having days off. He got bored and liked nothing better than being in the thick of things in the incident room.

"If you can just tell me where you all were last night." Michael got the response he'd anticipated. Frowns. Mouths dropping open. "It's standard procedure, nowt to worry about."

"Has something happened?" Charlene smoothed a fingertip over a well-plucked ginger eyebrow.

"There's been an incident, yes." Michael smiled tightly.

"On the pier," Ian stated. "We saw coppers, and people in here have been talking about everything being closed."

"Yes, there's activity down there," Michael replied. "So, where were you?"

Ian looked directly at him. "At my mam and dad's from six onwards. My sister and niece share a birthday, so there was a bit of a tea party."

"What time did you leave?"

"Eleven, something like that. I should have gone home earlier to be fair, what with the new time to start work, but Mam moaned it isn't often we all get together, so I stayed. God, the pressures of a parent." He grinned.

Michael wrote that information down, plus Ian's address when he supplied it.

Michael looked at Charlene. "And you?"

"I went to the gym about six, nipped to June's for a chippy tea, then went home and watched Netflix all night until about nine with my boyfriend, then we went to bed."

"And his name is?"

"That's me," Quentin said. "We live together."

"Did anyone else see either of you at your house?" Michael asked. *They could be giving one another an alibi.*

"Probably," Quentin said. "We never shut the living room curtains, so some bastard will have nosed in and seen us."

"What's your address?"

Charlene laughed. "Good luck speaking to our neighbours, if that's what you've got planned. Rough as a badger's arse, the lot of them."

Michael would send uniforms.

"Forty-eight Cove Avenue," Quentin said. "And while Char was at the gym, I was in the coffee shop there talking to a mate of mine. Joe Pitt, if you need to check. He lives in the new flats by Sainsbury's. Royal Gardens. Number fifteen."

That went down in the notebook.

Michael stared at them all in turn. None of them seemed agitated, as if they'd committed a crime recently. They were too relaxed, no micro-expressions to be seen, no legs bouncing or eyes skirting away to avoid him seeking out their secrets.

Should he tell them about Ortun? Just the basics? Carol had told him not to say anything about the death to his grandad, but this lot here were different, surely. They needed to know they might not have a job anymore.

He was undecided.

"Do you know of any plans Ortun has for retirement?" he asked. "Mainly what would happen to the *Nerys Angel.*"

Ian picked up his pint. "He's leaving it to George, although George doesn't know that. Ortun thinks he'll make a great skipper when the time comes."

Michael's skin prickled. Now *that* was something Carol needed to know.

He opted against telling them about the murder. They'd find out soon enough. Thanking them for their time and wishing them a good afternoon, he left the Little Devil, eager to tell Carol what he'd discovered.

CHAPTER EIGHTEEN

Undisclosed Location

Butterfly stared at their wet trousers. Warm piss soaked into the grey fabric, and shame flared on cheeks wet with tears. This was the ultimate humiliation, and it happened sometimes when they thought of the past. In recent months, guilt had brought on incontinence, and it was lucky they'd gone home when they had. Other people seeing this damp little accident would have resulted in a ribbing wicked enough to last a lifetime.

Butterfly couldn't shake the feeling that chickens were coming home to roost. It was a heavier sense than any time before, an ominous, cloying presence that had followed them since they'd spotted that big yacht drawing into dock yesterday. Why, though? Nothing had changed. Everything was the same as usual.

Maybe I really have got psychic powers.

It wasn't the first time Butterfly had thought that. Other people had commented on it, too. Times past, Butterfly had predicated many things, all of them coming true. Small stuff like: "They'll break their leg if they're not careful." A leg had broken. "That window's going to smash if he keeps swinging that bat the way he does." A week later, that exact thing had happened.

Butterfly had known, right from the night they'd first done what they had, things would come out into the open at some point, it was just a matter of when. A voice had whispered as Butterfly had run away that dreadful time: *"Karma will come for you later when you think you're safe."*

Safe wasn't on the cards.

I thought I was, but now . . .

Butterfly trembled. Maybe they should go and see a certain person, explain, omitting the true facts of what had occurred, have a chat about the result of their actions. It wouldn't go down too well with Butterfly's family, maybe not with the person in question either, but it had to be better than living on pins and needles, didn't it?

If I make up a story so what I did isn't viewed as evil but as a loving act, I could just about get away with it . . .

CHAPTER NINETEEN

Robottom Street

Carol's phone rang just at the point she was about to lead the way across the road, desperate for a wee after the tea they'd had at Hattie's. She stopped with one foot midair then lowered it, taking her work mobile from her pocket. Michael's name filled the bar on the screen, and she answered with, "What have you got?"

"I'm off back to the station. Just spoken to the crew of the *Nerys Angel*. They'd all met up in the Little Devil, seeing as they now have the day off. One of them said something interesting: Ortun planned to leave his boat to George."

"Bloody hell. That's motive. We've just left George's, and he said his reason for having the laptop was because he was looking at what I assume was a spreadsheet to work out where else they could sell. What if he was doing it for his own ends?"

"Hmm, but apparently, George doesn't know about the boat being his when Ortun retires."

"Who told you that?"

"A chap called Ian Yates."

"One of them could have informed him, or George could've overheard a conversation. He could've staged the burglary, like I thought earlier. This is frustrating as fuck not having all the facts. Listen, we're off to see if anyone nearby saw or heard owt last night in Mollengate. I know uniforms will have already done it this morning, but it's best to double-check. After that, providing nowt else turns up, we'll join you at the station and get our heads together again."

"What's the score with Hattie?"

"I'd bet my last quid it isn't her, but we'll see. Thanks for dealing with the crew. Speak to you later." She ended the call, slipped her phone away and told Dave the news. "What do you make of that, then?"

"Blimey, it's not looking all sunshine and roses for George in the suspect stakes, is it?"

"No, but sadly, we've got sod all to pin on him at the moment, and arresting him on suspicion now when we don't have any evidence will be a waste of time. It's a case of playing the waiting game to see what comes up during the rest of the day."

She paused on the kerb for a trio of lorries to thunder past. God, she hated them. They ruined the serenity of the village. Maybe she should find time to sign the local petition to have them rerouted.

She crossed the road. Splats of rain hit her face, so she rushed inside the Co-op and walked up to the counter. Stanley stood behind it reading a magazine.

"Is Liz in?" Carol asked.

He didn't bother to lift his head. "Yeah, out the back. Her office."

"We'll go straight through." She didn't wait for him to say anything else, although, going by his rapt interest in whatever he was reading, she doubted he would anyway.

Dave followed her down the staff corridor. "What a job he's got, standing there reading about nipple clamps. Did you *see* the headline of that article?"

"Er, no, and I'm glad I didn't."

"It was a sex mag. Surely that's not good when he has to serve customers."

"You can tell Liz, then, because I don't fancy her snark being directed at me. You know what she gets like."

"Err, thanks?"

Reaching the office, Carol tapped on the door.

"Come in!" Liz shouted.

Carol poked her head round the door and smiled. "Mind if we have a quick word?"

"Of course not. Park your arses." Liz gestured to the seats in front of the cluttered desk she sat behind. "What can I do for you?"

"It's about a robbery in our flats last night. Did you see anyone hanging around?"

Dave plonked himself on a chair, so Carol did, too.

"Uniforms have been in asking the same thing," Liz said. "What are you doing, checking up on them?"

"Nope. Thought I may as well ask again while we're here."

"Well, I've got nowt to report, but I've heard news from Scudderton." Liz stared at them knowingly. "About the pier closure."

"Hmm. More news will filter here eventually, but for now, if you've got nowt for us, we'll be off to the pub."

"Drinking on the job?" Liz winked.

"You know me better than that."

Carol left the room and waited in the corridor.

Dave leaned over the desk. "Stanley's reading. About nipples."

"You what?" Liz barked. "I've told him to do that on his break or at home!" She shot up and rounded the desk, storming from the room and thudding down the corridor to the shop.

"He's in for it now," Carol said.

Dave shrugged. "Tough. Kids could see what he's reading. There were pictures. Not good."

"No."

Carol and Dave followed Liz and walked past Stanley being chastised by Liz in her whisper-shout way. Thankfully, no customers were in, so her "*Fucking pervert!*" wouldn't reach the gossip mill.

They left the Co-op and popped to the Lord. Carol's bladder protested, so she nipped to the toilet first. She came out to find the landlord wasn't in — he'd gone to the cash and carry — so she chose the next best thing, the shift manager, Beryl Vones.

"I wasn't in earlier when the other officers arrived, but the boss told me about it. I had it in mind to phone the station once I'd topped the fridges up."

"Why, did you see something?"

Beryl lifted an eyebrow. "I did as it happens. Got up for a widdle about three. I've had such a bad water infection you wouldn't believe."

Christ Almighty, the shit people tell us. "Sorry to hear that. Remind me where you live, just so I can get a general idea of where you were."

"In the first cottage down the way there on the other side of the street. I heard a car. Surprising, given the racket the weather was making, but I heard it all the same. I opened my bathroom window and looked out. I thought it was my old man home early, see. He works away, stays wherever he has to go four nights a week. Salesman. Except it wasn't him. Someone rolled up in our parking space in a van, then got out. They had black clothes on, so that's not much help to you, but they had a hood up, I know that much because I ran through to the front to see where they walked."

"And where was that?"

"Up Robottom, towards your flats."

"I know it was dark, but a general idea of the van colour and size?"

"A small one, like a car but with no back seats, no windows in the rear, that sort. All I can tell you is it wasn't light-coloured."

"Did you see owt else?"

"No, I went back to bed. I had it in mind to go and stick a note on the windscreen in the morning, saying it was residents only, but it wasn't there when I got up."

"What would you say about the person's size and shape? How tall were they?"

"Beefy, so I'd say it was a fella. And about as tall as Dave there."

Dave chuckled. "Well, it bloody wasn't me."

Beryl smiled. "No, can't say I can imagine you putting on a hoody. So, someone got burgled, then. Is it something we should watch out for, be worried about?"

Carol shook her head. "I have a feeling this is a one-off, but it doesn't hurt to be careful, does it?"

With nothing more forthcoming, Carol and Dave left the pub, promising to come back later for their evening meal. As Hattie had opted to stay with Grumpy George, getting a taxi back to Scudderton later, there was nothing left to do but return to the station and see if they could get a few ducks in a row.

* * *

The Incident Room

Carol had done her part in bringing everyone up to date, and now it was time to go through Katherine's and Michael's discoveries and see if they could make any headway in this mess.

Katherine had a page full of notes on Nerys Bevan's murder case, and she'd doodled little stars beside each point she'd deemed interesting or possibly important. "She seemed to have disappeared into thin air at the time. Despite extensive door-to-door enquiries the first couple of days, only a shopkeeper and a resident saw her — they're both dead now. Her body wasn't discovered until a week later, which is odd, considering it was summer and a lot of people go and picnic by Scud Stream. Who the hell would sit there eating sandwiches with a body nearby and not say owt? I can't get my head around that."

"Unless she looked like rubbish or a lump of something from a distance," Michael said.

Katherine nodded. "True, seeing as not all of her was visible, and she *was* a fair way down from the usual picnic area. Hmm. That makes me feel better. I'd convinced myself several people had sat there and ignored her, didn't bother calling it in."

Michael sighed. "That's these days you're thinking of. People don't give a shit for the most part, but back then, folks actually cared."

Carol grew concerned. This job wasn't for the faint of heart and could get you down if you didn't watch yourself. "Do you need a break, Michael? A few days off?"

"Nah, just feeling a bit, I dunno, defeated. We've got all these suspects and no evidence against any of them. I'll be all right."

"If you're sure . . ." Carol would keep an eye on him. "So, Katherine, who found Nerys?"

"Ortun."

"Oh shit." Carol stretched her feet out under the spare desk. "That's bloody rotten, that is. No wonder he kept looking for who'd killed her. Finding her would have stuck in his mind, given him more of a push for justice."

Katherine tugged her earlobe. "He had a friend with him, some kid called Dan Nixon, now deceased."

"You don't leave any stone unturned, do you?" Carol smiled.

"I don't, because what if this Dan did it and Ortun killed him? The lad died age sixteen."

"Ruddy hell!" Carol sat straighter. "What happened to him?"

"He was found in Scud Stream . . ."

Everyone sat silently for a moment.

"Murder?" Carol asked.

"Misadventure, according to the report."

"In what way?"

"He slipped and fell. Banged his head on the same rock Nerys was found against. It has 'drunk' in his file."

Dave choked on derisive laughter. "Oh, come on. How could they imagine for a second Dan and Nerys weren't linked? They did check that, didn't they?"

Katherine ran a hand through her hair. "No. So I'll look into his death, too, shall I?"

"Please," Carol said. "So was anyone in the frame for Nerys?"

"Nobody at all."

"What state was she in?"

"Well, she'd settled against some outcropping rocks, her belly towards them. Half of her body was in the water, the right side, and her left poked out, so the expected bloating on the submerged parts and the usual on the other. She'd been beaten about the face and head. Eye socket damage, bruising, a gash to her temple which, according to the report, meant a severed artery, so lots of blood loss there, and she'd died of asphyxiation. Someone would have had the red stuff on them no matter how careful they'd been."

"Poor girl. Only young, too." Carol sighed. "So, with no suspects, the case went cold, and nothing's been done since. Right, this is what we face: is it linked to Ortun's murder? Did he poke about a little too close for comfort and our person got scared and offed him?"

Michael drank some coffee. "Despite the leanings towards George, and I admit, it does appear dodgy for him, wouldn't he have had some kind of love for Ortun, seeing as he treated him like a son? They must have been close for Ortun to even consider leaving the *Nerys Angel* to him. It's been in their family for years, my grandad said."

"Oh yes, tell me what you found out from him." Carol reached for her orange Fanta and sipped.

"Not a bloody lot that will do us any good." Michael consulted his notebook. "I rang him, asked him what he knew of Ortun. He basically said he's a nice fella, he'd known him for years since they were kids, and that was that. He did ask why I wanted to know, but I told him it was police business, so he didn't press. He wouldn't because he's too nice."

"Okay. Katherine, what have we got on the residents of Fisherman's Rest?"

"All of them are clean bar one: Edward Fields. Collared for stealing years ago as a kid but nowt since."

"If it wasn't for the word 'stealing', I'd ignore it, but we'll have to go and have a word."

Katherine held up a finger. "Helen's already sent in some notes about him, and Howard at the cordon got hold of me about a visitor Edward had this morning, some fella on a bike." She folded the top page of her notepad over. "Here we are. Helen spoke to Edward, and he said he'd been watching telly last night then went to bed. Didn't hear or see owt. Howard stopped Mason, the bike rider, when he arrived at Fisherman's Rest, and asked him what he was doing there. Mason replied he'd come to drop some cakes off for Edward. There was a Buns 'n' Bread bag in the basket on the front of the bike. He didn't stay long, and when he came out, he asked what was going on at Ortun's and mentioned he'd been to the marina to ask him for a job earlier but hadn't seen him. Howard didn't tell him, obviously, and he asked him if anyone would have a grudge. Mason responded no, everyone loved Ortun."

Carol sighed. "Except for Skipper. So apart from Edward nicking something years ago, where do we go from here? We've got a motive with the following people: Hattie because of Ortun having it off with Louise Roberts. The same for George, offended on his mother's behalf, plus he could have found out he had the *Nerys Angel* and the business coming to him and just happened to want it sooner. Skipper Kinnock, not wanting to play nice and share the cod — he's already poached June as a customer. Louise Roberts — her dabbling with Ortun got her kicked out and divorce papers on her doormat; we still need to speak to her. Callum Roberts — he's intimated it was his lucky day when his wife got caught playing away, but maybe he's good at lying, Hattie giving him an alibi." She looked at Dave. "Which one out of that lot do you have your money on?"

He puffed out air. "All of them have what they'd feel is a good reason."

"We should try another angle," Michael said. "Digi have sent over the messages they got off Ortun's phone. Still waiting on the details from his provider, though. He sent a message to his crew at twenty-two minutes past ten last night. He told them to be at work an hour earlier than usual as they'd be going to a different reef."

"So we know he was alive at this point, unless someone else sent the message."

Michael nodded. "The responses and Ortun's reply to those were deleted and didn't show up in the message app, but digi found them. He informed the crew a mate was there who'd told him about the reef."

"Shitting hell, we might just have got a break." Carol sat up straight. "Did he mention a name?"

"No, but it's more to go on than we had — we have someone at his home before the murder. What if the so-called mate killed him and that person isn't any of the names on our current suspect list?"

Carol got up and studied the whiteboard. Katherine had added more in their absence. "I see here that Ortun's friend circle is small. Who did you find that out from?" She turned to raise her eyebrows at Katherine.

"I rang Violet Kinnock. Michael told me you said she was chatty."

"And what did she say?"

"That he didn't have mates that he hung around with, more that he'd have a drink with people in the Little Devil. That's Skipper, believe it or not, Callum, Fred, Ortun's crew, another fisherman called Jason, and that's it."

"Is she really someone we can rely on, though? Skipper might not tell his wife everything, and she didn't strike me as the sort to sit in the pub or go to the marina and natter with everyone. That can be a job for you two after this discussion. Ring those people and asked them if any other friend is missing off that list. Owt else?"

Katherine flipped her top page over again. "We've had news back from Better Way Forward. Barney did go to Mrs Bamford-Fox's that day last week, and Hattie was at the front door as soon as it was opened."

"I thought that would be the case."

"And the last thing . . ." Katherine ran her finger down her notes. "Uniform at Mrs Bamford-Fox's spotted a dirty boot print in the mudroom. Estimated size eleven. Then there's the CCTV. A big man was caught on camera going down the side of the house and breaking the window, then going inside. In *daylight.* All in black, a balaclava and a hoody on. So that rules Hattie out on that side of things, doesn't it, unless she's got the ability to grow taller and wider, and has monster feet."

Carol laughed. "She's about a size four in shoes. Dinky hoofs. She's short and skinny. Dave, didn't we get a similar description for the laptop robber?"

"We did, but it's a standard outfit for those up to no good. Hoody. Balaclava."

"So could this be two unrelated incidents and we're looking at Barney for it?"

Katherine smiled. "You said I don't leave any stone unturned . . . I asked his boss at Better Way Forward for his description. He's about five foot, thin, and has small feet."

"So he's not the big man on CCTV. Right." A memory prodded. "Oh, also, can you have a nose at the reports for graffiti being sprayed at the pier yesterday? June would probably have phoned it in. It might be a link. Okay, to recap: speak to Ortun's mates to see if there are any more we're not aware of, follow up the graffiti, then add everything we've talked about to the board. Me and Dave will nip to see this Edward fella regardless of the PC reports on him. By then, it'll be nearly the end of our day, so unless you get owt that means overtime, go home."

* * *

1 Fisherman's Rest

Upon twigging they'd skipped a food break and the afternoon was drawing to a close, Carol wanted to get to the Lord and fill her belly. First, she and Dave had to speak to the man sitting on his sofa, Edward Fields. He was beefy like the fella Beryl had witnessed going into the flats last night, and the thief at Bamford-Fox's, but size didn't make anyone guilty until evidence presented itself. Look at the summer murder case. The killer had put on a padded body suit.

She'd keep an open mind.

"I realise the officer who was at Ortun's door earlier has already spoken to you, but I'd like to have a chat about the burglary you committed." She'd worded it that way on purpose to get a reaction.

"That was years ago. Bloody hell, I've been good ever since. You lot put the shits up me, all that talk of going to prison next time. I'd be mental if I did it again. I were only a young lad."

True. And his reaction had been the correct one, although he'd have surely schooled himself not to admit he'd done another robbery last night, plus whenever Bamford-Fox had been burgled. She glanced at Dave, who nodded minutely.

"Where do you work?" she asked.

"On the *Poisson Mort.*"

"Oh right. Were you there today?" She already knew the answer from Violet Kinnock, but he didn't need to know that.

"Nope. Had a dicky belly."

"Is that why your friend bought some cakes round?"

"Yeah."

"Where did you go this morning, then?"

"To my mate's. Mason's."

"When you're poorly?"

"Needed some fresh air."

"Do you know Ortun well?"

He didn't flinch at her throwing rapid-fire questions at him. "Yep, used to work on the *Nerys Angel* until he sacked me."

Ooh, what's this, then? "Why was that?"

"One look at his crew will tell you the answer. They're all young. He said me and Mason were getting on a bit and he needed to replace us."

"Mason, the friend you visited this morning, the one who brought you the cakes?"

"Yes. What's this, an episode of *This Is Your Life*?"

"You're going back a bit there with that programme. I used to like that." She smiled. "So are you a friend of Ortun's, or was he just your old boss?"

"He's an all right bloke. Doesn't have mates as such, just people he props the bar up with."

The same as Violet had said. "So Mason isn't his friend?"

"They get on fine."

"Any bad feeling because you both got sacked?"

He shrugged. "Why would there be? I got a job with Skipper pretty quick, and Mason doesn't need the money. His mam left him a shitload when she died."

"That's great. Thank you for your time."

"Look, what's happened? You don't have to be clever to know something's up. There's been people in white suits at Ortun's all day."

"I suspect it'll be on the grapevine later. Nowt stays quiet for long around here."

And he could take that whichever way he liked — a threat she'd find out he was guilty of something . . . or merely an observation.

* * *

The Lord

Food eaten, they were well into their second drink each when Carol's ex-lover walked into the pub. She groaned, wishing she'd never gone to him to scratch her sexual itch. He did that well enough, but his obsessive tendencies to do with cleaning and everything having its place had got on her nerves — that and him wanting to progress their relationship to something more. He'd implied in the summer that everything belonged in a box, and she'd told him she'd couldn't be placed in one. Never again. She'd lived her life pigeonholed as "Harry

Wren's daughter", not a person in her own right, and she was buggered if she'd let it continue now she was getting a handle on things in that respect.

"D'you think he'll come over?" Dave muttered.

"No idea. I hope not."

He did.

Bollocks.

"How are you, Carol?" He gave her a smile that was probably supposed to melt her. It didn't.

"Fine, thanks." If she asked how he was out of politeness, he'd take it as her being interested again.

"What are you up to these days? I miss you." He stuck his bottom lip out.

"Work, work, and that other thing, work."

"Right." His eyes lit up. "I bought a set of storage racks the other day."

Give me strength. "Lovely."

"It's amazing how much they hold. You should pop round and see them."

"It's not something I'm interested in."

"But you've been doing so well, cleaning your things out and keeping a tidy home. You learned from the best." He inflated his chest.

What the hell did I see in this knob?

He lowered his eyebrows at her. "Are you slipping, Carol, back into your old ways?"

The lie came quickly — she had to get him to be disgusted by her. "Yes, my place is a dump again."

He turned his nose up and shuddered. "Oh."

"Look, was there owt else, because we're busy," she said.

His cheeks turned red. "No need to be rude."

"There is, though, isn't there. I've told you we're over, yet you keep pestering me on the phone. Calls, texts, shit on Messenger and WhatsApp. And now here you are, in my space again."

Dave coughed the words, "Restraining order."

Her ex shook his head as though he pitied her and strode away to the bar.

"Some people." Carol gulped her wine.

"He's so bloody *weird*."

Carol grimaced. "Don't I fucking well know it?"

CHAPTER TWENTY

The Claxon

Steady still had the jitters from those detectives being at his place. He didn't need his equilibrium shot at the minute, could do without worrying if they were onto him, but here he was, thinking about it, letting it live in his head, some irritating sitting tenant. It had taken all of his acting skills to appear normal, but inside, he'd been bricking it. The woman had mentioned a robbery but not a specific one — had she been testing him, waiting for his mouth to spout lies, for his expression to prove his guilt? He'd kept a poker face, though, so sod her. And as for that fella she'd brought with her — what, was he supposed to scare him? He'd bet she hadn't expected his answer.

As if I'd be dumb enough to fall for her trick.

Another thought throbbed into life. Had his number plate been clocked last night when he'd gone to Mollengate? If so, why hadn't she said anything more about it? Why leave with her threat hanging in the air? She'd implied, bleating on that nothing stayed quiet around here, that she'd get to the truth eventually.

Maybe they're watching my place, got some copper hiding in Violet's bushes. Or they've probably asked her to keep an eye out, nosy cow that she is. Well, I'm not even at home, so that's their waste of time, not mine.

Then there was the visit from Mason earlier. Why the fuck had he broken one of his own rules, one he'd been so specific about it had got on Steady's nerves? He'd said they weren't to be seen together until the heat had died down about Ortun. He'd been well weird, giving him a bag of cakes — what the fuck for? — suggesting he had a few things to say to Steady at a later date. He'd mentioned the *Poisson Mort*. Did he know Steady worked for Skipper? Would he take offence to the point he'd kill Steady, too? Mason was unstable, that much had been made clear from their discussions about his plan, and Steady wished he'd never agreed to help him out. But he'd wanted the money, so he only had himself to blame.

When does he plan on giving that to me?

Whatever, it didn't matter now. Steady had decided he wasn't hanging around to find out what was going on. A plan of his own had formed, and he'd execute it later.

Once the coppers had left his place, he'd got in his van, ignoring Plod still standing at the cordon. He'd driven to Sainsbury's, stocking up on provisions, mainly processed shit and stuff in cans, then parked in the Backstreet, which wasn't allowed, but the traffic warden hadn't come by, thank God. He'd hunched down in his seat, keeping a low profile in the deserted road until it got dark. The passenger footwell had the evidence of his snacking to pass the time — empty crisp packets, a few Coke cans and something he *hadn't* eaten, the cakes Mason had given to him. How was Steady to know the bloke hadn't laced them with something? It wouldn't surprise him in the slightest.

Now he was below deck on the *Claxon*, the yacht moored beside Senor De León's. It wasn't as fancy as the one next door, but it was still swish enough. The interior was like one of those posh homes in magazines, everything cream, those smart lights and whatever. The owners were away in Bulgaria for a month. He'd earwigged last week, them saying they hadn't rented it out to anyone while they were gone.

He'd be safe to hide out here for the length of time he needed to remain out of the way. He'd already sent Skipper a message, lying, saying he'd been to the doctor and he had a gastric issue so wouldn't be in for the rest of the week — having the shits and handling food didn't mix, so Skipper could hardly insist he came in. Those few days would give Steady time to become established elsewhere, days with no one wondering where he was. By next week when he didn't show up on the *Poisson Mort*, yeah, tongues would wag, but Steady didn't care. He'd be a new man by then.

He wouldn't be going back to his home ever again, which was a shame in some respects, as he'd lived there since his divorce and had made it as nice as he could, stealing when he needed to buy something his wages wouldn't stretch to. The fridge, the cooker, that sort of thing. It amused him that so-and-so's bracelet paid for his stuff or some bloke's watch topped up the electric meter. But with his new life ahead of him, he'd be able to afford whatever he liked.

He had to get out of Scudderton, start again elsewhere, put this shit behind him.

Should I do an anonymous phone call and grass Mason up once I'm gone?

He ate his curry noodles and pondered that. It was all well and good dobbing his friend in, but what if Mason blabbed about Steady nicking the laptop — *and* that he'd known about the murder before it had happened? Steady could deny all knowledge of the murder, that was one thing, but the robbery was another. He could have left something of himself behind. A hair. But surely those coppers wouldn't have walked out of his bungalow if they knew he'd pinched the laptop. And would they even bother getting forensics in there for some cheapo device?

Or were they playing a game and waiting until they had concrete evidence? How long did it take for forensics to come back? Days? Weeks?

He'd be long gone before then, so his mad thoughts were pointless.

Steady mulled his movements over. Certain he'd taken the route to Mollengate with no cameras, he relaxed a little. All he had to worry about other than Mason were stray DNA and witnesses, and as far as he could tell, no one had seen him going down Robottom Street. He'd had a balaclava on, so who would have recognised him anyway, especially as he lived in Scudderton and didn't go to Mollengate if he could help it. Sleepy villages weren't his bag.

But if I stop robbing at the new location, behave myself, the police won't need to pull me up for owt, so my identity will be safe. There'll be nowt to match that DNA to. And I'll grow my hair, a beard. It'll be okay.

He finished his noodles and washed the fork up, placing the plastic pot in the bin. His holdall called to him, so he walked into the living area and took it over to the built-in cream leather sofa, moving his thief outfit aside to sit and look through the rest of the contents. Every item had a cardboard label attached with string. On them, he'd written the time of each theft and how long he'd have to wait to pawn them in the Leeds shop he travelled to so no one knew who he was. But he wouldn't be going to Leeds ever again. He had his sights on London. A fake passport — he'd arranged for it as soon as Mason had revealed his plans included murder — sat in his pocket, there if Steady needed to scarper. He'd become that person, start over, and forget this place with its gossips and closed minds.

The diamond necklace from that posh bint's place last week would be a bugger to shift, so he was better off removing the gems and selling them separately. With that piece, he'd get a shitload of cash on top of the other money he'd get his hands on.

The future was bright.

So long as he could pull his plan off tonight.

CHAPTER TWENTY-ONE

Kettlestone Rise

Mason stared at the man who'd shirked his parental duties for fifty-odd years. What a tosser. How could he have walked away from his only child? Ignored him his whole life? As far as Mason could work out, Eamon didn't have any other kids, the Spanish wife hadn't produced any, but then again, maybe he'd paid *other* bits on the side off, too, like he had with Mam, shutting them up about more buns in ovens. He thought nothing of throwing cash around to remove problems. Word had rustled through Scudderton once that he'd bought some bloke off a few years back, a man who'd complained about shoddy work in his house and had threatened to tell all and sundry by going to the papers. That little error had cost Eamon ten grand, Ortun had said.

Once again, in the light of his torch, Mason strained to see any resemblance between him and Eamon, just one little thing that would confirm his suspicions. Maybe they had the same shaped eyes, but that was about it, and the only thing personality wise Mason had gained from him was his ability to hold a grudge. Mam had said Eamon hadn't spoken one word to her since he'd hit her, blanking her if they happened to be in town at the same time. He'd avoided Woolies and Superdrug when she'd worked there, although Mrs Spanish Pants had gone in, probably oblivious to the fact her husband and Mam had been "acquainted".

He'd hardly want to announce to her he had a secret kid, would he?

And Mam's ramblings about "that man" being out the front of the cottage sometimes, staring in, made sense now. It must have been Eamon.

"Where's your ex-wife these days?" he asked, genuinely curious. "She just disappeared one day, and personally, I think that's a bit suss, especially as you've got a yacht. You could have thrown her overboard."

"None of your business."

"I could *make* it my business. I'd like to have a chat with her. Let her in on a few things."

Eamon had pooped himself earlier, literally. The stench, mixed with dried piss, was gross, but Mason had anticipated this happening, and a little discomfort to his nasal passages would be worth it in the end. When the DNA results came back, he planned to threaten Eamon even more about exposing his secret, then get him to change his will to include Mason. No monthly payments for him. He wanted the fucking lot as inheritance.

He had to get *something* out of not having a father and living with the world's shittiest mother.

"Got nowt to say?" He kicked Eamon's leg.

"How long are you going to keep this up for? People will be looking for me, wondering where I am."

"What, you think you're so important in this town that folks will give a shit that they haven't seen you poncing around? I doubt it. All you're good for to them is having parties, and as for those managers you brag about, the ones who run things on sites, well, they'll just think you've gone off on another of your jaunts, sunning yourself on the Continent while they slave away in England's shitty cold and rain."

Eamon wheezed. He didn't look too well. "If I'm not back in circulation by the next couple of weeks, there's a woman who might phone the police."

Who's that, then? Is he seeing someone? "Maybe she will, but being back in circulation is a ball that's in *your* court. Whether you agree to what I want when the test results come back is a return you really need to lob over the net."

"I won't agree to anything except paying you off."

"That's exactly what I thought you'd say."

Mason had relented earlier, giving the man one of the cinnamon buns. Feeding it to him had been grim. He wished he'd let him starve for a bit longer now they'd had this conversation. Eamon wasn't about to strut around town telling everyone he had a son no matter how much Mason pressed him to. No, he'd rather make it go away with money.

Well, he couldn't shut Mason up with zeroes in the bank, not unless he changed his will and Mason was there to witness it.

He stared at him, having given him a blanket, something he also regretted, and tilted his head. "I have to go out. Behave while I'm gone."

He laughed at Eamon's groan and left the cellar, opening the door at the top of the steps to stand in the kitchen. He ought to do some housework really, but funny enough, he hadn't had the time the last couple of days, what with his planning. He'd go through it like a dose of salts later; the slight mess was annoying and brought back unhappy memories.

He locked the cellar, then the cottage, and rode his bike towards town, his trailer jostling behind him when he hit a pothole. Mason had another bastard to sort out, but this one might be trickier than Ortun, considering his strength, but what was life without taking a few risks?

Boring, that's what it was.

* * *

Mason had been patient, waiting down the side of the pub for Skipper to come out. The earlier rain had stopped, but it was bloody cold, and a nippy breeze coming off the sea chomped on his cheeks. Good job he had a thermal vest on beneath his fleece, his poncho on top, then there were his gloves and woolly hat. He'd chosen those Toasty socks, the ones hanging on racks by the till in B&M, red with sticky pads on the bottom for people like Mam who tended to fall arse over tit on uncarpeted flooring. Still, he'd get warmer once he was on the move.

The door of the pub slammed, and that lot off the *Nerys Angel* walked past his hiding place, drunk as lords, laughing and joking.

"We might get a day off tomorrow an' all if Ortun doesn't show up again," Ian said.

"Here's hoping. If we do, shall we meet in the pub about eleven and do a repeat of today?" Charlene waved at a taxi approaching.

"Yep. Tarra." Ian staggered away towards the cliff path, where he lived in a caravan at the top.

Charlene and her boyfriend — what's-his-name, Quentin — got into the taxi.

Mason breathed a sigh of relief and waited some more.

Eight-thirty on the dot, Skipper left his drinking hole and wandered down the alley that led to Fisherman's Rest. Long rows of bushes lined either side, taller than them, and offered enough privacy. Skipper whistled a tune Mason didn't recognise. He must have drunk a few more than usual, as he weaved along, unsteady on his feet, seeming three sheets to the wind.

And on a school night, too. Blimey.

He followed Skipper.

Mason thought about the cluster of woodland where he'd parked his bike. It stood close by the estate on the opposite side of a main road, no houses in that part, no one to see anything, although if Skipper created enough racket when it came to death time, someone might hear. While the autumn had stolen some of the trees' leaves, pines still proudly displayed their year-round clothes, and that was where Mason would do the deed, behind five in a row. They'd be his accomplices.

The old boy didn't look over his shoulder at the sound of footsteps, ploughing on no matter that someone was right up his arse. He probably thought he was safe, seeing as he'd always had the rep for being someone you shouldn't cross. Well, Mason didn't give a runny turd about that, he'd cross the fucker if he wanted to, and no one could stop him. Skipper's fist in a fight against Mason's mallet . . . it was obvious who'd come out the winner.

He stifled a chuckle and darted forward, lifting his weapon high. Skipper turned at the point Mason brought it down in an arc, so instead of hitting him on the back of the head, he struck his brow. Skipper cried out, all gruff and manly, no high-pitched squeal going on here, and staggered backwards into the right-hand hedge, the prickly sort Mason had been thrown in by Mam as a child. Skipper held a palm to the wound, and in the dark, the dripping blood appeared black, snaking between his splayed fingers towards his wrist.

"Who's there?" he demanded, a little less sure of himself. Groggy might be the word for it.

"Only me." Mason stepped forward, hiding the mallet in his poncho pocket. "It was a good job I was on my way to see Steady. The fucker who hit you just ran off. I saw what he did. We ought to ring the police."

"What fucker? There *was* no fucker but *you*."

Mason gripped Skipper's elbow. "That knock to the head must be wreaking havoc, pal, because someone else *was* here."

"I don't understand . . ." Skipper sounded confused as fuck.

"Look, we'll sort out who did this another time. For now, you need help."

Mason tugged, but the hedge didn't fancy letting go of Skipper's thick yellow jumper. Mason used his gloved hand to pry the wool away, although a strand broke from the intricate pattern and clung to a thorn. Another pull or two, and Skipper was free from the hedge's clutches, swaying, dribbles of blood painting veins on his face.

"Let me take you home, eh?"

* * *

The Woodland

Mason guided an increasingly puzzled Skipper down the alley, checking behind them to ensure no one was coming. At the other end, they came out on a path opposite an estate, and instead of heading to the Rest — no copper or cordon at the entrance now — Mason led his adversary across the woodland on the left.

"Where are we going? Fucking hell, my head's banging something rotten." Skipper teetered, his hand slapping to his forehead.

"I think you need to sit down. Over here."

Mason took Skipper to his hidden bike, ignored his garbled ranting, and when they arrived at the correct spot, clapped his hands on the man's shoulders. He added pressure, and Skipper sank to the leaf-strewn, boggy ground, his legs straight out in front of him.

"That's wet," he muttered.

Mason laughed at the dampness from the grass soaking into Skipper's jeans. He must feel as uncomfortable as Eamon had when he'd pissed himself.

"You rest there for a minute."

"Phone police," Skipper muttered.

"Yep, I'll do that in a sec."

Mason moved to his trailer and peeled the tarpaulin back to take out a plastic storage tub, twenty-five by twenty-five inches. He set it on the ground beside Skipper.

"What are you playing at with that thing?" Skipper grumbled.

"You need to wash your face, yes? Violet might worry if she sees all that blood."

"I feel sick."

"That'll be the effects of that wallop."

Mason retrieved three water receptacles from his trailer, and while Skipper squeezed his eyes shut and moaned, Mason filled the box. Revulsion swirled through him at what he was doing, what he was about to do, but it was the only way he knew how to show these people how angry he was. The threat of drowning had always frightened him, but he'd known, as *his* head had been plunged beneath the water, that he'd gone too far and his mother had chosen this method to prove a point. *He* was proving a point now, except he wouldn't be hauling Skipper's head out just in time no more than he'd hauled Ortun out.

He tossed the empty receptacles to the far end of the trailer then turned and studied Skipper. His groaning had increased, and he retched, watery vomit landing on his jeans. That'd be the beer he'd sunk in the Little Devil. Mason chuckled, the sound low, and hummed while he waited for the older man to finish making a mess.

"Ugh," Skipper said. "I think I'm going to faint."

"Up on your knees, then."

Mason aided him and checked Skipper's eyes. They were closed again, so Mason straddled him from the back, on his knees, wet going through *his* jeans, too, and took a deep breath to do what had to be done.

"What the fuck are you doing back there?" Skipper slurred. "Get *off* me."

Mason had heard enough of this dickhead's whining. He gripped the bastard's hair and clamped his arm around Skipper's front, banding his victim's arms to his sides with the crook of his elbow and his hand. "Why don't you just shut up for good now?"

He smiled.

"Hold your breath."

He pushed Skipper's head into the cold water, using force to keep him still so the tub didn't tip over. Skipper thrashed and managed to lift his head out despite Mason pushing, the captain of the *Poisson Mort* gasping for air. Mason trying to dip Skipper's face in again resulted in a tussle, Skipper attempting to shrug him off. The tub knocked over, all the water oozing into the already drenched ground, and Mason saw everything through a red haze. He took his hand off Skipper's head and reached for his mallet. It got stuck in his pocket in his rush to take it out, and Skipper fighting to stand didn't help matters; Mason was losing his grip around the bloke. Fucking hell, this wasn't going as he'd planned.

Mallet finally free, he smacked Skipper's arm with it to stop him from bucking, the resulting grunt of pain satisfying. Mason let the fella go and stood quickly, wielding the mallet again, this time running around the front to lump him one in the nose. The squidgy crack that bled into the quiet told of a broken bone, Skipper's bellow of agony drowning it out. Mason hit him again and again, and Skipper slumped, silent at last.

Mason checked for a pulse. The fuckface was still breathing, so all wasn't lost. Plan B was in their future, but Mason would have to wait until after midnight, remaining in the woodland, both of them hidden beneath the tarpaulin.

Good job he'd brought his Kindle.

CHAPTER TWENTY-TWO

Kettlestone Rise

Steady had been watching through a window on the darkened yacht, thinking about the dangers of his upcoming mission. Mason could ruin it all, but Steady had reminded himself how clever he was at breaking and entering, how quiet, and if his so-called friend kicked up a fuss, he'd punch his lights out and scarper, trying again tomorrow night.

He wasn't leaving Scudderton without that money.

Mason had ridden past the marina earlier on his bike with that stupid trailer on the back. He'd headed towards the Little Devil then disappeared down the alley, so maybe he was going to Steady's place. Perhaps he had it in mind to tell Steady what had been bothering him earlier, then hit him with that mallet of his and load him into the trailer. He'd have had a shock when he got there because Steady wasn't in, but it was all the incentive needed to leave the yacht and run to the Backstreet, where he'd left his little blue van. With Mason away from home, Steady could do the business.

Now, in his thief getup, gloves and balaclava giving him anonymity, he stood in the rear garden of Mason's cottage. Even if Mason turned around and came home, Steady had just about enough time to do the job and get out before then. He'd take the long way back to the marina so he didn't pass Mason on the road, and the little twat wouldn't be any the wiser until he next checked under his bed. Steady had told him not to leave all that money there in the suitcase, but as always, Mason thought he knew best. He didn't trust banks and wanted the cash close to hand.

More fool him.

Steady inserted his pick and entered the kitchen. How divvy to not have extra security with all that dosh upstairs. It wasn't as tidy as it usually was, he'd noticed that when he'd brought the laptop here. Mason was slipping and had let the housework go, although it was a damn sight better than years past. It had been an awful state when his mother was alive, boxes upon labelled boxes of useless stuff hanging around, a bit like Ortun's spare room. She hadn't allowed Mason to clean up except for his bedroom, so when she'd snuffed it in the sea one night when she'd gone wandering in the early hours, he'd wasted no time in carting her boxes into the cellar.

That was a point. She'd had an American baseball card Steady had clapped eyes on one time he'd come here to pick Mason up for work. It had been in a box marked *Memorabilia*, and he reckoned it was worth a bob or two.

Every little helps . . .

Did he have time to go down there and nick that box? He could dump the other contents later if they weren't of any value.

He crept through the cottage and then upstairs. In Mason's bedroom, he got on his knees and reached beneath the bed, smiling, curling his fingers around the suitcase handle. He pulled, dragged the case towards him and lifted it to test the weight, then checked it wasn't empty. He stood and walked downstairs, listening for Mason coming back, prowling in search of him, but the cottage was just as quiet as it'd been when he'd arrived.

At the van, he dumped the case in the back and returned to the kitchen. A key sat in the lock of the cellar door, so he twisted it and took it out, slipping it into his pocket. That way, if Mason arrived and caught him, he couldn't trap him down there in one of his weird anger spurts.

Steady reached for the light switch, and a yelp of surprise echoed from below. What the fuck? There was no way Mason could have got here before him. Heart rate ramping up speed, Steady cautiously went down the steps and looked around. It appeared the same as when Mason had showed him his "gym", which was on one side, Mrs Ingram's boxes on the other, except . . . that was different. Mason had created an aisle down the middle of them.

Steady walked over there and stood in the gap.

From the far end, Senor De León screamed at him, eyes wide, and Steady remembered he had a balaclava on, so no wonder the old duffer had got scared. What the hell was *he* doing here? As far as Steady was aware, Mason didn't have a beef with him, just Ortun, Skipper and Fred.

"All right, pal, you're all right." Steady held a gloved hand up to calm him.

De León wiggled his legs, a blanket covering them. "Who . . . who are you? Where has *he* gone?"

"He's out. I came here to . . . do something. Shit, your face doesn't look too good. Did you have a fight with a concrete floor or what?" That remark reminded Steady of the floor in George's bedroom.

"He . . . he must have dragged me from the marina. He knocked me out, and I ended up here."

It was so odd seeing De León vulnerable like that, weak, his voice showing how unsure he was. Usually, the man gadded about as if his shit didn't stink.

"Coppers were on your yacht earlier. Uniforms. They arrived about seven o'clock and left at half past. What's that about?"

"I don't know. Maybe someone reported me missing."

"How long have you been here?"

"Not sure."

"It's the day after your party. Night."

"Is that all? Oh *God*, it feels like I've been here for *days*. Last night, he texted me . . ."

What hasn't Mason told me? "You were brought here *last night*?"

"Yes, after the party."

Jesus Christ, he was here when I nipped by with the laptop. "What does he want with you?"

"I can't say."

Well, that changed things. "Ah, so there's history there?"

"Please, just get these cuffs off me."

Cuffs? Bloody hell. "Err, I'm staying out of this. Not my circus."

"Please, please . . ."

Whatever De León had done, it might not even be bad. After all, Mason had killed Ortun just for sacking him. Then again, he *had* fucked up Mason's reputation a bit, spreading it around that he was a pervert for feeling that woman up, but death wasn't a justifiable action for either of those things, and Steady had tried to tell him that, too.

"Look, just give him what he wants, yeah? All he'll be after is for you to own up to whatever you did. I'm guessing that's what the issue is with you. He'll be happy if you hold your hands up, d'you get what I mean?"

De León stared at him funny. "I know your voice . . ."

Shite. Steady didn't need this, De León telling Mason who he was. Steady needed an hour or so to get himself sorted and away, but if Mason returned and this geezer opened his mouth . . .

He spied a hammer in a box in the left-hand corner, a stupid place to leave tools. If De León got out of those cuffs, he could lamp Mason one the next time he came down here.

Would that be such a bad thing?

Steady sidled past the man — *God, he stinks* — and snatched up the hammer. He turned to De León and advanced fast.

Ignoring the little voice in his head telling him to stop, he whacked him on the top of the head with it, the flat end creating a dent and a sickening thud of metal on bone, De León screaming, blood spurting. Shit, shit, this was nasty, but he'd started it now. Steady hit him three more times, De León's skull caving in, red stuff spattering the wall behind him and the side of one box stack. He left the tool embedded, eager to get the hell away and forget what he'd done. He rushed up the stairs, fuck the baseball card, and used his clean left hand to put the key back in the lock and turn it. Next, he whipped Mason's boat key off the little rack on the wall and stuffed it in his pocket, his heart beating too fast for his liking.

At the back door, he took the time to use his pick to secure the cottage — Mason knew his trick of leaving doors open to scare residents and would guess it had been him who'd stolen the money. Prior to getting in the van, he stripped off his gloves and balaclava, throwing them in the footwell on top of the litter, then jumped in the driver's seat.

Time to fucking go.

* * *

The Claxon

In his haste to get going, Steady had forgotten he was supposed to go the long way so he didn't pass Mason. Luck was on his side, though. No one had been around, so he'd avoided the roads with cameras and parked again in the Backstreet, taking the suitcase out. A quick scout of the marina area had shown no one appeared to be around, so he'd walked casually across the street and onto the *Claxon*, hoping he'd forgive himself for killing Scudderton's most prosperous man.

He couldn't think about that now, though. He dropped the case on the floor and stripped out of his clothing, bundling it up and stuffing it into a reusable shopping bag he found in the cupboard under the kitchen sink. In the shower, he washed any trace of blood off him, then bleached the walls and door with a sponge he'd found on the soap rack. He used that to clean the bathroom floor, too, then went over everywhere else he'd walked, checking for any blood smudges. He found one on the lino in the kitchen and wiped it away, stuffing the sponge in the bag for life.

Dressed, he removed the noodle pot from the bin and put it in with the clothes, then took all the forks as he wasn't sure which one he'd eaten from. He opened the case, spied all that money, and grinned, cramming the provisions he'd bought in Sainsbury's beside all the ten- and twenty-pound notes. A deep breath, and he closed the case, grabbed it, his bloodied clothing bag and his holdall with his burglary spoils in it, clicked the lights off and left the yacht, using his pick to lock it.

He looked around at the other boats and the visible part of the street. No one. Quickly, he threw his stuff onto the jetty, cringing at the loud *donk*, and climbed down the ladder, gathering his shit and boarding the *Jar*. Steady stored his things in the cabin. One last job to do, and he was out of here.

He took one of the many fuel canisters Mason kept on his boat and walked across to the Backstreet. His van went up in flames within two minutes, then he was back on the *Jar*, excitement ripping through him. Engine fired up, he sailed away from the marina, planning to go down the coast as far as Cleethorpes. His trail would go cold there, after he'd withdrawn his grand retirement fund from the bank then snapped his debit card and lobbed it in the sea on his way to Felixstowe. He'd make the phone call there. Dob Mason in. They'd likely do him for De León's death as well as Ortun's. Steady would ditch the *Jar* there and get on a train, which would take him to London and his life with his new name, far away from the murder he'd committed.

He was a new man now.

Hello, Roland Tweed. Nice to meet you.

CHAPTER TWENTY-THREE

The Coldwater Estate

Fiona, on a swing at the park, listened to Ortun asking Dan Nixon questions that really didn't need answers. Everyone knew Dan was a weakling, so why keep on at him? She glanced about. They were the only three there at seven in the evening, Fiona not wanting to go home until her curfew at nine else Mam would ask her questions incessantly before bed: "Are you sure you're all right? You look pale, so something's wrong, and you haven't been yourself for days . . ."

Fiona wanted everything to stop, for time to rewind, for things to go back to how they were, where she avoided Nerys because she was such a cow, and the only bad things in her life were her periods and their dog dying last winter. Fiona would never have gone to the moors with Eamon if she could do it all over again. Nerys would be alive, being nasty to people in her usual way, and although Eamon would still have gone to Spain, Fiona wouldn't have this god-awful ratchet in her belly, hacking at it until she had to throw up. She wouldn't have to keep things to herself, the only one shouldering the burden.

Shouting from the lads had her jumping, a sick feeling crawling up her throat to settle as a too-wide lump. She should go home, get away from them, tell Mam once again she was okay, then go to bed and hide, praying that sleep took her quickly and she didn't have any nightmares.

Poor Dan. While he was three years older than them, he was a puny kid, short, and looked about ten. Mam said he had stunted growth. Mam said he hadn't eaten enough greens when he was little. Mam said . . .

Ortun towered over him. The words coming out of Ortun's mouth had been cruel so far, and she wished he'd pack it in. Dan wasn't the sort to kill anybody, not even an insect, yet she could hardly say he hadn't done it and she knew who had.

More than ever since that horrible day, this secret was too heavy to hold.

"Your mam saw her, she told the police," Ortun said with a poke to Dan's chest. "She saw her after she'd been to the sweet shop. You followed Nerys, didn't you? You went to the stream and hurt her, killed her."

"I didn't! I had nowt to do with your sister going missing — or her murder. God, Ortun, you've been accusing everyone, and I'm telling you, it wasn't me. I was in my bedroom."

"You might have been in your room, but I'm willing to bet you saw Nerys through the window and went after her. She told me what you said that time, asking her out to the dance. She told you no, but you kept on. What was it, an act of revenge or what?"

"You can think what you like, but I'm not taking the blame for it. I'm going home."

Dan stormed off, and Ortun followed, clomping after him, his hands balled by his sides. Fiona had a horrible feeling this wasn't going to end well and Ortun would clobber him before Dan even reached his house.

She debated what to do. Stay on the swing in the lovely summer evening or follow?

She chose to go after them. Ortun sent a barrage of accusations flying towards Dan's back all the way down Blenheim Street, the satchel on his shoulder swinging, bringing back in sharp relief the sandal she had in hers beneath the bed. What did he have in his?

Dan didn't respond, and Ortun ran ahead to stop him from walking farther.

"Look, how come you knew where to go that day we found her, eh? You said to check Scud Stream because the police hadn't. They thought it was too far away so didn't bother, but you? *I remember every word you said."*

Fiona stopped to sit on someone's front garden wall. If Ortun saw her, he didn't show any sign. He was too busy getting in Dan's face.

Dan whined, "My dad said about it, wondering why the police hadn't even been to check. Yeah, it's a couple of miles away, but it was an obvious place because of it being summer."

Ortun's fight seemed to go out of him. "Fine. I believe you."

"Really?"

"Yeah."

So that was it? The arguing was over?

A calculating look swept over Ortun's face. "Let's go and get drunk."

"What?" Dan squeaked. "My mam wouldn't like that."

"Neither would mine, but I stole a bottle, put it in my bag, so we may as well drink it." Ortun poked his head around Dan. "You coming, Fi?"

She stood and walked over to them. "Only if you're going to stop rowing, and I have to be back by nine else Mam will worry. You know, because of Nerys. She said the killer's still out there and might be going after girls."

Fiona hadn't told her the only monster girls around here had to worry about was Eamon. That would be stupid, especially as he wasn't even here anymore. Not only that, Fiona would be carted off to a kids' home for her part in it.

"I get that." Ortun nodded. "So we'll go to Scud and drink on the bank, for Nerys, yeah?"

"But it's ages away," Fiona said. "We'll have to come back soon after we get there. It takes half an hour to reach."

"So? That's an hour drinking on the bank, and anyroad, we can walk faster." Ortun checked the watch his father had bought him last year. He was lucky to have it. Not many kids owned one.

"Fine," she said. "Come on, then."

* * *

Scud Stream

Fiona hadn't let a drop of that whiskey pass her lips. Ortun had taken it out of his bag the second they'd sat on the bank close to where Nerys had been. He'd let Dan have far more swigs than him, and now, half an hour after the first sip, Dan was slurring his words and laughing a bit too much at every joke Ortun told.

Uncomfortable, Fiona once again wished time would rewind. She'd have said no to coming here, and even though it was still light out, it gave her the creeps being where Nerys had been dumped. It brought back terrible memories of Eamon throwing her in the water, of everything that had happened.

She'd changed her mind. She'd have a drink. "Right, I'm going to try some."

"It burns at first," Dan said. "But now I feel great."

Ten minutes later, most of Fiona's worries had scampered away, the alcohol chasing them from her mind and heart, and the tummy ratchet had disappeared. She felt good, carefree — until Ortun stood and smacked the bottle on Dan's head, shocking her silly. Amid Dan's shouts of protest, he pushed him backwards and sat on him.

Had he stolen the bottle on purpose, planned to get Dan drunk?

Ortun punched Dan's cheek. "She was strangled, but you know that because you did it, so now you're going to die."

Ortun bent over and pressed his hands over Dan's face. Ortun's weight and strength easily overpowered the smaller kid, who slapped his arms on the parched grass and thrummed his heels, fighting for breath. Fiona caught up to the enormity of all this after a few seconds of watching, her mind too addled at first for her to have reacted immediately. This was Eamon all over again, except it was Ortun being the aggressive bully this time.

She shifted over there on her bum. "Get off him."

She smacked at Ortun's head, but it didn't bother him. Unable to stand being a party to this, to anything bad ever again, she grabbed the whiskey and ran off, heading towards Scudderton, her sobs catching in her throat. She drank the alcohol to the point of gagging, then worried about how she'd get it into the house to hide it in her satchel with the sandal. She couldn't leave it here because of fingerprints.

Ortun would stop it soon, he'd realise what he was doing was stupid. There was no way he'd suffocate Dan for real.

She had to believe that.

But first, she had to ignore Ortun calling her, concentrate on getting home and hope Mam didn't smell her breath.

* * *

Outside the Sweet Parlour

"Fiona," Ortun said. "Wait."

She stopped walking and turned to him, a bag of sweets clutched on one hand. She hadn't seen him since that evening, avoiding going anywhere he'd be. "Keep away from me. I don't trust you."

He held the top of her arm. "Listen to me, I need you to say we were together at the park the other night."

"But we were."

"I know, but all *night."*

He sounded like Eamon, cooking up a plan, and she didn't like it.

She planted her hands on her hips. If she got him to think she wasn't afraid of him, he'd leave her alone, but she was *afraid. "Why, will you murder* me *next if I don't?"*

"What? And keep your voice down, for Pete's sake. No, we need to have been together. Like, we didn't leave the park until home time."

She whispered, "But someone would have seen us all in Blenheim Road, stupid."

"I didn't think of that."

She had to know. "You killed him, didn't you?"

"No! I didn't!"

"You told him you would. You said—"

"I was teaching him a lesson, showing him what I'll do if I find out for sure he hurt my sister."

"So what happened after I went, then?" She dug her fingertips into her hips until it hurt.

"I got up and left him there after you ran off. I called you, but you wouldn't stop running. He was fine, only groggy. It's just . . ."

"What . . . ?"

"He didn't make it home. My dad knows his, and he told him he'd gone out and hadn't come back. He called the police, and they think a kid killer is out there, just like your mam said to you."

Fiona didn't know whether to believe him or not, but the look on his face seemed genuine. "Do you swear you didn't do owt else to him when I ran? Swear on Nerys's memory?"

"I swear."

"Then where can he be?"

"I don't know, but the police are going to the stream today."

"Oh God . . ." The world seemed to spin, and she wished she had some of that whiskey to push everything away.

"Please, say we were together until we both went home for nine. I didn't do *owt, I promise you."*

Maybe she was a fool for swallowing his words, but she did. If she told herself he was telling the truth, it meant something else had happened to Dan, someone else had hurt him.

That afternoon, the police found Dan's body, and for the first time, Fiona stole a few gulps of sherry from Mam's Christmas cupboard.

It shooed her fears away.

CHAPTER TWENTY-FOUR

The Backstreet Entrance

Butterfly had left the Little Devil to see what all the commotion was. A loud bang and the noise of glass exploding ten minutes ago had shit the life out of everyone in the pub. Shouts had filtered in there a few minutes ago, and people had rushed to the exit, one of them coming back in to say there was a fire down the Backstreet but the emergency services had been called. Fifteen minutes after that, Butterfly had walked down there, a fire engine parked at the end of the road, chugging noise into the air and grating on the nerves. The vehicle had been put out, one fireman holding his hand up to keep everyone at bay.

Butterfly's sixth sense said this was related to them somehow, that those roosting chickens they'd thought of before were indeed threatening to come back home. Why, though? Why, after all this time?

"It's Steady's van," a fella said.

"What's it doing parked there?"

"Maybe he's on one of the boats."

"But he'd walk here. He only lives in the Rest."

"Shit, I wonder if he was in the van when it went up . . ."

Butterfly turned away and trudged back to the pub to ponder why this ominous voice in their head seemed to think Steady's van had something to do with them. It didn't, but as sure as Butterfly knew they'd done wrong for many years, they knew there was a connection somewhere.

I just need to find it. Make it go away. And if I can't?

Oh God.

CHAPTER TWENTY-FIVE

The Marina

The scent of smoke in the air puzzled Mason. At half past midnight, he parked his bike down the Backstreet and frowned. Something was off, but he couldn't put his finger on it. Everywhere was quiet, no lights on in any of the boats opposite, but a strange feeling persisted. Maybe he ought to take Skipper home and kill him there — in the cellar so Eamon could watch and know what was coming to him if he didn't play ball.

A patch of the road and some of the path didn't look right, even in the dark. Was it wet, stained? He dared not put his torch on to check. He caught the shadowy sight of his bike and trailer tyres, thick with mud. Fuck it. He hadn't thought about the boggy ground in the woodland creating a problem. If only he hadn't used all of the water. He could have washed them on the path. Then again, there would have been more chance he'd be spotted. Fuck all he could do about it now.

To take his mind off his faux pas, he checked beneath the tarpaulin. Skipper was waking up, although he wasn't with it at all. His head was a bit of a mess, lots of dried blood since so much time had passed, so maybe his brains had scrambled. It might be a job and a half to get him to the *Jar* if he couldn't walk; Skipper had been heavy when he'd lugged him into the trailer earlier, heavier than Mason had estimated, so how the fuck would he get him over the road in good time?

Mason had to be quick. Violet must be going out of her mind by now, phoning around, and who knew whether she'd get a search party together and they'd all coming storming along here at any moment, fishermen and their wives to the rescue. She was still in love with Skipper after all these years, and she'd know him not coming home wasn't like him.

Everyone knew it. The man did everything like clockwork.

Mason had a moment of sorrow for the woman then swiped it out of his mind and heart. No one had cared for *him* and what *he'd* been going through all his life, so why should he care about her?

He secured the tarpaulin again and ran across the road, hoping Skipper didn't find his way out while he was gone. On the jetty, Mason jogged over the planks with the intention of steering his boat behind Eamon's yacht so he had less distance to drag Skipper if it came to that.

The *Jar* wasn't there.

"*What the fuck?*" he whispered.

His guts rolled over, and he flitted up and down, frantic, looking for it. Someone must have moved it, but why and how? He supposed they could have tugged it using another vessel, but there was no reason to do that, was there?

Or is that smell of smoke from my boat? Did it catch fire? Has it been taken away for the police to check it over? Shit, would they have gone to the cottage to tell me? Was that what the bang was earlier?

There was no time to worry about that now, not when he had an injured man in his trailer, plus Fred Collerton could wake up, come out on deck and spot Mason. He'd have to drown Skipper another way, take a massive risk.

Mason rushed to his bike and checked on Skipper. The man had gone back to sleep, loud snores coming out of him, so at least he was alive to feel the vicious burn of water in his lungs. Mason got on his bike and rode towards the pier. You wouldn't be able to tell any police had been there today, all of them packed up and gone. *Should* he risk it? Or should he take Skipper down the beach and hold his head beneath the water like he'd done to Mam?

No, he didn't reckon he'd get away with that a second time.

He rode up the boards as far as the fairground and parked behind the Beach Hut Café. Quickly, he took his muddy boots off and flung the tarpaulin back, rooting around Skipper for the longer lengths of rope he'd cut when he'd been preparing for Ortun's death — he'd ensured he had more than he'd needed in case things had gone wrong. Glad of his foresight, he tied the ends to Skipper's ankles then dropped the tailgate on the trailer. He pulled the man off and let him drop to the boards, giving himself a moment to check all around him for any nosy parkers.

He doubled over and dragged Skipper to the railings, smears of blood from his head creating stains. He didn't dare to smack the struts out with his mallet this time — the echoes of thuds might be heard so close to shore. He knotted the other ends to the top railing then peered over to check the height of the sea. The ropes should be the right length. The sea was high enough, so Skipper's head would immerse, even though his body wouldn't. On his knees, he slapped Skipper's face, pleased it only took a few cracks of his palm to bring the man round.

Skipper groaned.

It was clear that having a conversation with him wasn't going to happen, the mallet had done some proper damage, but he spoke anyway.

"If you'd given me a job after Ortun sacked me, if you'd believed me when I said I wasn't a pervert, none of this would be happening."

He stood and grabbed Skipper beneath the armpits. It took a lot of effort to get him on his feet and lean him belly-first against the railings, but he managed it, puffing and panting. A dip of his knees, and he pressed his head into Skipper's lower back to keep him in place, then reached down for his ankles. A surge of energy pushed through him, and he lifted the legs, moving his head away. Skipper's top half bent over the railing, Mason gave one last heave, and the body went south.

"For the last fucking time, dickhead . . . Hold. Your. Breath."

A splash, and Mason stared down. Skipper's head and shoulders had submerged, and the man struggled half-heartedly, his arms waving through the water. His position meant that unless he had enough upper body strength to haul his torso up, grasp the ropes and pull himself to safety, he was stuck there, drowning his way to Hell. The mallet had done too much to that head of his for Skipper to rescue his own sorry arse, and Mason closed his eyes, imagining the salt water going into the bastard's lungs, filling them up, suffocating him.

Marvellous.

It was time to leave a message on the side of the café, and he chortled at the owner having to get someone to paint over it again. She deserved the expense, the frigid bitch. Were the police aware of his first lot of graffiti? It had been covered by the time he'd brought Ortun here. Mason had done it the night before killing him to see what came of it, but there'd been nothing except a few grumbles about kids having no respect for other people's property.

He got a spray can out of the trailer and got to work.

Yes, fucks did equal death. If Mam hadn't gone with Eamon, if she hadn't got pregnant with Mason, then none of this would be going on.

It was all their fault.

Lastly, he ferreted in his trailer for his little present then ran up the pier in his socks, searching for a suitable place to put it. Pleased with his location, he tied it to the handle of a wheelie bin and smiled.

* * *

After cleaning the bike and trailer tyres, Mason stripped his clothes off in the garden and entered the cottage, placing them and the poncho in the washing machine, setting it on an hour-long cycle. His detergent claimed it could get rid of blood, so anything that had transferred from Skipper's broken head would be gone soon.

He went for a shower, something he'd had installed after Mam's death — he never wanted a bath again. He skimmed through his memories of the evening. He'd so wanted to drown Skipper in the woodland and drag him to the edge, the body in full view. A neighbour walking their dog would have found him come the morning, or maybe sooner if Violet had decided to go looking.

Must bleach the plastic box.

They might know he'd gone missing by now, the police, unless Violet had gone to bed early and still slept, unaware her husband hadn't come home. He couldn't see it, though. She'd have waited up for him like the dutiful wife she was, worried, phoning the landlord to see if her husband was still there with a beer in hand. Once she'd been told he'd left at half eight, panic would have set in.

Mason had perfected that scenario when Mam had died, talking to the police. Calling them when he'd "found" her bed empty, telling them she'd been odd lately, wandering the streets, forgetting where she lived, saying she wanted to end it all because the demon drink had ruined her life. They'd arrived to get details from him, and he'd paced up and down the living room in front of them, pulling at his hair, acting the distraught son.

It had gone down a storm.

He couldn't believe it had been two years already. Two years of living without fear of a tongue-lashing, no more shame heaped on his shoulders by her for existing, no more being called "the Jar" in her drink-addled voice. That had been the final straw, her not explaining why she'd chosen to call him Mason, why the nickname.

That night, he'd decided to get rid of her. He'd lost his job on the *Nerys Angel* the week before, and his camel's back had broken.

But he still had that weight, though, in the form of people being wary around him, thinking he was a perv. Life wasn't fair at all.

Must clean my boots.

Well, she was gone now, and once he'd dealt with Fred Collerton, the last of the bastards who'd turned him away for a job, he could finally move on. Yes, he'd still have people looking at him funny because of the rumour, but he hadn't touched a woman since, and that had to count for something. A few folks would say he was behaving himself these days but was a letch underneath, but some would think about how well-behaved he was now, *and* before he'd touched the woman up, so maybe his version of events was true?

Anyway, with the three main fishermen gone, the flames of gossip would die down. Yet . . . it had lasted two years so far, and Mam's nasty dead-woman voice whispered about people having long memories and not forgetting.

Mason would show them. Next week, he'd be the one providing their cod from June's Chippy, and they'd thank him for hiring a boat and saving the day. Jason didn't bring enough in, and anyway, he sold elsewhere. They'd forget all about Mason's hand on that woman's arse, him asking her if she wanted to go home with him, and he'd be forgiven. Yolanda had ignored him since that night, so everything was okay there. She hadn't fuelled the rumours, but she hadn't disputed them either.

Maybe I shouldn't have chosen her café to ruin with graffiti.

Of course I should have. She didn't exactly fight my corner, did she?

Did a small part of him blame her for this, too? If she'd have gone with him, you know, let him have sex with her, none of what followed would have happened. No one would think he was a deviant.

He shut the shower off and dried himself. Put his pyjamas and monster-face fluffy brown slippers on. As he was so buoyed up from the drowning, so awake and *alive*, he'd spend the next hour or so doing housework, then go and check on his captive.

Cottage clean and tidy, the washing machine finished, he hung his poncho to dry from a hook on the wall above the hallway radiator and stuck his clothes in the tumble dryer, draping the extraction hose out of the window. He collected the plastic box from the trailer and his boots from the patio and washed them in the shower. The plughole got clogged with mud. God.

Everything sorted, he approached the cellar door. Something caught his eye. His boat keys were missing from the rack on the wall, and his heart all but somersaulted. He checked on the floor in case they'd fallen off but found nothing except a toast crumb he'd missed with the hoover. Fear pervaded him, fear of having been robbed, and he rushed upstairs to check under the bed.

The suitcase was gone.

Oh fuck. Had Eamon got free of the cuffs? Had he managed to leave the cellar? Taken back all that money and stolen the keys? Gone off on the *Jar*? But why would he need either of those things? He had his own cash, his own boat. It didn't make *sense*.

Mason pelted downstairs, pain gripping his chest. The key to the cellar door was still in the hole, but that didn't mean anything. He turned it, and the click of unlocking didn't mean anything either. Eamon could have secured it before he'd left. To trick him.

Shit, what if the man was with the police now, telling them Mason had kidnapped him? What if they'd already been here when he was out? They could blame him for Skipper, he wouldn't have being in his cottage as an alibi.

This couldn't go wrong. It wasn't *allowed* to.

No, Eamon would be downstairs. He had to be.

Mason switched the light on. Nerves, a pinch of terror and a lot of anger propelled him down the stairs, and he stopped short at the entrance to the aisle.

"Oh God. Oh shit . . ."

Eamon had a hammer sticking out of his head.

Mason ran up the aisle and stopped in front of him. Blood drenched Eamon's face, wet and sticky in places, dried in others. How long ago had this happened? And who the fucking hell had killed him?

Someone had been here, in the safe haven he'd created after sending Mam to Hell. They'd entered his home, taken his money and the boat keys, and discovered Eamon.

The only person Mason knew who could get into a building without any hassle was Steady. Had it been him? Had he fucked off with the money on the *Jar*?

But another realisation slapped him around the face.

With Eamon so clearly dead, he couldn't write a new will.

Mason had possibly lost out on his inheritance unless he proved he was related through the DNA test.

He screamed at the ceiling, and the devil in him took hold. Mason punched Eamon repeatedly, anywhere and everywhere, his dreams and aspirations turned to ashes because of someone else. Again.

Someone he'd thought of as a friend.

The second betrayal regarding Steady stung more than words could say.

CHAPTER TWENTY-SIX

The Pier

Protective gear on, Carol and Dave stood in a tent between the edge of the fairground and the side of the café. Prior to their arrival, Skipper Kinnock's body had been pulled up from where he'd been dangling by rope from the railing, all the in-situ photographs and gubbins done already. A woman, Yolanda Rubio, had called the death in at 6 a.m.

Carol couldn't believe they were here. Someone had the audacity, the *balls*, to come again so soon after Ortun's murder, even spending time leaving more graffiti on the side of the café.

Questions thrummed through her ever-working mind. Didn't they care about being seen? Caught? Or was that the main thrill, hanging around afterwards, pushing their luck, their bodies alive with the anticipation of someone coming by and seeing what they were doing? It was a damn shame no one who worked on the pier had had time to get CCTV put up since the police had gone yesterday. Did the killer even give a shit about being captured on film?

They're probably in a disguise, a balaclava at least.

Was the café linked to this case? Why leave the weird message on it otherwise, twice? Annoyed with the merry-go-round in her mind, she pinched the bridge of her nose to stop the incessant queries and concentrated on the body.

Skipper, fully dressed, a stark contrast to Ortun, lay on his back on top of a plastic sheet. Once again, rope had been tied to his ankles using the same knots, and his head injuries were visible. He'd been hit on the side and top of his head, and Carol had yet to find out if he'd also been smacked on the back of it.

His yellow jumper, heavy with water at the shoulders, the tops of the arms and partway down the chest, clung to the dead man as though it wanted to hold him tight. His jeans, relatively dry, had blood on them and another type of stain on the thighs, larger, one that had spread. Dirt coated the knees. Boots covered his feet, and the treads had mulch in them, a squashed leaf clinging to mud.

At last, something for forensics to get their teeth into. Soil samples, organisms and microscopic bugs, and that leaf could be identified by the tree it had fallen from. They'd have a chance to narrow down where he'd been from all of those findings.

Rib, kneeling on an evidence step, scrunched his nose. "He was sick before death." He leaned over and took a big sniff of the jeans.

Carol groaned. "That's such a gross thing to do. Bloody hell!"

"Part of the job. Did you know, I can identify thousands and thousands of scents off the cuff? Even mixed ones. I'm proud of that. I'd say he was sitting when he puked as he has mud on the bum of his jeans."

Carol bit back a heave. The smell, although faint, likely from the body being outdoors all night, had reached her nose regardless the moment she'd stepped inside the small tent, and she'd recognised it as the same stench that pervaded their home after Mam had left. Her father, throwing up from drinking sessions. It was an aroma she'd never forget, and the faintness of it now reminded her of the times she'd scrubbed the mess off the carpet, only for it to linger for days afterwards.

"Alcohol," she stated.

"Definitely, so he'd either been to a pub or drank at home, possibly in someone else's."

"Violet called in to report him missing, Joy told us when we got into the station, then Miss Rubio found the body, and here we are."

Dave folded his arms. "It's looking like this is something to do with the fishing after all. That someone wanted to stop Ortun and Skipper from bringing it in."

Carol nodded and took her phone out. "It's such a lame reason to kill, though." Despite that, for safety reasons and to cover their arses, she rang Richard Prince, who once again stood at the front of the pier turning people away, denying them their chance to earn a living at the arse end of the season, denying others their fun. "Rich, can you do me a favour and organise for someone to go and see Fred Collerton? I think it's wise he goes and stays elsewhere and keeps out of sight for the time being."

"He'll be out on his boat," Richard said, "but I can ask the marina manager to get hold of him via radio and advise him to come back, then send Pitson along to have a word. Explain things."

"Thanks. Can you also sort the other fishermen — warn them, too. I'd rather be safe than sorry. How are you diddling?"

"Lots of annoyed people, as to be expected."

"Good luck with that. See you on our way past. We'll need to speak to Miss Rubio quickly then go and visit Violet."

"Helen May is with her at the minute. Violet's been told a body's been found, just not who it is."

"Okay. Poor woman."

"Hmm. Do you want me to get Whitney round there? Violet might benefit from a family liaison officer, seeing as she's now on her own."

"Get Helen to ask her first. I don't want her having a FLO if she doesn't want one. And besides, I don't think Violet needs watching or spying on, not like Gary last summer."

"Leave it to me."

Carol tucked her phone away and looked down at Skipper, saddened they hadn't caught who'd killed Ortun before they could move on to this man. "Whoever's done this is warped in the head. Killing people to stop them fishing? Is that *really* what we think? It's nuts — *if* that's what's going on."

"True, it does sound crackers," Dave said, "but do you remember that old boy who killed his neighbour because he'd lopped off some overhanging bushes on his property? People only have so many straws, and for him, that was the last one. But it could be a coincidence and there's something else going on here. The graffiti suggests having sexual intercourse results in death, so we *could* be going back to the affair business — Hattie, Louise, Callum."

She was about to answer when Todd poked his hooded head inside the tent.

"Carol, did you get a chance to look at the report I sent through last night?"

She spun to fully face him. "No. What was it?"

"A wooden plaque of sorts, roughly cut, cable-tied to the railing behind the Sweet Parlour. Someone had written the word 'die' on it in white paint. It's with forensics now, but I don't hold out much hope of getting any prints off it. I'm guessing the plaque was made before the weather turned to shit, otherwise all that rain would have washed the word away if it had been done just after the murder."

"Was a paintbrush used, d'you think, or a spray like the graffiti?"

"Spray."

"So that's definitely something to do with this."

Rib chuckled. "If it isn't, it's a pretty weird thing to do just for the fun of it."

Todd cleared his throat. "We found another one just now with the word 'you' on it. Tied to a bin behind the gift shop. We may get lucky with prints on that one."

Carol shook her head in disgust. "So we have someone who's spelling out a message for us. How original of them." She left her sarcasm hanging. "Okay, so we're to expect another death, then, another word to complete the sentence."

"Yep, afraid so, unless this is it, two deaths, and it spells 'You die'." Todd's head disappeared through the tent flaps.

Carol sighed. "Okay, do you have an estimated time of death, Rib?"

"Rigor is present, Bird. So sometime during the night." He laid a hand on Skipper's belly and stared at the top of the tent, thinking, gauging. "Between eleven and two."

Dave grunted. "It's a bit of a risk if the killer came here close to eleven with people leaving the pub."

Rib stood. "Some enjoy the thrill. Note the blood smears, as if the body was dragged." He lifted a finger. "I also sent you a report last night. Ortun died of drowning, not the blow to the head. I suspect the same can be said for Skipper. Ortun's Bermuda shorts have been sent for analysis to see if we can determine what the brown stains are on them — the soak in the sea didn't get rid of them all."

"Brown stains? I didn't notice any yesterday."

Rib's eyes crinkled above his mask. "You should have gone to Specsavers."

"Very funny. Did his bowels evacuate?"

"Yes, but *these* brown stains were on the front and aren't shit. It's a drink."

"Ah, I get you. The stains on the chair and the wall in Ortun's living room."

Rib nodded. "One of Todd's lot said they smell of hot chocolate. Given the liquid spatter pattern, we think it was poured on him."

"Ouch," Dave said.

"Ortun's scalp was burnt," Rib confirmed, "and he had a small blister at the point of contact."

Carol twitched her nose. "So this 'friend' of his who went there to tell him about the reef . . . We suppose they tipped a boiling-hot drink on him to get the upper hand?

Then what? They took him into the bathroom and clobbered him on the head?"

"Sounds about right to me," Dave said.

Carol let out such a long, forceful breath her lips wobbled and grazed her mask. "Okay, we need to go and see Violet as soon as possible, much as I don't want to. I hate this bit."

"Me, too." Dave moved to the tent flap. "But it's got to be done. The woman deserves to be put out of her misery *before* we speak to Miss Rubio."

Carol's mind whirred yet again. They still had to talk to Louise Roberts, too, but it had become abundantly clear this was no longer about an affair.

Or was it?

Fuck, I don't bloody know!

* * *

Fisherman's Rest

Today, Violet had on a pair of blue jeans and a pale-yellow jumper. Carol marvelled at the human mind, the subconscious. Had she unknowingly opted for that colour, that outfit? Skipper had the same on. Was her mind telling her it was a way to feel close to him?

They sat at her kitchen table again, Helen May making tea. Violet whittled her fingers, her eyes red raw, her nose the same. Scrunched tissues lay on a circular wicker placemat beside her phone.

"Out with it," she said, her Irish accent more pronounced today. "I don't want ye beating around any bushes with me. Either it's him or it isn't."

"It's him," Carol said. "And we're so very sorry."

"So am I, a *mhuirnín*, so am I."

Carol had no idea what that meant, but it sounded sincere and kind. "Tell me what happened last night."

"He'd gone to the Little Devil, as usual. He always leaves at half past eight, so he does, and I was waiting on him. By nine, I didn't think much of it except that he'd only ever been late twice in all our years together, and they were for good reason, not him playing me about. So I told myself something had happened and he'd stayed to help. I'd heard a bang later on, so I put it down to that."

Carol glanced at Dave then back to Violet. "A bang?"

"Yes, and sirens. I'd say it was a fire engine."

Helen turned from pouring boiled water into the cups. "A van caught fire in the Backstreet. Howard told me about it, but that didn't happen until well after half eight when Skipper normally leaves the pub."

"What kind of van?" Carol asked.

"A small blue one."

Carol's stomach all but dropped into her feet, that horrible yet wonderful pull of realisation giving weight to her bones. "Excuse me for a moment."

She got up and walked down the hallway to the living room. Stared out of the window across to Edward Fields's place. His van, the one she'd clocked when they'd visited yesterday, wasn't there. Could it be his that had gone up in flames?

She put in a quick call to Joy. "Hi, it's me. That van last night, the one in the Backstreet. Who is it registered to?"

"Two secs." The clatter of keys being tapped, then Joy's response: "Got it! Edward Fields, number one Fisherman's Rest."

"Bugger."

"Owt wrong?"

"No, but I have a feeling someone's just slipped through our net. Okay, I'm in a delicate situation here. Can you get hold of Michael or Katherine for me and ask either of them to search ANPR and CCTV? I want the last captured location of that van, plus ask one of them to find out where the van was towed last night. Forensics might need to go over it. I want them to go over Edward Fields again, too, and see what else crops up."

"Will do."

"Thanks."

She returned to the kitchen. "I apologise for that, but it may well be linked to Skipper's death."

"Ye do whatever ye need to," Violet said. "I want the bastards who killed *mo shíorghrá*."

"What does that mean?" For all Carol knew, she could be calling someone a big fat pig.

"My eternal love, and that's what he was, ye know. My everything."

Carol had never loved anyone like that so couldn't begin to understand the depth of grief Violet must be enduring, but from the woman's expression, filled with pain and longing, of utter *loneliness*, she'd do whatever it took to lessen this woman's suffering by finding who'd murdered her husband.

She'd have to tread carefully. "How well did Skipper get on with his employees?" Better than saying the name Edward outright, which would alert Violet to exactly who Carol was leaning towards for these murders.

"Well enough. No animosity, if that's what ye mean."

"Did he ever mention a specific person he wasn't as fond of?"

Violet speared Carol with a knowing gaze. "Ye think someone who worked for him did this."

"I don't know, that's what I'm trying to ascertain."

"I can't see his crew being involved. I heard about Ortun, finally. I popped to Sainsbury's last night about six. Bumped into Hattie. She'd been with her George, so she had." She pondered something. "Two fishermen dead. There's a connection there, ye know that, don't ye?"

"We do. So, back to last night. You were at Sainsbury's."

"I was. When I got home, I put the shopping away, and at some point a bit later, after Skipper hadn't come home, I heard the bang. Couldn't tell ye what time it was. I went out the front to see what was going on, although it wasn't in the street, I knew that. Too far away. No one else was around, they were out, apart from Ortun, the poor fecker. I rang the landlord because that was a bit too late for Skipper to be hanging around, but he said he'd left at half past eight. So then I got to thinking the bang was something to do with him being hurt. Ye know how ye mind goes. I took a walk around there, down the alley over the way there, ye know the one, and people were outside the Devil, smoking, talking of a van going up, and the firemen were chatting to folks."

"That must have frightened you."

"It did. I thought my Skipper was in the hospital by this point, and I wasn't listening to a word Kingy was saying to me. I got home and phoned the hospital, but no one had been brought in burnt, not that Skipper would have been in the van in normal circumstances, but ye just don't know, do ye? By midnight, I'd worried myself enough and phoned the police. I had a terrible night, I can tell ye. I couldn't sleep. When Helen came about the body this morning, I knew. Truth be told, I knew around ten to one. Part of me died."

Carol had heard of this, people knowing the moment their loved one passed, and she supposed, having been in tune with Skipper for many years, Violet had a connection to him that was deep enough for her to feel things when they weren't together. If it turned out he'd died around then, Carol would never dismiss such a bond again.

Violet's eyebrows drew down. "Now, I know ye won't mind me saying this because it's said with the best of intentions, but ye won't be drinking my tea. Feck off out of here and find your man."

Relieved, Carol stood. "We'll get whoever it is."

"I know ye will. Go on. Out!"

* * *

Mayflower Gardens

Yolanda Rubio, who ran the Beach Hut Café, sat on her sofa, black hair in a high ponytail, make-up on point, and her skinny jeans and tight pink camisole top showing off her enviable figure. She was around forty, give or take a few years, although she may well have had surgery — not many crow's feet.

Maybe she's just got good genes.

"I am thinking of going back to Spain early with what has happened," she said, the words heavily accented. "It is not safe around here anymore."

"I know what you mean, but I don't think this is owt for you to be concerned about." Carol smiled. "The deceased are fishermen, and we believe their murders are connected, so once we find who we're looking for, things will return to normal."

Yolanda rubbed her upper arms. "I know, but finding him . . ."

"You said 'going back to Spain early'. Tell me about that." Carol couldn't discount the fact this woman might be responsible, had finished her bout of murdering, and was about to bugger off.

"I was brought up in Cadaqués and live there during the winter with my mother."

Carol relaxed. "That sounds lovely. Here just for the tourist season, are you?"

"I am. I live in a caravan on the cliff from May to October."

"Why did you choose Scudderton to live during those months?"

"I wanted . . ." She stared off into space and sighed. "I wanted to get to know my father."

"And who is that?"

"Senor De León, but he will deny it if you ask him. My mother was married to him, and . . . and when she fell pregnant, he sent her back home."

Carol frowned. "Are *you* married?"

Yolanda smiled. "The surnames do not match, I know. I have my mother's maiden name. They are divorced. He did not want children. I have discovered this for sure in the years I have summered here — I believed my mother but wanted to see it for myself. I have spoken to him, and he denies everything. I have not told anyone but you two about our relationship. Too ashamed to admit my father does not want me."

Carol thought about his yacht being empty and unlocked with his wallet left behind. No one had got back to her on that, so she'd assumed he was okay. She glanced at Dave, who nodded and walked out into the hallway, closing the door.

"What is he doing?" Yolanda asked.

"Just checking something for me."

"What, you do not believe me, that Eamon is my father?"

"I have no reason not to. Dave's looking into a query that cropped up yesterday morning. Your father's yacht was left unattended." She explained, then said, "So I want someone to follow up on it and see if he's turned up yet."

"You think I did something to him." A statement.

"God, no. It's loose ends. They annoy me."

"I do not dislike him, you know, even though he does not want to acknowledge me. I have come to terms with that. Although . . . him not wanting me in his life will not chase me from Scudderton. I have made a summer home here, and I belong. My mother told me many stories about this place as I was growing up in Spain."

"No grudges, then."

"None at all. How can you miss what you never had?"

Dave came back. "No sighting."

Yolanda frowned. "Have you been to his house?"

Dave sat on an armchair. "Uniforms went up there last night after another check on his yacht. He's not there."

"That is not like him," Yolanda said. "He has a pattern. I have watched him. He comes back from his working trips, has a party, then stays up on the cliff for a week, seeing no one, not coming into town. Maybe he just does not want to answer the door. For the week after that, he gets some shopping and he . . ." She blushed. "Then he goes off again on his travels."

"Why have you gone red?"

"I . . ." Yolanda waved as if that meant she didn't have to answer. "Something is wrong."

It certainly seemed like it. "Do you know of anyone he'd be likely to stay with instead of being at his house?"

"This is why I blushed. There was a woman. She is dead now, but I do not think they were friends. He used to stand outside her cottage at night during the second week he returned to Scudderton. Every day for a week he would do that, staring from his car."

"You've been following him?"

"I wanted whatever part of him I could get back then. I know it sounds wrong, but as I said, I have accepted it now and moved on."

"No, I understand, but it could be classed as stalking or harassing, so please, stop doing that."

"I stopped two years ago when the woman died."

"Who was she?"

"Fiona Ingram."

Dave wrote that down.

Carol drew a circle on her knee. "Let's switch to your movements this morning when you found Skipper."

With the tale much the same as June's regarding Ortun, except Yolanda had left the body hanging where she'd found it, Carol got up to leave.

"We'll let you know if we find your father, save you worrying."

"Thank you."

"We'll see ourselves out."

In the car, Carol turned to Dave. "What a can of worms that was. Blimey, De León with a kid? And what a callous bastard to send the mother packing once she was up the duff."

Dave shrugged. "Maybe they had an agreement before they got married. No kids. To some, it's a deal breaker."

"I know, but to ignore the child when she comes looking for you years later? A special kind of bastard."

"I agree. Sounds like he didn't even give her the time of day."

"She's better off without him, if you ask me. However, now we have *three* men in the mix. Two are fishermen, but all three have boats. Is *that* the connection, not the cod?"

"What, you think De León could be another victim?"

"It's not impossible."

"So why hasn't he been tied to the pier or elsewhere for us to find?"

"Life is full of unanswered questions. Maybe he's been dumped in the sea." She massaged her temples, a headache threatening. "Right, while I drive, get hold of Joy to arrange for a couple of uniforms to actively search for De León — I want to know who Fiona Ingram is, too. Message Michael or Katherine to add her to their snoop list. I mentioned loose ends to Yolanda, and we still have one. Louise Roberts. If we get her name in the clear, we can concentrate on speaking to Skipper's crew."

* * *

Gingham Avenue

Louise Roberts perched on the edge of a mustard-coloured wingback armchair. Carol had spotted it in IKEA the last time she'd browsed there, and upon seeing it here had decided to get it for herself next week. The footstool that came with it would agree nicely with her weary legs after a long day at work.

Louise had wittered on from the moment they'd been shown inside. Tea handed out, she'd lost no time in gassing, as if she rarely had people visiting and couldn't get the words out fast enough. She kept giving Dave the eye like he was a piece of meat she wanted to devour. Did Carol dare to cast aspersions? Not out loud, no, but the woman looked and acted flighty, a tart, sounded rough as arseholes, and she'd already admitted she had sex with anyone who'd have her. That she'd come out with it, no prompting, proud as punch, told Carol that Louise may well have made choices Carol wouldn't in sleeping around, but that didn't make her a bad person. She was far too honest, so hiding things clearly wasn't her style.

The visit had been a waste of time other than for Carol and Dave to use the toilet and to settle Carol's mind that this woman hadn't killed Ortun, nor had she had anything to do with Skipper if her alibi was rock solid. She'd been at the Little Devil last night, giving an in-depth version of events regarding the van fire, then copped off with a man called Lionel and spent the night in his "stinky-arsed" caravan. Carol had held a hand up to stop her from giving them too many intimate details. Apparently, Ian Yates, one of Ortun's crew, had seen her entering the caravan and leaving this morning. They'd walked down to the marina together, then she'd left him and returned home.

Carol made another decision, nothing to do with the mustard chair. She'd action uniforms to go and speak to this Lionel bloke, plus Ian, then they'd talk to Skipper's crew. *Then* they could go to the station and hash things out.

There were too many threads jumbled together, and it was doing her head in far more than she liked. What the fucking hell was going on here?

CHAPTER TWENTY-SEVEN

The Little Devil

Mason sat in the pub, his belly quiet now he'd munched his greedy way through a full English breakfast and three slices of buttered toast. The yolk in his fried eggs had been runny, something that bugged him, he preferred them hard, but everything else had been perfect. He'd had a long night, staying awake to dispose of Eamon's body. His legs ached from riding his bike so much, and his head had pounded until he'd downed a cup of strong coffee.

The landlord approached, inspecting the table to see if Mason had finished. Reg tended to linger, didn't like his tables staying messy for long, which was why Mason had taken his sweet time eating his breakfast to wind him up. He was sick of people orchestrating his life, their actions affecting his.

The man stopped opposite Mason and claimed the plate and cutlery as though he'd been worrying he'd lose it. "Terrible about that van, isn't it? Fancy parking it where you think it's safe and some jumped-up little prick decides to have fun with it."

Mason frowned. He hadn't heard anything regarding a van. "What are you on about?"

"Steady's. Went up like a firecracker last night, it did. Ah, you weren't in here, were you? I did wonder why. You're usually at the bar every night. Poorly or something?" He grinned. "Or did *you* torch the van?"

"No, I fucking didn't. I just had a night in front of the telly, that's all. I don't always have to be here, you know." Mason fumed inside. Why did people insist on knowing shit about him then telling him so? Why couldn't he get on with his life without people poking their bloody hooters in?

Steady's van. Things made sense now, especially because he remembered what Steady had told him once — if he ever thought he'd get caught for robbing again, he'd disappear. Was the heat too much for him this time because murder was attached to it? Had he fucked off? That can't be the whole story, there was much more to this. He must have nicked the money, the *Jar*, and pissed off into the sunset. What other explanation was there?

And he killed Eamon. Took away my chance at having an inheritance. A dad!

Mason acted calm for the benefit of Reg, plus William King at the next table, who was clearly listening in as usual. Probably so he could skitter off and tell his pig grandson Mason's business.

"Blimey. Was Steady inside it?" He didn't believe that for a second but felt it best to ask, to seem worried. *William can report that back an' all.*

Reg shook his head. "Nope. I spoke to a copper early this morning when the draymen were here. He came round to get a statement. They've seen neither hide nor hair of him. They went to his place last night, but he wasn't there. D'you know where he could be? You're in each other's pockets, aren't you?"

Mason hated Reg now. Hated him so much he could snatch that fork off him and plunge it into his eye. He'd become a nosy bastard like everyone else. But at least he hadn't barred him for feeling Yolanda up, so he had that going in his favour.

Mason tamped down the rage, tucking it away. "Well, we get on, if that's what you mean, but I wouldn't say we're in each other's pockets. That's going a bit far." Had it been obvious they'd colluded with one another recently? Mason had thought they'd acted normally while planning the laptop theft, but obviously not. "He wouldn't tell me if he was doing an insurance job on his van, if that's what you're getting at, and I wouldn't condone it if he had."

"But he'd tell you if he was going away somewhere, surely," Reg pressed.

I'd have thought so, but he fucking didn't, did he? "Nah. He's his own man. We're not buddy enough for him to say shit like that to me."

Reg shrugged, and the knife fell off the plate. He stooped to pick it up. "I told the police you were pals, though, so they might want to talk to you."

Mason's hate for Reg returned, and he battled to keep it hidden. "Fine."

It wasn't fine, it could ruin everything, and it also wasn't fine that he couldn't kill Steady now. The man was out there, with knowledge in his head about Mason, and taking the bloke out to drown him at sea wasn't an option anymore.

Sod it, he'd go for it and admit something he'd previously decided to keep quiet. "Well, I'd like to speak to them myself because my boat's been nicked."

Reg's eyebrows shot up. "Oh. You don't think . . . ?"

Mason warmed to the theme. "Makes sense, doesn't it? His van's on fire, he's not at home and my boat's missing."

William piped up. "I agree with that. Suspicious."

Mason nodded. "Yeah, we all know Steady got nabbed for robbing years ago, so it's obvious what he's done. What a wanker."

"I thought he'd stopped that rubbish." William drank some coffee. "I should tell my grandson, he might be able to help."

Mason thought about that. "No, don't bother him. He'll have enough on his plate, what with all this weird stuff going on." He hadn't heard anyone talking about Skipper being discovered yet, but he must have been. Mason had ridden past the pier to get here, and it was closed again, that copper in the hi-vis prowling. Maybe he ought to bring it up, see what they said. "I'll tell the plods my boat's gone, they can deal with it."

William shrugged. "Up to you."

Yes, it is. "Does anyone know what's going on at the pier now?"

William nodded. "I saw the police down there so went along to find out. There's another body, that's all I could get out of them."

Wouldn't your grandson tell you? Mason widened his eyes. "That's terrible, that is. What's this place coming to?"

The door slammed against the wall, and he looked that way. Two uniformed police officers waded in, heading straight for Reg.

"Ay up, here comes trouble," Reg muttered from the side of his mouth.

William grunted. "Look lively, they're coming this way."

Mason wanted to get up and run but had to stay put. It'd seem well dodgy if he walked out now. Why had he come here for breakfast instead of making his own at home? Christ.

"Morning," the blond one said.

"Someone's already been about the van," Reg informed them.

"We're not here regarding that. Did anyone notice owt going on at the pier after the fire?"

William put his cup down. "No, I went home shortly after the fire engine left. Why?"

"There's been another incident."

Reg's eyes lit up. "Oh, fuck me. Like with Ortun?"

Confused, Mason eyed the landlord. If Reg knew about Ortun, why hadn't he said? Now was the time for his best performance. "What's up with Ortun?"

"Murdered," Reg said. "Hattie came in last night to let us all know. Bloody awful business."

"Murdered?" Mason hoped he'd sounded like he gave a shit. "Poor man."

The blond officer glanced at his colleague. "When was the last time any of you saw Skipper Kinnock?"

Mason kept laughter at bay. "Yesterday morning. I spoke with him on his boat. Asked him for a job."

"And you are, sir?" The brown-haired fella took a notebook out of his pocket.

Fuck it. "Mason Ingram."

"How did he seem to you?"

"His usual moody self. Said he didn't have any work for me at the moment. While you're here, I need to report my boat missing. Seems weird with Steady's van catching fire and him not being around, and now there's been a murder . . . Well, what if he's done a runner?"

The officers gave each other a look, one that said Mason might have a good point there.

"You could be right," Reg said. "It's iffy that he's not around." He addressed the policemen. "If you're asking about Skipper, does that mean . . . ?"

One of them nodded.

"Fucking hell, so when Violet rang last night to ask where he was . . ." Reg straightened the cutlery on the plate. "Who'd want to kill him, though?"

Mason couldn't stand being there any longer. He had ants in his pants and needed to get away from two pairs of piggy eyes giving him the once-over. "God knows, but I need to scoot. So, about my boat." He gave them his details then stood. "If that's all you need from me, I've got to see Jason about a job." He hadn't begged him yet, but he needed to be on the marina to listen to the chatter and stare across at the pier.

"You in later?" Reg asked.

"Yep." *I've just got Fred to kill, then I can celebrate, although what the hell I'm celebrating now is anyone's guess. I've got nowt left.*

He exited the pub and got on his nice clean bike, minus the trailer, and rode across the street and down a bit. He propped the bike against a lamppost and chained it up.

Steady might get caught if an alert was put out for the *Jar*. *And* because Mason had implied his "friend" might have something to do with the murders. He could get away with this, scot-free, if he played his cards right.

* * *

The Marina

Mason walked down the jetty and stood at the post where the *Jar* used to be moored. The space was a big one, Fred's trawler not there either. It sickened him that his little boat had been taken. The cheek of it, the presumption that it didn't matter, that the thief's need was greater than his.

What am I meant to do? I have no boat to go out on to make me feel better, no money to buy a new one, and no cash to hire a trawler.

It hit him properly that all this had been for nothing. How could he take over the fishing and selling now? He couldn't, and it pissed him off. His dream had been snatched away, but why was he surprised? All his life he'd been cast aside, seen as worthless, and now wasn't any different. He'd fought for what he'd wanted and hadn't got it.

Why did I brag to Steady about the money?

All that was left was the DNA test, proof he had a claim on the yacht, the house, all the assets as the only child of Eamon De León. Once the results came back and his body had been discovered, he could step up and announce he was Eamon's son. Yes, he'd have to wait for probate to go through, survive on Jobseeker's until he could sell the yacht, but maybe it wouldn't be so bad. He didn't have a mortgage to pay, and he could use firewood to keep warm instead of using the rads and racking up a massive leccy bill. He'd taken around a thousand out of the suitcase yesterday and popped it in his bedside drawer, his monthly spends, so unless that had been filched, too, he'd manage for a bit if he went back to being frugal.

He cast his gaze to the far end of the jetty. Jason's smaller boat was coming in, he could tell by the shape, another behind it, likely Fred's. Mason estimated them to be two miles out, so he'd wait for them to dock, even though no one else was around for him to earwig their conversations. It was eerily quiet until someone on the *Poisson Mort* shouted for a hose, and he peered that way. Skipper's crew stood on deck, stiff brooms in hand.

Footsteps on the planks had Mason turning. *Fuck*. Those police officers were heading towards him. The ones who'd been on the news. They'd probably come to speak to Skipper's lot, and he hadn't factored that in.

Shit.

They stopped, and the woman smiled.

"Can I have your name, please, sir?" she asked and held up her ID.

Mason's stomach didn't feel right. "Mason Ingram."

"Ah, the same Mason who's friends with Edward Fields?"

"Yep, although we're not *close* friends."

"We wanted to speak to you."

Oh God, this is it . . . "Oh right. What can I do for you?"

"Edward. Have you heard from him since you took cakes to his place yesterday?"

It bothered him that she knew what he'd been doing. *I bet that plod at the cordon told her. That's who he must have been ringing.* "I haven't, as it happens. He said he was ill, so I didn't stay long. Didn't fancy catching whatever it is he has. I was in the pub for breakfast just now, and there's talk of Steady's van being on fire."

"Who is Steady?"

"Edward. You know, Steady Eddie. Have you found him?"

"No. Would you have any idea where he's gone?"

Mason barked out a laugh. "Not where he's gone, no, just that he has. I think he's nicked my boat." He gestured at the empty space. "My keys were missing off the rack at home, and he came to mine yesterday morning to collect some eggs, so I reckon he took them."

She frowned. "Eggs?"

"I keep chickens," he lied. "Free range, and they sleep in my bushes in the back garden, but the foxes got the lot of them around midnight. I was out shooing the bloody things away for ages. Didn't get to bed until about three." That was his alibi for Skipper sorted. "I was surprised he'd come over, seeing as he had tummy issues."

"Even more surprising you went to his place after he'd come to see you, knowing he was poorly. You already said you left his because you didn't want to catch it. Double exposure in one day. A bit odd, don't you think?"

"Well, now you put it like that, yes. I thought the cakes would cheer him up, that's all, and anyroad, he didn't tell me he was ill until I gave him the cakes."

"How well do you know him?"

"He's a pal of sorts, or I thought he was, but he said a couple of things that didn't make sense at the time, but they do now. About Ortun, Skipper and Senor De León."

The man copper glanced at the woman, and she raised her eyebrows.

"What about them?" she asked.

"Just that they needed taking down a peg. They'd naffed him off for some reason, he didn't say what, and I didn't ask. I've just left the pub, and what was said in there is a bit concerning. I found out Ortun's dead and now Skipper, and De León's gone missing. That bothers me. We've got a DNA test on the go."

"Who, you and Edward?"

"No, me and De León. I found a letter left to me, written by my mam. She's dead, see? She said De León's my father, so we're getting a test sorted to see if it's the truth."

The coppers looked at each other, communicating stuff without words. Did they know something he didn't?

"You were saying?" she said.

"Yeah, he let me take a sample from him the day he got back. Trouble is, Mam acted as if she had dementia at the end, so she could have been having a false memory. If he's gone missing, that's a worry."

"Who told you he'd gone missing?"

He shrugged to hide his error in saying more than he should. "Just chatter in the Devil. I was listening in. Don't know who said it."

"What makes you think Edward took your boat?"

"Because he told me if it looked like he'd get caught for robbing again, he'd be off, and he'd pinched someone's laptop recently. Don't know whose it was, but I didn't want owt to do with it. He's on his own if he's doing that crap again."

"A laptop?"

"Yeah."

"If you can give my colleague here your address and phone number, that would be great, and if you hear from Edward, ring the station."

"Will do." Mason smiled.

"Oh, and while we're here. Do you know why Mr De León would go to your mother's and watch the place?"

Who the fuck's been talking? "Maybe because he's my dad? Maybe to catch a glimpse of me? I dunno."

"Did you report your boat stolen?"

"Yeah, I told the policemen in the pub."

"Good. Hopefully, it'll be found."

She walked towards the *Poisson Mort*, leaving Mason with the man. Details given, Mason strode back up the jetty towards his bike. If he hung around to see what was said on the *Poisson Mort*, he'd appear suspicious, so his next stop was riding past the pier for a gander then going home.

He had a cellar to scrub.

CHAPTER TWENTY-EIGHT

The Pier

Carol and Dave climbed aboard the *Poisson Mort.* Incensed the crew were scrubbing the deck, thick foam everywhere, she stalked over to the man closest to them, one with bleached hair and bushy eyebrows.

"Stop!" she shouted. "Put the brooms down *now.*"

All the men stared at her, some of them grumbling.

Callum Roberts strutted over, a frown firmly in place. "What's the problem?"

"Forensics will need to go over this boat."

"What?" He gawped at her. "Why?"

"Did you go out for fish earlier?"

"Yeah, Violet said to carry on. She mentioned Skipper didn't come home last night; she knocked on my door once I'd got back from the pub to see if I knew where he was."

She didn't tell us that. "What time?"

"About midnight. Got me out of bloody bed."

So the murder's unlikely to have been Callum's doing if he was out drinking then at home. "Right. So you used the *Poisson Mort.* Carry on."

"We went out and got a good catch, came back, sorted the fish below decks."

His dig at her about using the processing room and not the deck wasn't lost on her.

He cast his gaze towards the road. "The bloke who delivers it is out in the van, and now we're cleaning up like usual. I saw police on the pier when we came back, so June won't be taking her delivery, then?"

"No. Was everything the same as normal when you went on board this morning?"

"Yep." He paled. "Fuck, are you saying what I think you're saying?"

"We'll talk on the jetty. Get all the men off this boat, please — and I want their wellies left on deck for forensics."

She and Dave climbed down and the crew followed, all of them in waterproof overalls. The overalls would need to be bagged, too, but for now, the men could keep them on until forensics arrived.

She spoke to them at length, going over their movements this morning and last night. Predictably, all said they'd been in the pub, their main focus the van fire, then they'd gone home.

"What's going on at the pier, then?" one of them asked.

"I'm afraid it's bad news." She'd already informed Violet and she needed to be truthful to get the answers she wanted. "Skipper has been found. Murdered."

"Fuck me." Callum palmed his bristly chin. "What the *fuck*'s going on?"

You read my mind. "Do you know of anyone who'd have a grudge against him?"

Everyone said Ortun.

"Well, it can't be him, so who else?"

A few more names cropped up. Old crew members who'd rowed with Skipper over the years. Everyone seemed to have had a run-in with him at some point. The man had a short temper.

Dave wrote everything down.

Carol changed gears. "Has anyone seen Mr De León since he docked?"

An older gentleman held his hand up. Seventy-odd. Wispy white hair and a scraggly beard that had hints of his former colour in it, ginger that stubbornly remained, fighting the passage of time. "I was at his party the night he got back. Took the wife."

"What's your name?"

"Zeb King."

"Any relation to our Michael?"

"Yep, I'm his great-uncle."

"Okay, Zeb, how did Mr De León seem?"

"Annoyed we were there, to be honest, and I thought that was odd, seeing as he'd thrown the fucking . . . er, the party himself. He does that when he gets back from securing his deals. Likes to show off, does Eamon. He's been like that since he came back from Spain."

She thought of Yolanda and what the story was prior to her being conceived. Carol acted thick. "Spain? What's that about, then?"

Zeb folded his arms. "Thirteen, he was, when his mam married this Spanish fella. Joaquín De León, his name is. Rich man. He swept Eamon and his mam away. Eamon came back when he was eighteen, Spanish accent, acting all posh. Joaquín gave him some money to start his own business." He laughed. "We all thought he was a dick for it, how he behaved. He threw his first party, on a smaller yacht he owned, and told everyone he'd made it big. Ever since, he's had one every time he docks, bragging, letting us know we got left behind while he's travelled the world. We don't take no notice, just let him go on. We get free food and drink out of it, so there's that."

"Do you know owt about his wife?" Carol was interested in the age gap between Mason and Yolanda. Or maybe she'd guessed the woman's age wrong and she was older than she appeared.

Zeb nodded. "He met her while he lived in Spain. Brought her here and stuck her up in that big house of his on the cliff. She was a lonely sort. Used to see her in town, doing a bit of shopping and the like, and she looked sad. Next thing we know, she's gone and they get divorced. Odd business, but none of us pried as to the reasons. No point. He wouldn't have told us owt."

"Who has a grudge against him?"

Zeb cackled. "Everyone. You must have heard, surely."

She hadn't, but then town gossip didn't interest her unless it pertained to a case. De León had never come up in any of her previous enquiries. "Why do you say everyone?"

"It's the way he acts. High and mighty. You know what it's like here. We're all friendly. People like him tend to stand out. Has something happened to him an' all?"

"We don't know, although he appears to be missing."

"Shame Fiona's dead. She might have known, they were thick as thieves when younger. Saying that, they had a falling-out years back. Dunno what it was about, mind."

"Fiona . . . ?"

"Ingram."

"Mason's mother?"

"Yeah."

Why did they fall out? Was she having an affair with De León, told him she was pregnant, and they had a row? Was he married to Yolanda's mother at the time?

Mason appeared to be in his fifties. Had Fiona been pushed aside for the new wife? Yolanda had said De León didn't want children. Maybe, with both of his women telling him he was about to be a father, he'd lost the plot and broke it off with them. Why hang around outside Fiona's, though? Was it as Mason had said, he'd wanted to see his son? That didn't add up if he didn't want kids.

Carol would keep the information about the DNA test to herself for now. She wouldn't air his dirty laundry in public.

"What was this falling-out, do you know?" she asked.

"I don't know exactly. Fiona liked the drink, and she was in the Devil one night, crying into her vodka. She'd come staggering in, see, drunk already, her blouse ripped; one of the buttons had been yanked off. I asked her what the matter was, and she said she'd had a row with De León and he could die for all she cared, then she sank a few more vodkas and left."

"When was this?"

"I can't remember, but it wasn't long before Mason was born, I know that much. Always did wonder what it was about. I took a punt that it was to do with him having a wife and he told her he was bringing her over. Everyone thought Eamon and Fiona would get married, seeing as they were together all the time as kids."

Now Carol wondered what the matter had been. Mason's name had come up a few times, and she'd be a fool to discount that. Yes, he was Edward's friend "of sorts", but with the van being on fire and Edward going missing, not to mention the possibility he'd fled on Mason's boat, and now this little story involving Mason's mother and De León . . . But what was the connection? Why had Ortun and Skipper been killed? Or did she have two cases on her hands, Ortun's and Skipper's murders, then De León's disappearance?

Taps on the jetty boards alerted her to SOCO arriving.

"Okay, I'd like you to take off your overalls. Forensics are going to need them."

"Why?" Callum asked. "Ortun's crew didn't have to give up theirs."

"Because they didn't get on his boat after a murder. You lot did. We have no idea yet whether Skipper was killed on his, and with you cleaning the decks . . ."

"Shit, that's nowt suss. We didn't know owt had happened, otherwise we'd never have gone out to sea," Callum said. "Violet told us business as usual."

"I'm not blaming you." Carol put on a smile, although it was tight and felt odd, as if it didn't belong there. "Just do as they ask, okay? All of you, give DS Waite your full names, addresses and phone numbers, and we'll get back to you later on if we need to."

She walked towards Ben Asher at the front end of the jetty, who'd likely be lead SOCO here while Todd was still on the pier. She explained about the overalls and wellies, and the deck being cleaned. "There might be sod all to find, but it needs doing just the same."

Ben nodded. "Not sure if you know, but Todd's lot have found some muddy tracks at the pier. They fade farther along the decking, but the cordon's being widened. The tracks come from the alley beside the Devil."

She turned to survey the street. Officers were marking off a two-metre-wide gap either side of what she presumed were the tracks, blocking off one half of the road.

"I didn't spot those this morning," she said, more to herself than Ben. "Umpteen cars will have driven over them by now."

"Todd didn't see them either until he did a proper walk-along on the pier. Looks like three bicycles."

Bicycles? Didn't Helen report to Katherine that Mason used a bike? But Ben just said there were three, so . . . "So this could be three people committing murder, or the tracks are from yesterday, kids visiting the pier."

"It rained a bit yesterday, stopped in the evening, so the tracks were made after that. Todd's taken scrapings. If they match what's on Skipper's boots and jeans . . ."

A sliver of elation wiggled in her gut. "Sounds promising. Are officers following the tracks to see where they originated?"

"Probably."

"Me and Dave will do it. If this is connected to Skipper's death, we may as well." The bike thing bothered her. "Do you know a Mason Ingram?"

"Not off the top of my head, no."

"Okay, well, we'll get going. I'll leave you to it."

She strode to her car and got in, phoning Katherine to get her to look into Mason. Carol wasn't prepared to dismiss him as being something to do with the De León issue, no matter how nice he'd seemed, and with bicycles now being involved, she couldn't discount him regarding Skipper either. Martine and Harry Smith from the summer murders had seemed nice, too, yet they'd been guilty as sin. Mason might not have anything to do with the murders, him having a bike could be a coincidence, but he could be linked to De León in more ways than being his potential son. An argument over his parentage? Yolanda had already said the man didn't want to acknowledge her, so why would it be any different for Mason?

Unless De León's one of those tossers who prefer sons over daughters. That could be why he stood outside Fiona Ingram's place.

Dave joined her and put his seat belt on. "You've got the look."

"Reminds me of that song by Roxette. I used to love that."

"I did an' all. Christ, I feel old. Anyroad, what's up?"

"Something's niggling me."

"To do with?"

"Mason and Yolanda."

"The fact De León's spent his whole life pretending he hasn't got kids?"

"Yes, plus Mason has a bike."

"What's that got to do with owt?"

"Muddy tracks on the pier, although Ben said there are possibly three bicycles involved." She glanced towards the other end of the jetty. A small boat docked, but a larger one loomed behind it. "I wonder if that's Fred. Come on, we'll speak to him." She got out of the car and phoned Michael. "Can you do a search on a Yolanda Rubio, please, Beach Hut Café. Also, can you let Richard Prince know we don't need Pitson to speak to Fred Collerton, just the other fishermen? I can't see anyone else, so I assume they've gone home. Also tell him we're going to follow the tracks. He'll probably know what you mean."

She thanked him and slid her phone away, then she and Dave waited in the gap where Mason's boat was supposed to be, Fred bringing his vessel round. He climbed down to secure it to a post and gave them the side-eye.

She held up her ID.

"Here to explain why I had to come back early?" he asked gruffly. "I was farther out than usual today. Got a couple of nice ling as well as cod."

Carol had never heard of ling. "Yes, there's been some bad news."

He folded his arms. "Out with it, then."

"I'm going to advise you not to sleep on your boat at the moment. Is there somewhere else you can stay for a few days?"

He tutted. "What the bloody hell *for*?"

"Skipper's been murdered."

Fred's cheeks bloomed red. "Well, fuck my old boots." He tweaked his beard. "I could stay at the hotel, I suppose. I don't have to ask why. Ortun, Skipper. Then there's me. Are Jason and the others in danger?"

"We don't know. Do you have their addresses?"

"Jason lives in the street beside Fisherman's Rest. Horton's Way, number six, and I don't rightly know where Ken lives at the minute. He's been kicked out by the wife, maybe she'll know."

Carol glanced at Dave to see if mention of a wife throwing her husband out bothered him, but he remained impassive, writing the address down. Maybe he was over what his missus had done to him.

"Where does she live?" Carol asked.

"She's in one of the houses behind the pub."

"Dave, can you pass that info to Richard, please?" Carol asked. "He can tell Pitson where he needs to go."

Dave wandered away to make the call.

Fred regarded her through slitted eyes. "So someone's picking off fishermen, eh? All of us, or just captains?"

"It appears to be captains."

"I suppose I'd better get my haul off and pack a bag, then, hadn't I? I'll have to gut them elsewhere, and that's a sodding pest."

Dave returned, nodding to her. Carol nodded back. While she had sympathy to do with the disruption to Fred's day, finding a killer was more important.

"Where were you last night?" she asked the old man.

He grunted. Or it could have been a bark of derisive laughter. "I was waiting for that. On my boat. I'm usually in bed early, but there was a bang, so I sat on deck to watch the fire and all the palaver that went with it."

"We heard about that. Any idea where Edward Fields may have gone?"

"Nope, but I saw him taking the *Jar* out after the bang. That's Mason Ingram's boat. And Steady's been snooping on the *Claxon*, the yacht beside De León's. The owners are away. He took a holdall on there. When he got on the *Jar*, he had a suitcase an' all, so your guess is probably the same as mine: he's scarpered. I bet he's your man."

Carol hoped so and would double-check the boat theft had been filtered down the line for other ports and marinas to keep an eye out. She thanked Fred then led the way to the car.

Settled in her seat, she phoned Michael again. "I need Edward Fields's financial footprint. I want to know if he's drawn money out since last night when his van caught fire."

Hopefully, he had, and they'd have a location. She sighed, knowing someone else in another division would have the pleasure of collaring him. Still, he'd be brought back to Scudderton, and she could interview him, see if he confessed to the murders, but with no evidence they'd be strapped for time before they had to let him go.

For now, there was nothing for it but to follow the mud tracks.

CHAPTER TWENTY-NINE

The Woodland — Coldwater Estate

The chill in the air had Carol shivering. A light mist hovered at roof height, the sun struggling to penetrate it. By this afternoon it would be clear, but at the moment, it gave an ominous feel to the area. Odd that just a short walk away on the seafront, there wasn't any mist. It was likely rolling inland.

She studied the scene. The tracks of mud stopped at the edge of a path, but divots in the water-clogged grass, which had disturbed the leaves, showed the bikes had also been there. Slipping booties and gloves on, Carol and Dave walked a metre out either side of the tracks towards some pine trees, the ground wet and spongy. Carol trod carefully.

Dave stopped. "If this was three bikes as the tracks imply . . . People don't ride in a dead straight line all the time, and riders don't stick to this exact formation at all times either. These are uniform. There's the front track, single line, then there's two either side but wider, as though they have thicker tyres."

Carol paused to study them. "You're right, and if you look at the thicker ones, they're deeper, so to me that indicates heavier riders."

They continued on, and Dave pointed behind Carol. "There are more over there."

She turned. "So an entry and exit route."

"Could be."

The tracks farther out had veered to create the shape of a curve-handled walking stick then stopped by a line of pine trees. The wider divots were much more indented here, as if weight had been applied to the back bikes. The tracks then carried on at an angle, stretching to the path alongside the main road, so yes, a definite entry and exit, creating a wonky, elongated horseshoe. The question was, had anything happened here?

Dave carefully moved closer to the trees. "Um, blood. On the leaves — the same sort of leaf Skipper had on his shoe. And there are impressions in the mud, a patch where someone's been. Shoe soles, and marks where a person's possibly knelt. At least that's what I think it is, and it tallies with the filth on Skipper's jeans."

Carol sighed. "I'll phone Todd."

They squelched away from the potential crime scene, keeping close to the edge, Carol calling Todd along the way. They waited on the grass in front of the path, Carol staring ahead at the estate of streets. One of them was Fisherman's Rest, the one next to it Horton's Way, where Jason lived, and the others she couldn't read the signs as they were too far away. Each end house was side on to the main road with no windows, so anyone going upstairs to bed wouldn't have had a glimpse of someone, or three someones, out here last night.

Did Mason Ingram have two pals who also owned bikes, and they were all in on this together? But what about Edward fucking off last night?

With Skipper living in Fisherman's Rest, had he walked this way to come home and been waylaid, then taken to the trees? She turned to look at the grass behind her again.

"Footprints. Someone went on foot to intercept Skipper — which tells me they knew his movements, that he'd be on his way home from the pub at eight-thirty — then they led him across the grass."

"Everyone who goes to the pub would be aware of that, though. The time, I mean."

"Hmm."

They chatted about the case for five minutes or so, then Carol brought up the footprints in the alley and a piece of yellow wool caught on the hedge. She'd slid a small evidence bag over it from her pocket on the way here. It reminded her to phone Richard.

"Hi, it's me. We need an officer to come down the alley and put a cordon up. The one beside the Devil needs blocking off both ends, plus the woodland opposite the estate." She told him what they'd seen.

"So the wool's likely to be from Skipper's jumper, then."

"Seems so. There's blood on some leaves. Might be where he was hit on the head. I've got to go. SOCO's here."

"That'll be Todd. He passed me not five minutes ago. I got the messages about Piston and the fishermen, and he's en route. Tarra for now."

"Thanks."

She slid her phone in her pocket and approached the van. Todd got out along with four other officers. Carol explained everything, including the wool on the hedge.

"We'll leave you to it, but you'll see the pattern of the tracks and where people have walked." She pointed out their own footprints. "The others belong to someone else."

"The ground's boggy, so no wonder the tracks lasted all the way to the pier. The tyres must have been caked in mud when they left here."

"Yep, it's pretty messy by those trees, as if someone moved around a lot and churned the earth up. Which begs the question: why weren't there any footprints on the pier? The blood smears indicate that Skipper was dragged, not something someone could have done while sitting on a bike. They'd have had to put their feet down at some point."

"I agree. Right. We'll get on with it, then."

Carol and Dave strode on the left of the cordon in the road towards the car. Thankfully, she'd parked away from the marina this time on the pub side. More officers were in attendance, sorting out people who were on their way to the Devil. That'd be fun, telling them they couldn't go for breakfast just yet in case evidence was nearby.

In the car, she started the engine while Dave buckled up, but her phone ringing stopped her from driving away. Joy's name appeared on screen.

"Hi," Carol said.

"Where are you?"

"Just about to come in to catch up with Michael and Katherine. We're at the marina."

"Well, get yourself off to Braithwaite's farm. He's got a body for you."

"Oh, fuck me . . . Any idea who it is?"

"Mr De León. He's had his head bashed in."

* * *

Braithwaite's Farm

Mr De León had been placed behind the farmhouse, sitting propped up against the back door like a drunkard who'd lost his keys and couldn't get in. The hammer in his head wasn't pleasant viewing, and the blood dribbles down his face had dried and turned a rusty brown. Bruising marred his cheeks and one eye. Carol couldn't help but be reminded of the summer killings, the hammer the weapon of choice back then. This wasn't a mallet, as with Ortun and Skipper, so was De León's murder committed by someone else?

Had Yolanda Rubio been a bloody good actress when they'd spoken to her? Had she been rebuffed by her father again and finally snapped, attacking him with a hammer? Or had Mason done it? *Was* the De León business anything to do with Ortun and Skipper?

Carol and Dave, their protective suits rustling in a sharp wind that had picked up since their arrival, stood staring at the deceased. Carol, her mind on the verge of blanking because of the overload of information, sighed and walked away to where a skinny, ruddy-cheeked, brown-haired Braithwaite leaned on the bumper of his green tractor at the corner of the farmhouse, his flat cap askew. Dave caught up with her, and they accepted the cups of tea Braithwaite had brought out for them, which he'd placed on an upturned wooden barrel.

Carol shuddered. The stark reminder of her childhood ripped through her, and she saw herself as a child, freezing in the water, her father watching from behind the back door. He'd called her a little rat, and it was only now, as an adult, that she knew why. She'd overheard a conversation he'd been having with a friend out in the front garden. He'd been seeing another woman. Carol had gone straight in and told her mother.

Mam had left them after that.

So it was my fault.

Stop it. Focus.

She snapped back to her previous thoughts, although it took a bit of doing. Braithwaite had explained earlier that he'd emptied his barrel yesterday — it was for decoration, not punishing children, but all the flowers that had been inside it were dead — and as far as he could tell, it hadn't been moved.

With Rib en route, Carol may as well get the interview over and done with. "So when did you find him?"

"About forty minutes ago. I called it in immediately. Me and the dog had been out in the sheep field a couple of miles away since five o'clock, had to move them yonder, see, and when we came back, the missus asked me to bring the clothes in off the line because they reckon it's going to rain later."

"Didn't she see the body when she hung the washing out?"

"No, the washing line's at the side of the house, so she used that door. She'd have had her back to where he is. Anyroad, I came out from the rear of the house, saw him, and that was that."

"Did you touch him?"

"Nope. Recognised him straight off, knew he was a goner. Who wouldn't be with a ruddy hammer in their head?"

"Did you know him well?"

"Only that he's a jumped-up old prat. My dad went to school with him. Dad's dead now, but he used to say De León thought he was better than everyone else. I've seen him about town, when he's not away, like. Never had any reason to speak to him."

"So you wouldn't know of any grudges or whatever?" Carol sipped some tea.

"Nah. We keep to ourselves out here. Don't listen to gossip."

Dave glanced back at the body then to Braithwaite. "So did you hear owt at any point yesterday evening or during the night?"

Braithwaite shook his head. "I'm dead to the world as soon as my head hits the pillow, but my wife might have. Hang on." He went to the back door and called indoors.

A blonde woman of about forty, her hair in a high ponytail, came to stand on the mat but didn't come out.

"They want to know if you heard owt last night," Braithwaite said over his shoulder as he walked back to the tractor.

"Only your snoring." She smiled then changed her expression, probably thinking the joke wasn't appropriate.

"No vehicles or owt?" Carol asked.

"No, sorry."

A van on the main road came into view, followed by Rib's vehicle. They turned onto the long track that led to the farmhouse, and the woman went back inside.

"You can go in, too," Carol said to the farmer. "They'll have to put a tent up and whatnot."

Braithwaite nodded. "Will they need a cuppa an' all?" He jerked his head in the direction of the track.

"That'd be lovely. Thanks. Just call out when it's done, and I'll come to collect it."

"How many will you need?"

"Two secs." Carol peered at the vehicles parking and everyone spilling out. Rib, the photographer, four forensic officers and a PC. "Seven, please. All with sugar. If they don't like it, they can go without." She left him to it and waited for Rib to approach after he'd signed the log with the uniform.

He stared over at De León, an evidence step in one hand, his bag in the other. "Oh, fuck me. That must have stung."

He togged up and walked over with two techs carrying a tent. While they put it up, Carol and Dave continued drinking their tea, watching the photographer take snaps of the area leading to the body. The uniform was stringing up a cordon with one of the remaining SOCOs while the other inspected the track verge.

Dave glanced at the sky. "Looks like a second storm's coming."

Carol eyed the clouds. "Hmm. Can you believe so much has happened since yesterday? I mean, I get up to my neighbour bitching about being robbed, and now, here we are, three murders later, contemplating the bloody weather."

"It's certainly been busy." He drank some tea, his cup bearing the image of Homer Simpson holding a doughnut. "I signed the divorce papers before work."

If Carol thought he'd appreciate it, she'd have squeezed his arm, but other people were around. "Sorry."

"I'm not. That bloke's welcome to her. She's pregnant."

Shock punched Carol in the gut. "Fucking hell, Dave!"

"Hmm. She rang to tell me last night after me and you had been to the pub."

"Why didn't you say sooner?"

He shrugged. "Needed time to process it."

"How do you feel?"

"Shocked at first, but I'm all right now. Glad she kicked me out. She's changed. Not the same woman I married. Spiteful. Blaming me for everything."

"That should pass."

"Here's hoping. The sooner the divorce comes through the better."

Braithwaite appeared in the doorway with the tea, and Carol took the tray from him and placed it on the barrel. She called out that there was a brew to be had and finished hers.

"Come on, let's get back to work."

At the now erected tent, Rib glanced up from his usual kneeling position beside the body. "Didn't you bring my cuppa?"

"Fuck's sake." Carol turned to ask Dave to collect it.

He tromped off, returned with a blue mug, chipped on the rim, and passed it to the pathologist.

"Thanks." Rib put his mask beneath his chin, took a swig and gestured to the body. "Hit on the head a few times with that hammer. Markings on the face; I can't tell if that's from before or after death yet, but it indicates a beating or a kicking. The blood wouldn't have fully coagulated, so any smacks to the face after he died would still create bruises. He's stiff as a board, so in full rigor or on his way out of it. So, dead from around ten to fourteen hours ago. He's shit himself, pissed himself — I won't gross you out again by sniffing — but he's pungent enough to smell it without leaning over him. Odd choice of clothing. A raincoat and pyjamas."

"So he was ready for bed the night before last, which is when we assume he went missing. It could have been early morning, I suppose. Any sign of his phone on him?"

"I've looked in the pockets. Nope. Question is, is that his coat or did the killer put it on him?"

Dave entered the tent. "I've seen him in that coat."

"Wonder where his slippers are," Carol mused.

Someone shouted through on their way past. "Pair of abandoned dress shoes down the side of the farmhouse. Look expensive. Hidden behind a bush."

"Cheers," Carol called. "So he left his boat with shoes on. Given the weather, that's not surprising, but why go out at all? What got him off that boat? Or who, should I say." She took her phone out and rang Michael. "Hi, sorry to keep bugging you when you're busy, but can you get on to Ben Asher at the marina and tell him De León's yacht is another potential crime scene? Also, put in for De León's phone records. I need to know if anyone phoned or messaged him about leaving his yacht to go out in the storm."

"Ah, Joy let us know he'd been found, so Katherine's already poking into him. I had a feeling you'd ask."

"Thank you, that's a weight off. We also need to know who was at his party, so phone your uncle for me."

"Which one?"

"Zeb. We spoke to him today, and he said he was there with his wife. Maybe he'll remember who else attended."

"I'll get on that now. Will you be in at any point today so we can go over everything?"

"Yes, after we're finished here." She ended the call and held her phone by her side. "Fuck me, my head's spinning."

Rib stood and gulped some of his drink. "Hangover?"

"Bog off. We only had a couple last night." She smiled behind her mask. "I meant about this case. So much going on."

Rib nodded. "You'll figure it out, Bird, you always do."

Touched by his faith in her, considering six months ago he'd have said something cutting, she swallowed an unexpected lump in her throat. "Here's hoping."

CHAPTER THIRTY

Bay Crescent

Fiona couldn't get over the letter in her hand. It was from Eamon, and he'd asked for her banking details. He wanted to give her some money. It was 1967, and he'd come back from Spain to start a new business last week. She wondered what he looked like now, an eighteen-year-old man instead of the teenager she'd last seen. Rumours had flown around already. He was different. Very different.

The letter obviously didn't have anything incriminating in it, but it stated he "owed" her, and she wasn't stupid, she knew what that meant. The monthly sum he'd written down had staggered her as soon as she'd read it, and it proved he was paying her off, paying for her silence. She'd accept it, she needed to get out of this house, find a place of her own. Mam was sick of her drinking, and Dad had shaken his head earlier, saying it was no way to live a life, addicted to booze. They'd asked her to leave, and she'd been worrying how she could do that on her wages.

Eamon's offer had come at the perfect time.

She'd manage on her own. She didn't need anyone.

All she needed was for the nightmares to stop.

* * *

Time had passed since Eamon had sent the letter. He shouldn't have come here, but a force had dragged him this way. In the time since he'd settled into the big house on the cliff that Joaquín had rented for him, he'd done nothing but worry about Fiona opening her mouth, despite her taking the money. He had to speak to her face to face, to know for sure she'd keep silent. Yes, she'd done so ever since that day on the moors, but still.

Eamon loved the house on the cliff so much he'd promised himself he'd buy it one day when he'd made his millions, and he was well on his way there. Ambition and bragging rights had brought him back here to Scudderton. He'd learned everything he needed to know from Joaquín in Spain, and he was already conquering the housing market. Building from the ground up, renovations to current properties, whatever he could snag as jobs. Joaquín had secured workers, men he'd had dealings with when he'd first come to Scudderton all those years ago, so everything had been in place for Eamon to grow his empire.

He stood in Bay Crescent, where Fiona lived in a little flat above a butcher's shop, alone. She worked in Woolies, he'd seen her there. He'd asked around after her, and some mentioned she was always drunk, staggering about and slurring her words. He couldn't believe it, not Fiona, and now he was about to find out for himself.

If she'd see him.

Maybe he'd left it too long.

He walked down the alley between the butcher's and the betting shop and turned the round handle on the blue gate. Behind it, a small yard, covered with a wooden structure which created a sort of room with a couple of stripy deckchairs, an old coffee table between them. A fat church candle with a black wick sat on the table, wax drips hardened on the outside, a box of matches beside it. To the right, a front door with no glass in it. He closed the gate and went to the door, knocking on it.

A minute or so passed, then it opened, and Fiona stood there. He already knew how much she'd changed in the intervening years because he'd been watching her recently. Her red blouse and matching skirt indicated she was ready to go out on the town, as did her black high heels and stockings, suspender straps pressing against the skirt fabric. She looked older than twenty-one, as if life hadn't been kind to her, and he internally winced at that.

Her mouth dropped open, and she narrowed her eyes. "What the fuck do you want?" She'd already been drinking, evident by her lengthened words, a drawl that wasn't a good sound on her. "Why are you here?"

"I came to see you."

"It's been years. Had to pluck up the courage, did you?"

She was nothing like the woman he was marrying soon. Fiona was all hard edges and a grating tone, whereas Valeria was soft, gentle, her voice lilting. Once upon a time he'd thought he'd marry Fiona, a childhood promise of theirs, but what had happened on the moors and at the stream had changed things, not to mention him moving to Spain.

He didn't think Fiona would marry him now if he paid her even more than he already was.

"I didn't know what kind of reception I'd get," he said.

"I heard you'd taken to talking funny, and now I know."

Ah. His accent. It had been so easy to slip into the Spanish way of speaking, to adopt their ways, their mannerisms, and it had benefitted him to change from who he'd been to someone new. Joaquín had adopted him, so even his surname wasn't the same as before. How could he remain the old Eamon, someone who'd amount to nothing? Rage had come over him that day on the moors — he'd been sick of Nerys's taunts, her jibes, and her encroaching on his time with Fiona had been the last straw. He hadn't gone into a fugue, he'd known exactly what he was doing, his hands around her neck, her struggling to breathe, and it had felt good. He'd had the power, not her. It had been wrong, yes, but did he regret it? No.

The only thing he regretted was not keeping in touch with Fiona. Before that day, he'd planned to write to her every week, then come back and marry her, but life had taken another path with him meeting Valeria, and here they were, strangers yet not, neither of them really knowing much about what the other had been through since they'd last seen each other.

"Can we talk?" he asked.

"Got nowt to say."

"How have you been?"

"How do you think?"

He held up a bottle of vodka — someone had said she preferred that — and her eyes lit up.

"Shall we chat about old times?" he asked.

"Only if you cut the poncy accent. Fucking hell. And you're not coming into my flat. We'll drink outside."

"It's fucking cold."

"So?" She flapped a hand at the deckchairs. "I'll get something for us to drink out of."

She closed the door, and Eamon walked over to the chairs and sat. Placed the bottle on the table. She was lucky to get a flat with a garden, even if it didn't let the sun in. He supposed it'd been used by the butcher at some point. Storage. Since Eamon had come back, the butcher had expanded into the old greengrocer's next door.

Fiona returned, closing her flat door, and tottered across in her heels, tossing her bag on the ground beside the other chair. She placed two mason jars on the coffee table then plonked herself down, releasing a gust of air from between her painted lips. A root around in her bag produced a packet of cigarettes, and she lit one using the matches on the table. Drinking and *smoking? No, she definitely wasn't the Fiona he'd known.*

Eamon poured, and she snatched the jar and drank greedily, not wincing at the burn. A seasoned alcohol abuser, then.

"How long have you been drinking?" he asked.

"Since just after Ortun and Dan found Nerys."

This was why Eamon was really here, to find out what had happened. There was no one else he could talk to about the murder without appearing odd. It had been painful, him wanting to know but not daring to ask. "Talk to me."

And she did, telling him everything that had happened since he'd been gone. How she'd convinced herself Ortun had killed Dan, not that the lad had got up, drunk, and wandered to the stream, falling and striking his head. Drowning.

"That's what the police put it down to." She stubbed out her cigarette. "But no, it was him. Ortun. He said it wasn't, but it was. I know." She tapped her chest with her pointer finger. "I know a lot of things."

"Like what?" He topped up her drink.

"Like how you've been able to move on, leaving me behind, while I'm stuck inside my head."

"You could leave town."

"But the memories won't go away."

"They do if you try hard enough."

"Maybe for you, what with that new country and everything being different. I'm still seeing Ortun, his mam and dad, how broken they all were. Are. They're still wrecked from it."

His true reason for being here poked at him. "What did you do with the sandal?"

She smirked. "I've still got it."

His stomach rolled over, and he had to fight hard to hide his alarm. "I thought you were going to get rid of it. Why did you keep something like that?"

"In case you thought you could come back here and give me hassle. I've got proof if I need it, then there's all that money you're paying me off with. I only spent a bit to rent this place."

"What proof, that you were there as well? It wasn't just me, Fi."

"I didn't kill her!"

"If I hadn't strangled her, she'd have died from that rock you threw."

Fiona closed her eyes, and a tear plopped out and down her cheek. She opened them again and glared at him. "If you didn't hit her, I wouldn't have thrown the fucking rock, so don't go blaming it on me. D'you know, this has ruined me. I can't sleep, I can't breathe, and the only thing that makes it go away is drink. Mam and Dad kicked me out because I'm such a mess."

"That's not good for you, booze and fags."

"You pious bastard. D'you think I don't know that? You have no idea what it's been like for me. Not only Nerys but Dan, too. I believed Ortun at the time, but not now. I'm scared of him, do you get that? He looks at me funny down the Devil."

"Don't go to the Devil, then."

"I'll go where I fucking well like, thanks."

She ranted on for another hour, and all the while, Eamon plied her with drink. When she was close to blotto and crying, he stood to stretch his muscles from where they'd cramped, bored of her going on. He peered at the garden roof and caught sight of the darkened sky through a knothole.

"Where's the sandal?" he asked quietly.

"None of your fucking business." She got up and teetered, the empty mason jar clutched in one hand. She staggered a bit and dropped the jar. It smashed against the ground, and she laughed wryly. "That's what my life is. Smashed. Wrecked."

She headed towards her front door, which stood slightly open. She couldn't have closed it properly earlier like he'd thought.

Eamon followed, leaving her bag on the ground.

She stepped inside, and he crowded her, entering, shoving her towards some stairs.

"Get out." She spun to face him, her cheeks mottled in the darkness. "I didn't say you could come in here. Piss off, go on."

"The sandal." He had to have it. Couldn't risk her keeping it.

"Fuck off." She pushed his chest.

"The sandal." He pushed her back.

"I mean it. Leave." She raised a hand to slap him.

He got there first and punched her in the stomach. "The. Sandal."

She stared at him, a hand to her belly, her eyes watering, widening in shock. Fear. What was she thinking, that he was about to do the same to her as he did to Nerys?

"No, never." Fiona turned and stumbled up the stairs.

Eamon gave chase and caught her at a bedroom, a lamp on in there, and she turned, about to close the door on him. He shoved at it, the momentum sending her backwards onto a single bed, and the anger he'd felt on the moors returned. He dived on her, pinning her down, and stared into her eyes.

"You will give it to me," he snarled.

"No."

"Yes."

"No."

Something came over him, a need to possess her, to have her, like he would have done if Nerys hadn't happened, him and Fiona together as a couple. And he wanted to show her he was the boss, he called the shots, like Joaquín had taught him. The man had educated Eamon in all aspects of business, and this was the same. A business transaction. The sandal for Fiona's freedom.

"If you don't hand it over, you'll end up like Nerys."

She breathed heavily, blinking, blinking, blinking. "What?"

"You heard me."

She fought to get up, and he couldn't contain his rage. Sexual desire flared through him, the same as it had with Nerys. He punched Fiona in her sides until she stopped struggling, then he did what he had to do, using a condom from his wallet.

She was a virgin.

* * *

Fiona cried on her bed watching Eamon rooting through her things, the space between her legs seeming to scream that he'd violated her and she'd let him, blaming her for his actions, like she'd blamed herself about Nerys. What else could she have done to get free of him, though? He'd been too strong, too heavy, a man now, not the Eamon on the moors. Even back then he'd been a maniac, and she hadn't been able to get him away from Nerys.

He found the old school satchel in the back of her wardrobe and crowed with happiness, wrenching the flap over and staring inside. His grin sickened her, his triumph at finding the only thing she had as evidence against him, and he held it up, his trophy, his get-out clause. Why didn't he wonder what the whiskey bottle was doing in there?

"Not a fucking word about what just happened," he said, pointing at her. "Nor about Nerys. If you tell on me, I'll kill you. Do you understand?"

His accent was so affected it was laughable, but she couldn't laugh for the life of her. None of this was funny in the slightest. She knew he'd carry out his threat. A pain shot up into her abdomen, and she winced, gritting her teeth so he wouldn't know she still suffered from his actions, that she'd always suffer.

"Then again, no one would believe you," he continued, the sandal clutched in the hand he'd punched her with. "I heard you're always on the drink. No one listens to a drunkard."

He walked out, and she went after him, desperate to snatch the sandal back and reclaim her insurance. On the stairs, he elbowed her in the place he'd so recently breached, and she thumped down onto her backside, tears burning. He rushed down the rest of the steps and outside, so she forced herself to stand and follow.

In the yard, the roughness of the ground reminded her that her heels had come off when he'd . . . when he'd . . . and she sped across to the gate and down the alley, coming out in the street.

Eamon had gone.

Crying, her sobs hurting her throat, she returned to the yard and grabbed the bottle of vodka, sinking onto a deckchair. She lit a cigarette, her hand shaking. Her blouse was damaged from where he'd wrenched at one of the buttons to get to her breasts, but she ignored it. Put the bottle to her lips. Tipped it back. And drank in the darkness.

Sometime later, oblivion calling, she got up, intending to walk around to sober up. She wanted to go to the Devil. To see people. Be safe. But she dropped to the ground in a stupor, her tailbone sparking with pain.

The gate opened.

She blinked to clear her hazy vision but couldn't make him out properly. He closed the gate and advanced towards her. Was he weaving? As drunk as she was? Had he gone and stashed the sandal then sunk a skinful in remorse? Had he come to say sorry, to beg her to keep yet another secret, the latest one where he'd raped her?

"You've got your legs open," he said, losing the Spanish accent. "Asking me for it."

He stopped and stared down at her, then kicked her chest so she flew onto her back. "You're a tease. You want it, you know you do."

He planted his feet inside her legs and undid his trousers, the sound letting her know exactly what he was doing.

He lowered onto her, his breath heavy with alcohol.

Oh God, he was back for another go.

Only this time, he didn't use a condom.

CHAPTER THIRTY-ONE

The Incident Room

Carol sat at the spare desk and stared at the notes she'd made. She could strike each thing off once they'd discussed it, then they'd get their heads together to see if they could pare down the suspect list — she had Edward in her mind for this, with maybe Mason as one of his accomplices. But who was the other one? Three bike riders, three killers.

"Okay, let's start with Ortun's drinking buddies. What did you get from Callum, Fred, Ortun's crew, and Jason?"

Michael sighed. "They said there's no one else other than a man called Ken."

Carol nodded. "We heard about him."

Michael opened a packet of cheese and onion crisps. "I spoke to him. He said him and Ortun got along well enough. Pitson got hold of me — he's had a chat with Jason and Ken and told them to stay elsewhere for a few days. Both men were okay about it, and they have solid alibis."

"Glad they've decided to take our advice," Carol said. "Although, I suppose Ortun and Skipper being murdered helped them make that decision. They could be next. Katherine, owt on the graffiti?"

"Only that it was sprayed before Ortun's murder. June called it in and arranged for it to be painted over." Katherine doodled on her pad.

"What did you discover about Dan Nixon's death?"

"Not much more than I told you before," Katherine said. "Misadventure, although Michael spoke to his grandad again."

Michael finished chewing a crisp and swallowed. "Yeah, residents thought it was odd, with Nerys and Dan being dead so close together, not to mention him being found in the stream as well. The police might not have wanted to follow up the link, but people talked. Grandad said word went round that it was a kiddie killer and they'd stopped after Dan in case they got caught."

"Or maybe they moved away," Katherine said, "which is why, once news came in about De León being murdered, I poked into when he moved to Spain. It was just after Nerys's death but before Dan's."

"De León was definitely out of the picture for Dan," Michael said, "but Grandad said he'd always suspected Fiona for Nerys. Apparently, Fiona went weird after the murder."

"A kid killing a kid?" Carol pondered. "It happens. It could tie into Ortun that way. He'd recently worked out who it was, waited for De León to dock so he could question him about Fiona's involvement, then they had a row and Ortun came off worse."

"So who killed De León?" Dave asked. "In an ideal world, it would be Fiona, to shut him up if she'd confided in him about the killing, but she's already dead."

"We need to look into how," Carol said.

Katherine lifted her notepad and flapped it. "I've already done that. She was found on Cove beach. The report said she'd taken to wandering in the last few years of her life, suspected dementia. She'd drowned."

"A water theme," Carol said. "Nerys and Dan in Scud Stream, Ortun and Skipper in the sea. De León . . . fuck knows where he fits into this. Okay, moving on to the next point before I lose my shit — this is so frustrating. Michael, Edward Fields's van. Any sightings prior to the fire?"

"Last one captured was in Sainsbury's car park last night. Internal footage, which they kindly gave up without a fight, shows him buying some canned goods, a few Pot Noodles and whatever. Food for hiding out?"

"Could be. Any news on the *Jar* being spotted?"

"Last known docking was in Grimsby this morning," Michael said. "He withdrew one thousand and forty pounds from a Lloyds in Cleethorpes — I assume he took the bus or a taxi from Grimsby. I spoke to the bank manager, and she said he closed that account."

"You two *have* been busy." Carol smiled. "So he's definitely on the run, then. Where was the van taken?"

"Forensics. It's looking like arson at the moment."

"That works. He torched it before leaving. Why? To hide evidence? Are the bike tracks some kids like I thought, and the van was used to transport Ortun and Skipper?"

Dave sat forward. "That doesn't work for Skipper. Fred Collerton said Edward had gone off in the *Jar* way before we estimated Skipper was taken to the pier."

"So we've got a duo again?" Carol said. "Edward buggered off through fear of being caught and Mason continued their plan? They were both sacked by Ortun . . ."

"So why kill Skipper?" Katherine asked. "None of this is adding up. As for Mason . . ." She consulted her notes. "This is from Michael's grandad again. Mother, Fiona Ingram, who never married. She lived with her parents until she moved into a flat above a butcher's shop, which is now that posh hairdresser's in Bay Crescent. She had Mason when she was twenty-one. From there, when Mason was three, she moved to a cottage just outside town called Kettlestone Rise. Mason still lives there."

"Rented or purchased?"

"Purchased."

"Any mortgage?"

"No," Michael said. "Grandad mentioned her buying it outright, and people wondered how when she just worked in

Woolies at the time. She never said how she'd come to pay for it so . . ." He glanced at Katherine.

She picked up the thread. "I took the liberty of looking into her financial footprint. The bank were very helpful. Fiona had regular payments going into her account since nineteen sixty-seven up until she died. She withdrew it over a period of time before her death from ATMs. Guess who was paying her?"

Carol held her breath.

"De León." Katherine raised her eyebrows.

"For Mason?" Dave said. "He told us about a DNA test."

Carol nodded. "That could be why they rowed. Zeb King mentioned them having a falling-out. She got pregnant and must have refused to get rid of it. De León didn't want kids so paid her to keep it quiet."

"It was a lot of money over the years," Katherine said, "even went up with inflation, but it can't just have been for Mason. She'd been paid three years before he was born, enough to buy the cottage, then it went up when the baby arrived."

Carol mulled that over. "So she could have been his mistress before the birth." She rubbed her forehead. "Talk about a complex web, and we still don't know if it's all linked. Okay, so Fiona was getting money. Would Yolanda's mother have been paid, too?"

"I'm still waiting on De León's financial footprint," Katherine said.

"Let's talk about Yolanda Rubio, then. What did you get on her?"

"Nowt much for the UK, but I can contact police in Spain if you need me to," Katherine offered.

"What has the UK got on her first?"

"She's been trading at the café for a few years, rents the building. No criminal record, although Michael's grandad helped us out again. One of the reasons Ortun sacked Mason, as well as being classed as 'too old', is Mason was a bit . . . well, he tried to get Yolanda to have sex with him, and Ortun didn't like it. He spread rumours that Mason is a pervert."

Carol burst out laughing. "That's a bit rich, considering Ortun fucked about with Louise. Double standards or what? And why would Ortun care whether Mason approached Yolanda like that?" It hit her. "Oh God. They could be half-siblings. Nasty . . . So maybe Ortun knew De León was Mason's father. He would have been disgusted."

"So what are we saying," Dave asked, "that Mason killed Ortun for keeping the truth from him? What about Skipper? Where does he come into it?"

Carol felt like screaming. "I don't *know*. Let's check off the other points then revisit that. So, owt yet about evidence on the *Poisson Mort*?"

"Nowt untoward so far. Ben said it all appears normal, bearing in mind the deck was being scrubbed." Katherine tapped her pen on the desk. "Nowt untoward on De León's yacht either. Ben left his team on Skipper's boat to go and have a look at the yacht himself. What he did say, though, was there's a lot of fingerprints, but he had that party so . . ."

"Owt on his phone records?"

"Yes, the company got back to us quickly there, which is more than I can say for Ortun's supplier. Digi are going through them. De León's phone is currently switched off, but the last pinged location is the marina."

"Fuck, that doesn't help." Carol sighed. "Right, so who was at the yacht party?"

Michael scrunched his crisp packet up. "I spoke to my uncle. He was there with my aunt and grandad." He listed all the other people. "They're from De León's schooldays, people he knew before he went to Spain. I spoke to all of them on the phone, only twelve in attendance other than De León, and no one saw owt dodgy or a guest who wasn't usually there. My uncle said it's highly unlikely any of them would have killed De León. They're good family people."

"That means nowt." Carol got up to stretch her legs and wished she'd gone to the same school as Mason. At least then she'd have more of an insight as to who he was.

Her phone rang.

"Hi, Joy," Carol said, aware she sounded defeated.

"I've got an Edward Fields on the line."

Carol's tenacity returned. "Shit. Put him through."

"Hello?" he said.

"This is DI Carol Wren. What can I do for you?" She played it cool, not wanting him to think she knew he'd made himself scarce.

"I know who killed Ortun, and I think he's going to kill Skipper, too."

Already done that, pal. "Who is it?"

"I . . . look, I've had to do a runner because I'm scared of him. I think he might go after Fred next, then me."

"Why do you think that?"

"Because of the job thing."

"What job thing?"

"We were sacked. I got a job after, he didn't . . . and I never told him. I reckon he's going to kill everyone who wouldn't take him on for work."

"Are we talking about who I think we are? Someone who owns a bike?"

"Yeah, and he has a trailer he puts on the back, too. He said he was going to put Ortun in it."

A trailer with two wheels? It'd seem like three bikes. Fuck . . . "He told you this?"

"Yeah. He's been planning it for a while. Mason. I went to his cottage to nick his boat keys, and I found . . . I found Senor De León dead in his cellar."

So they are *linked.* "Why would he have killed Mr De León?"

"I don't know. Got to go. Bye."

"Wait!"

But he'd cut the call. Carol took a second to process what he'd said. Mason. So it hadn't been about the cod or an affair. It'd been because he couldn't get a fucking *job*?

Dave stood. "I take it we need to go somewhere?"

Carol nodded. "Kettlestone Rise, Mason Ingram's cottage."

CHAPTER THIRTY-TWO

Kettlestone Rise

Fiona blamed everything on her son these days. It was better than blaming herself. For not getting an abortion. For being tied to Eamon forever, even if he didn't have anything to do with the child. Since moving to the cottage, she hadn't spent a penny of the money he gave her for Mason. It was tainted, and perhaps her cottage was, too, as she'd bought it from what Eamon had given her.

Nothing had gone right since that day on the moors, and she often contemplated ending it all. Removing herself from this hideous life. Days like today, when it all became too much, she wished more than usual that Mason wasn't around, this terrible tether to the past. She couldn't help herself, disliking him. His name, something she'd thought fitted at the time, grated on her nerves now. Throughout her pregnancy, she'd remembered that bloody mason jar, the one that had smashed, and how it had resembled her. Broken. Useless. No good to anyone. She'd called him that as a reminder of everything she'd been through, so that every day she'd have it right in her face that Eamon had violated her twice. A self-imposed punishment for not being able to shove him off her.

Mason had been weird from day one. She'd gazed down at his scrunched face after the birth and hated him. He'd looked so much like her father. Her dead father who'd joined her mother in Heaven. It reminded her of the American baseball card she'd found in Dad's bits and bobs after his death. She'd placed it in a box labelled Memorabilia *among his other things. Mam's personal possessions were in another box, one she'd spitefully called* Bitch *then had changed her mind and scribbled it out, writing* Mam *instead. How could she berate her mother for throwing her out when Fiona treated her own child even worse?*

Fiona was truly alone apart from the brat.

Mason was eight now, and earlier in the evening, Eamon had come to stand outside the cottage again. Watching her. Letting her know he was keeping an eye out. She'd moved from the flat to the cottage, thinking she could get away from him, but he'd found out where she was, and each time he came back from his travels, there he was.

Life was unbearable. She'd had to take on cleaning jobs to top up her shop wages. There was no way she'd touch his money now.

Just moments ago, she'd warned Mason to hold his breath if he wanted to live, and she held his head beneath the water in the bath now, him splashing, fighting, trying to push himself up, but his hands slipped on the soapy bottom and he remained under.

She'd become Eamon, in charge of whether another person lived or died, and it sickened her. This always happened. She took her hand away, moved back from the tub, and watched her child breach the surface, gasping, crying, looking at her as if she were a monster.

Which she was.

The past and the drink had turned her into one.

This must be about the hundredth time she'd tried to drown him, and she suspected there'd be many more to come. Each time, she bottled it, her breathing ragged, her vodka-addled mind whispering that she was a bad mother, a bad person. The booze didn't shoo away the memories anymore, no oblivion to be had, and the only thing she had left to make herself better was trying to kill the Jar or hitting him, pushing him over, tripping him up.

Yes, she was broken. Could never be fixed. And at this point, she was so far into the madness guilt brought on that she didn't want to be put back together again.

Maybe one day she'd succeed. Kill the kid.

For now, she hissed at him to get out of the bath and go to bed. A merry-go-round, her life was, the same thing happening over and over.

Tomorrow, they wouldn't talk about what she'd done, and she'd cycle to work, he'd walk to school, then things would build and build until the next time she pushed his head beneath the water.

It was the only time she allowed him to have a bath, when she wanted to kill him, so he knew what was to come if she called him upstairs. He must hate her, fear her, yet at the same time he was loyal. Loving his abuser. Trying to please her, get her to smile, to for once say a kind word to him. She never did. She didn't deserve his adoration, yet oddly, perversely, she enjoyed it.

It meant someone gave a shit about her.

CHAPTER THIRTY-THREE

Undisclosed Location

Butterfly paced the room. News had come. De León had been found dead. Three men who Butterfly had known their whole lives, gone. So was this nothing to do with the past, just someone killing old people? Had Butterfly's sixth sense been wrong?

I'm grasping at straws.

There had been no visit to the person Butterfly had planned to speak to, to plead their case and beg for forgiveness. Shame had once again prevented them from stepping forward to talk. They hadn't wanted their good nature to be in disrepute, for anyone to know Butterfly's life since that dreadful time had been a carefully crafted lie. What they'd done had been so wrong on many levels, and admitting it to another soul might break them. Taking what you wanted when someone was unable to stop you was a bad thing, but Butterfly kept doing it. Creating a façade and pretending to be a good, decent citizen all their life had taken a toll, though. Butterfly now understood people's need to bare all on their deathbeds. To purge, to speak of sins, to ask for absolution.

Maybe that was the thing to do. Visit the Catholic church and spill everything to Father Matthews. He'd find an answer, the man of the cloth who'd accepted Butterfly's money, placed on a silver tray Sunday after Sunday. Could Butterfly cope with the scorn, though? Even Father Matthews must have a limit. His compassion would be tested with what Butterfly had to say. No one could condone what had occurred.

No, there would be no confession. The words were too wretched to say out loud.

The phone rang, and Butterfly's heart panged at the name on the screen. Such a good boy, the caller. Someone Butterfly looked up to. A diamond.

I'm seen that way, but inside, I'm not who they think I am.

And that was the hardest part, the deception. The dual personalities. In patches of time, Butterfly *had* been a diamond, could almost convince themselves that they actually *were* this person they presented to the world, but the whispers, seeing certain people they'd violated, brought them back down to earth with a solid bump. Fooling oneself always caught up with you in the end. There were other times after the first, when Butterfly had allowed the demon inside to run free, again and again. The prowling through the streets in the dark, the bang of their footsteps, the fear inspired, then the inevitable conclusion. It was a wonder they'd got away with it for so long.

Butterfly ignored the phone. Eventually, it stopped ringing, then a minute or so later, a message arrived: *It's Mason Ingram! Apparently, De León is his father. Will talk to you later.*

Butterfly sank onto a chair. Didn't know how to process this turn of events. De León? What? How could that be true? Fiona hadn't been anywhere near the man apart from that argument the night she'd come into the Devil with a button missing on her blouse, Butterfly was sure of it.

Tears formed and fell. Lungs constricted. A cold chill seeped.

Butterfly looked around the room, and memories came. Of Christmases, of their children, their late partner, everyone so happy. At present-opening time, every year Butterfly had wondered about another household, how different it was to theirs. No Yuletide cheer there, no tree, no turkey for dinner. Fiona had said so. She'd said a lot over the years, thinking of Butterfly as no one to avoid, and why would she? It had been clear from the start she hadn't suspected anything. The secret had been safe, and Butterfly had been her confidant at times, her spewing out hatred for her child, how she couldn't stand to look at him.

I can't hack the voices anymore.

It had finally become too much.

The time had come to end this once and for all.

CHAPTER THIRTY-FOUR

Kettlestone Rise

Mason should have known they wouldn't leave it. Wouldn't let him live his life without interference. Those coppers were here, getting out of a car. They had a uniformed officer with them, too, and he didn't reckon that was a good sign. But maybe they'd found Steady and wanted a word. It might not be anything to worry about. If he acted normal, everything would be fine.

He waited for the knock on the door then went to open it. "Oh, hello."

The woman held up her ID, which was stupid, seeing as he'd spoken to her on the jetty. He knew who she was, and her treating him as if he didn't, that he was a thicko, got on his nerves.

"DI Carol Wren, DS Dave Waite and PC Alan Pitson. We need to have a chat."

"Come in, then. Got some news on Steady, have you? My boat?"

She didn't answer, so he led the way to the living room, nervous from the silence at his back. Was he supposed to offer them a cup of tea? No, that'd mean they'd stay longer, and the sooner they left the better. He had things to do and was tired from what he'd been up to earlier.

He sat on the sofa and looked up at all three of them standing in a line. They didn't appear friendly.

"We have heard from Edward, yes," Wren said. "And he claimed you killed Ortun and may go for Skipper Kinnock next, and that he found Mr De León dead in your cellar. What have you got to say about that?"

Mason laughed. "So he's blaming me for what *he's* done. Typical. You can go and look in the cellar if you like. No skin off my nose. There's nowt weird going on. I'm telling you, he killed them all and buggered off. I discovered he even stole my mam's money from under my bed. It was in a suitcase."

"That would be an ideal situation for you, minus the money being taken, but Mr Kinnock wasn't placed on the pier until after Steady had stolen your boat."

"How do you know? Has anyone come forward to say they saw Skipper being put there earlier in the evening, about the time the van was set on fire?"

She gritted her teeth. "No, they haven't."

Ah, got you there. "Well, then. You'd best be asking around and getting your facts straight. I'm not taking the rap for something that little shit's done."

"Do we have permission to look through the whole cottage?" she asked.

"Knock yourselves out."

He hadn't thought she'd actually do it, but there she was, walking out with the bloke in the suit, leaving Mason with the plod.

"This is bloody nuts," Mason said. "Steady's done me up like a kipper."

Plod didn't respond.

"I mean, why would I want to kill all of those people? Especially De León. He's my dad, for fuck's sake."

Still no response.

"Not the talkative type, are you?" Mason sat back, getting comfy. "Ah well, we can't all be a Chatty Cathy." He stared across to the window, working out if there was anything the other coppers might find. They'd said they wanted to look in the cottage, not anywhere else, so he was safe.

Wasn't he?

* * *

Carol and Dave stood in the cellar by a yellow wingback chair. Carol had changed her mind, she wouldn't be buying the one from IKEA now. If she did, every time she sat in it, she'd be reminded of this room, this case.

A faint smell lingered, bringing back memories of the odour in a house during the summer murder case, where a woman had cleaned her home constantly. Had Mason been getting rid of evidence down here?

Ahead was a gym of sorts, and to the side, stacks and stacks of boxes, each with labels on them. Three caught her eye: *Kitchen Equipment. Her Bedroom. Memorabilia.* An aisle went down the middle of them, and she led the way along it. At the end, a space. Copper piping on the wall with scuff marks on the metal. A tool bag in the corner. She approached it and crouched.

"No hammer," she said. "Doesn't everyone have one of those, especially if they have everything else? There's a screwdriver, a chisel, a box of nails and screws, a hacksaw."

Dave came and stood next to her. "It's likely to be the hammer in De León's head if Edward's telling the truth and he found the bloke here."

"True. But what everyone *doesn't* have in their tool bag is a set of cuffs."

"What?"

"There, look."

Carol stood so Dave could bend and see them better.

"Fucking hell," he said. "De León was cuffed down here?"

"We can assume, going by the scratches on those pipes. But Mason's right, there's no blood, but he could have washed it away." She inspected the boxes. She'd have to retract what she'd just said. "Scrap that. This stack of boxes is damp, like they've been wiped, and there are slight stains on them. Dark splashes."

Dave joined her. "Spatter, more like." He glanced at the ceiling. "What a prick. He missed a bit."

Carol looked up. "That's the thing with some people. They forget castoff spreads all over. We'll have to get SOCO here." She took her phone out and messaged Todd, asking for assistance at Kettlestone Rise.

At some point, she'd have to let the DCI know what was going on, although he'd made it clear he didn't want to hear from her until she'd brought someone in. She wasn't used to doing things that way with her former boss, but so long as she played by the book in all other aspects, she supposed she could deal with not running things by her senior officer. It wasn't like she didn't know what she was doing.

In the kitchen, Carol nosed around while Dave went upstairs. Nothing seemed wrong, although it had been cleaned recently, because that smell was in here, too. She waited for Dave by the back door, pondering, then a bike and a trailer on the patio snagged her attention. The trailer had two central wheels and a contraption on one end, similar to that on a caravan. The bike had a towing mechanism on the back, and her mind went to the muddy tracks. Not three bikes, just one and the trailer, although the tyres of both were clean. Silt marred the patio, though. From where Mason had scrubbed the mud away?

Dave entered, and she pointed to the garden.

He came over and peered outside. "Oh."

"Hmm." She took a pair of gloves out of her pocket and put them on, then turned the key for the back door. Outside, she waited for Dave so he could witness anything at the same time as her and peeled back the tarpaulin on the trailer.

"Okay . . ." Dave said. "I wasn't expecting *that*."

The naked body lay among lengths of rope, a plastic box with a lid, empty receptacles, a mallet and a rough-cut square of wood with drilled holes in the top corners, the word "bastard" on it in white spray paint. That completed the sentence: "Die, you bastard." Cable ties rested nearby. Old blood stained the base of the trailer either side of the corpse, fresh crimson seeping from wounds in the battered head — recently killed, then. The lips had pulled back in what Carol assumed was a grimace of pain, two front teeth missing. It was clear there was no life left, but Carol pressed her fingers to the side of neck anyway, a neck patched with strangulation marks.

"Deceased," she said.

"Thought so."

Petechiae spotted the skin around the eyes, blood vessels had popped in the whites, and the fists were clenched, as would be expected for someone who'd died fighting for air. Gouges in the wrists indicated the need to subdue, and Carol shuddered at the recall of those cuffs in the cellar. Had they been used, or was it something else?

She took her phone out and messaged Rib.

"I have no words, Dave," she said.

"I do. He found out what we were told."

"He must have."

Carol perused the rest of the body. Bruises on the stomach, thighs (especially the inners) and the tops of the arms. A bite mark on the chest. What a foolish thing to do. Did Mason not realise they could match that to his teeth? Or maybe he hadn't planned to ditch the body for the police to find this time. Perhaps this one was a secret, but it wouldn't have remained so for long. This person would have been missed, their absence noticed by many.

"What a waste of a life," she murmured.

"We'd best go inside."

Carol nodded, took her gloves off inside out, and put them in her pocket to hand over to SOCO when they arrived. She entered the kitchen, walking down the hallway and into the living room. Mason smiled at her as though nothing was wrong. She glanced at Pitson next to her, who immediately reached for his cuffs.

Dave came in and stood on her other side, forming a wall of authority.

"Mason Ingram, I am arresting you for the murder of Yolanda Rubin. You do not have to say anything. But it may harm your defence if you do not mention when questioned something which you later rely on in court. Anything you do say may be given in evidence. Do you understand?"

Mason didn't reply. Instead, he glared at her, hatred in his eyes, and she supposed that was done to scare her. She bit back a laugh. If only he knew how pitiful and pathetic he looked. He couldn't scare a fly.

* * *

Interview Room Three

The game was up. He'd been caught, and Mason couldn't believe it. He'd *really* lost everything now. The only thing he'd had left, his freedom, had been taken away the moment the plod had cuffed him. If only these two opposite hadn't gone snooping in the garden. If only he'd left Yolanda in her caravan to rot instead of taking her to the cottage.

It was always the way, wasn't it? Hindsight came knocking, pointing out your failures, laughing at you for them, bringing on such a blush you feel your cheeks might burn off.

It was the day after his arrest, and with a duty solicitor beside him, some bloke Mason didn't know called Kevin Dobbs, his rights had been read to him again, recorded for posterity on camera, the bloody thing pointing down at him from the corner behind the coppers. Plod stood by the door, hands clasped in front of him, but at least they'd given Mason a cup of tea. Steam rose from the Styrofoam cup, and he'd bet he'd been given that one so he couldn't smash it, slice them with a shard. Slash the plod's neck and escape. Where could he run to, though? He had no money, no boat, didn't even own a car. He'd get nowhere fast on Mam's bike.

He'd just admitted to Ortun, Skipper and Yolanda, it had been pointless claiming otherwise now they had forensic people scouring the cottage. But he wouldn't admit to De León, no fucking way.

"So you maintain Mr De León wasn't anything to do with you but that it was Edward Fields?" Wren confirmed.

"Yep. He did him in when he nicked my boat keys and money, had to have done."

"So is that the money your mother withdrew each day for a significant period of time before her death?"

Mason didn't like them knowing his shit. "Yeah."

"That's quite an amount."

"It was." He imagined Steady spending it and boiled inside. "He's got no right to it. That's my inheritance, my child support."

"From Mr De León. Yes, we're aware he was the one making the deposits."

"Have you been snooping at Mam's bank books and statements?"

"No, we were aware of the transactions before we searched your cottage."

Mason held back his temper. So they'd been poking into him before Steady had phoned them? Fuckers. Why? How had he slipped up enough for him to be on their radar? He'd spent all morning in the holding cell today before being brought here, thinking, churning it all over in his head, and he'd swear he'd covered all bases. Apart from Yolanda.

"What we want to know now is why your alleged father killed Nerys Bevan."

Mason blinked. "What?"

"Diaries were found in the storage boxes in your cellar. Your mam's."

Fucking hell, Mason hadn't gathered up enough courage to read those and had stuffed them in a box when he'd cleared away all her stuff. He hadn't wanted to read her rants about how shit he was, how she wished he'd never been born.

"Pardon?" He couldn't get over this. His dad, a killer?

"Your mam claimed he strangled Nerys. She witnessed it, which is why she turned to drink."

"I . . . I didn't know owt about that. This is the first time I'm hearing it."

"There was mention of Ortun killing someone called Dan Nixon. Your mam was there, too. She wrote that Ortun had frightened her for years, watching her in the pub, and that she feared for her life, that he'd kill her next, not to mention Eamon also saying he'd kill her if she ever told anyone what he'd done." She paused. "Not only to Nerys but on the night you were possibly conceived. She'd been raped. Twice. Is that why you killed Ortun and Eamon?"

"What? No!"

"What part did Skipper play in the past? There's nothing in her diaries about him."

"You've got it all wrong. I killed them for myself, not *her*." Smugness overtook him, and he blurted, "I killed her, too, and she bloody well deserved it."

Wren nodded, seemingly unfazed. "I had a feeling that's what happened. We looked into your mother's file. I have a theory. Everyone is linked by water. Nerys and Dan died in Scud Stream, your mother in the sea, Ortun and Skipper in the sea, too, and Yolanda . . . well, we just had confirmation from the pathologist that she was drowned in tap water. What does all of that mean?"

He shook his head, couldn't tell them about the baths, what Mam had done. It was still too raw. "No comment."

"Did you kill Yolanda because you were worried you'd have to share Mr De León's money and assets upon his death?"

She was getting right on his tits now. "What the fuck are you on about, woman?"

"Oh, didn't you know? Yolanda was Mr De León's daughter."

Cold sluiced Mason from head to foot, and he needed to punch this bitch who'd just told him a big fat lie. "What? No . . . That's not possible. I . . ." The room seemed to swirl around him, because they'd know, *they'd know* he'd raped his sister before he'd killed her. He was his father's son, all right. Eamon had raped Mam, something else Mason hadn't known. *Oh God. Oh fuck.*

He threw up between his legs, everyone else scooting their chairs back to get away from the splash. The voice in his head whispered that Ortun must have known and that was why he'd branded Mason a pervert. Like father, like son. Ortun hadn't been a hypocrite, he'd been disgusted that Mason had asked his own blood for a shag, touched her up. Had Yolanda known? Why hadn't she *said* they were related?

The solicitor grasped Mason's elbow and guided him to his feet. Plod must have left the room, because he returned with a bucket and mop full of steaming water, getting on with the business of cleaning up the liquid on the floor. Just tea. Mason hadn't had eaten today, refusing the breakfast then the sandwich they'd brought for him in the holding cell. Wren muttered something for the benefit of the tape, and the interview was called to a halt, something about getting a doctor to see to him and give them the go-ahead to continue later.

Mason stared at the mop strands moving back and forth, and it reminded him of Mam's white hair wavering in the sea. He'd killed her with water, the same way she'd tried to kill him so many times in his childhood, and he didn't regret that one bit. Other regrets, though, they crowded his mind, and he sank to the floor, leaning on the wall, and cried. Life had never gone well for him, and he'd been a fool to think he could change that. Like Mam had said, he'd been a fuck-up from the moment he'd been born, and today he wasn't any different.

* * *

The Incident Room

Three hours later, the second interview complete, Carol and Dave sat at Dave's desk, coffees in hand, their feet stretched out beneath. Michael and Katherine had gone home, the room filled with pregnant silence without them there. No clattering of keyboards, no exclamations of either annoyance at a lead slipping into nothing but mist or triumph at discovering a new clue.

Carol and Dave had done a lot of paperwork well into the evening, Carol suggesting they sort the majority of it now before they headed to the Lord for their dinner. Rib said he'd join them there about nine, and they'd congratulate themselves on a job well done and raise a glass or two to the deceased.

Carol waded through her thoughts. It was a shame she had no family members to inform about Nerys, everyone dead and gone, never knowing who'd killed her. The copies of diary excerpts Carol had read prior to speaking to Mason had explained everything, but what she couldn't stomach was the in-depth ramblings of a woman who'd hated her son. Mason had been an innocent product of the rape, he hadn't deserved to be brought up the way he had been, and he most certainly hadn't deserved being near-drowned in the bath. Fiona had written about it all, seemed to have no remorse, steeped in guilt for Nerys instead, and fear of either De León or Ortun coming to kill her.

I dread to think what else she wrote about. I only saw the highlights.

Her work mobile rang, and she glanced at the screen. "Ay up. It's Todd." She swiped to answer. "Got some more hideous shit to tell me?" She laughed.

"That can wait. We've found an envelope that must have scooted under the shoe rack in the hallway at Kettlestone Rise this morning. I wouldn't normally be bothered, would just bag all the post and send it in, but it's got a logo on the front. Thought you might need to know what's inside as I assume you may want to speak to Mason again."

"What is it?"

"A DNA company."

"Wow. Okay." She wasn't sure what to do. Ask Todd to open it or give Mason the privilege? She said as much to Todd.

"We'd normally inspect any mail ourselves in case it's evidence," he said. "I don't really want him touching the envelope, even with gloves on. You know I like to keep my chain of evidence as clear as possible."

"You look, then."

The rustle and rip of paper came down the line, then Todd spoke.

Carol digested what he'd said. "Right. Thanks." She slipped her phone away and told Dave the news. "So we'll go and see Mason now."

Dave sighed. "Why do our coffee breaks always get interrupted?"

"Because we're coppers, my friend, and our work is never done."

* * *

Holding Cell

Mason's long hair hung in his face, and Carol couldn't see his expression properly. She stood in front of him with Dave, Pitson hanging around by the door, and Mason finally brushed the strands away.

"An envelope was found at the cottage. It arrived this morning," she said. "I'm informing you that the DNA results came back, and Mr De León is *not* your father."

She didn't think she'd ever forget the sound of Mason's scream.

CHAPTER THIRTY-FIVE

Scudderton Cove

Butterfly stood at the edge of the remote part of the cliff in a spot where no caravans or houses were around. There was no need for anyone to see what was going on and rush out to stop it. News had come about Fiona's rape via a message on the phone from the same person who'd said Mason Ingram was the killer. Butterfly hadn't responded, they'd been on their way here after getting all of their affairs in order for the past few hours.

Butterfly had visited old haunts, reminisced, but had avoided family members and friends, unable to stand seeing them for a final time. The red-rimmed eyes would have given it away that Butterfly was upset, and questions would have come, ones they were unwilling to answer.

The night sky held the menace of more bad weather, although a second storm hadn't been predicted, just rain. Maybe that would wash away the sins when Butterfly's body landed on the outcropping of rock halfway down. They'd picked that as the terminus to their final journey because a path led from it to the beach. Easy access for their removal. No winches from helicopters needed. The thought of costing the taxpayer money poked a hole in the psyche, and they'd thought of swallowing pills with alcohol and ending it that way, but something like that may not have been a success.

Butterfly had used their smartphone, given to them by the grandchildren — they'd clubbed together to get it one Christmas — and Googled the height of the cliff and the distance to the outcrop, then searched for whether the speed of the fall and the subsequent smack into the rock would result in death.

It'll be on my search history.

That was good. It meant Carol Wren would know it wasn't another murder inquiry.

Butterfly lifted one foot, ready for the drop. They stepped into the air, their body pitching forward, their other foot leaving the safety of the ground. And they sailed downwards, fear of pain taking hold once they hit the outcrop, fear that this wouldn't work, but most of all, fear of their secret being exposed. The rock came up in greeting, a white shape in the gloom, and one last thought came before the impact.

Will Mason ever find out I fathered him?

CHAPTER THIRTY-SIX

Scudderton Cove

Such a grim thing to do, viewing the body of someone you knew, knowing you'd have to visit the next of kin, someone you also knew. Carol stood beside her loyal partner on a shelf of rock the day after she'd informed Mason about the DNA results. The early morning air held a wicked chill and the remnants of the rain that had come down overnight.

"Got to be murder," Dave said. "There's no way this one would be a jumper."

"Well, it can't be Mason's doing," Carol said, "so we've got another killer on our bloody hands. I'm not amused."

"No, not with who we're going to have to tell."

"I know."

The expanse of rock was large, somewhere people came to eat picnics or watch the dolphins, sunbathe, maybe have a little sit and think with nothing but the sea and gulls for company, so there was enough room for the usual officers to get on with their work. Photos had already been taken.

Rib gazed down at the deceased, shaking his head. "Nice guy. I can't believe it."

"I doubt anyone will." Carol sighed. "No idea who'd want to kill him."

"I'll know for sure from any marks on the back where they could have been pushed. I have to say, it looks like a classic jumper to me at the moment, given what I found on his phone." He explained why it hadn't broken in the fall and what he'd discovered. "So unless a killer did a Google search to make it look like the deceased had done it . . . I'm leaning towards him taking his own life. What on earth would he want to kill himself for?"

"Terminal illness?" Dave suggested.

Carol nodded. "Could be. Maybe he'd kept the diagnosis to himself. Whatever the reason, it's a bloody shame." She turned to Dave. "Come on. Let's go and get this over and done with."

"Are we going straight to the NOK and not . . . ?"

"We are, yes, but I've asked you know who to be there as well. We owe him that."

"Yeah, I agree. Fuck. This is going to be a tough one."

You're telling me.

* * *

45 Windmill Lane

Glenda, the eldest child of the deceased, sat with her son on the sofa. She looked afraid of what they'd come to say, but her son appeared all-knowing, as if he could read their faces and minds. Carol thought it best to just get on with it, put them out of their misery.

She addressed Glenda. "I'm sorry to have to inform you that your father's body was discovered this morning."

"What?" Glenda glanced at her lad. "What?"

He paled and shook his head, letting her know he hadn't been aware of this. Tears streamed down Glenda's wrinkled cheeks, and Carol shifted her sights to the son, asking for silent permission on whether she could continue, whether Glenda could handle the facts or if things needed to be sugar-coated for now.

He nodded.

Carol took a deep breath then dived in. "He was found on an outcropping of rock by a jogger who'd stopped there to rest. From initial evidence at the scene, it appears he'd been there since last night."

"Fuck," the lad said and held his mother close as she wailed. "Foul play?"

"The pathologist thinks not but will know more when he performs the post-mortem."

He nodded again, then gave Glenda a quick glance. "We don't need to be told what state he was found in."

"No." It hadn't been pretty. Lots of blood and limbs at odd angles. She imagined what else she'd seen and winced. *The pain. Christ.*

"I wondered why he didn't answer my phone call in the evening," Glenda said. "I thought he'd gone to bed."

"He had his phone with him," Carol said. "He'd wrapped it in a tea towel so it wouldn't get broken, then put it in a carrier bag in his coat pocket. Messages were checked in case it was a suspicious death, and two were found that he hadn't responded to." She pointed her gaze at the son.

He blushed. "I sent them."

"I know," Carol said. "And I understand why, so there won't be any recriminations."

"Thank you."

"What we also found was a recent search which came up on the last Chrome page he'd looked at." She stared at Glenda's boy, letting him know with her eyes that it may not necessarily have been the deceased who'd opened that browser.

He appeared to understand.

Carol continued. "He'd searched height of the cliff and the distance of the fall."

Glenda moaned, her grief taking over, and she buried her face in her hands. "Why would he do that?" Her words came out muffled against her palms. "I don't understand. It doesn't make *sense.*"

"Was he ill, perhaps?" Dave asked.

Glenda raised her head, her eyes red. "Not that I know of."

"We'll find out for you," Dave said gently. "We'll do all we can to work out what happened."

Carol swallowed and gave the son a sad smile. "It would be better if you remain here with your mother for a few days, don't you think?"

"Yes." He cleared his throat. "I . . . I'll take the rest of the week off work."

"Whatever you need."

They talked for a while longer, then Carol had the urge to get out, to suck in some fresh air. The house was stifling.

At the front door, Glenda remaining in the living room, Carol placed her hand on the son's shoulder. Tears pricked her eyes. "I'm so sorry, Michael."

Her beloved detective constable blinked back tears. "The butterfly finally flew away."

Carol frowned. "What does that mean?"

Michael smiled. A sad one. "He'd been called that since he was a kid. The story goes, when he was about seven, his class were studying butterflies. They came to the monarch, and someone said that was another name for king. Well, with grandad's surname and everything, butterfly stuck."

She smiled sadly, too. "That's a nice memory."

Better than the one I have of him, a sharp spike of rock going through his temple and coming out the other side.

CHAPTER THIRTY-SEVEN

The Cliffs

Three months later, Carol stood alone on the cliff one lunch break where William King had come before his death. She'd needed half an hour to herself to prepare for the task that lay ahead of her. This case had an unexpected strand, a letter found in an envelope after officers had spent weeks going through Ortun's things, all those boxes in the spare room, more in the loft. Carol hoped this was the end of it at last, the final piece of the puzzle, then she could move on.

Winter's frosty feet had stomped all over the grass, dusting it with white speckles, each blade rigid with the chill. She hunched into her thick padded coat, hands in pockets, and took a moment to breathe now all the paperwork had finally been completed, a big red bow on top of a job well done. Seagulls swooped, riding the icy air current, squawking at her as though she had no right to be there. It reminded her of when she'd watched them with Gary Cuttersby in the summer, the husband of a murdered woman, and she smiled, recalling what was said about the birds.

Fucking things. Size of cats, some of them.

She pondered whether the big bastards or the smaller ones had been the culprits that had pecked at William's eyes, leaving a mushy mess in the sockets, the piercings of their beaks creating holes on his cheeks and chin. The family had been spared as much horrific information as possible, but of course, Michael being Michael, he'd come back to work the Monday after and looked at the file.

Some things you should never be privy to, but he'd thought he knew best, then it had played on his mind, the images, and he'd ended up taking the rest of the month off, especially after a search through his grandad's phone had revealed a list in a note app. There had also been an explanation of what all the names and dates meant, and it seemed William King had been raping women for years. He believed Mason Ingram was his son. Michael had been understandably crushed, needing time to get over it, if he ever would. A small team of two officers were looking into all the rapes and visiting the victims.

Michael was back at work now, forever changed, a different person to who he'd been before. She missed the old Michael, but maybe one day she'd see glimmers of him coming back.

She mulled over the last few findings that had come through from forensics. The mud on Skipper's jeans and boot soles had matched that of the woodland, and microscopic evidence of it found on Mason's bike and trailer wheels had also been confirmed. The blood in the trailer and on the mallet belonged to Ortun, Skipper and Yolanda — no traces of De León present there, although it had been found in the cellar at Kettlestone Rise. More blood had been discovered in the fibres of a poncho, even though it had been washed.

A digi sweep on Eamon's phone had revealed a message from a pay-as-you-go on the night Mason had abducted him. Mason had admitted he'd sent it. Rib had discovered bruising and a break on Eamon's arm during the post-mortem, and Mason had said he'd hit him there with the mallet. He hadn't been able to explain why an empty whiskey bottle had been found in a satchel in one of the packing boxes, though. It had been traced back to the sixties, so she'd believed he'd told her the truth there.

With him still claiming he hadn't killed De León, but admitting he would have done when the DNA results came back negative, just so De León couldn't tell anyone he'd been kidnapped and incarcerated, the hunt for Edward Fields had been more vigorous. The *Jar* had been found abandoned in Felixstowe, and from there, he'd vanished without a trace.

Carol would find him one day. She'd never give up.

It was time to go. To face the final hurdle.

She turned from the black-looking sea and headed towards the car. Dave sat inside, waiting patiently, and she smiled at him through the windscreen. He'd had a breakthrough regarding his feelings for his recalcitrant wife, knowing he didn't need her anymore, although he still got naffed off when mention of affairs came into the conversation. Now he could start again properly, like Carol planned to.

She slipped into her seat and popped her safety belt on. "Do you reckon you could stand living with me?" She turned to look at him.

"Eh?"

"You heard."

"Probably. We spend all our time together anyroad. Let's face it, I only really sleep in my flat and have a shower. I'm either at work, in the Lord with you or in your flat watching telly."

"So that's a yes, then, is it?"

"Well, yeah, but I don't understand what you're getting at."

"My dad's money. I thought of using some to buy a static caravan and—"

"I'm not living in a fucking van, Carol."

She laughed at his indignation. "You didn't let me finish. I'd rent the van out, maybe stay in it myself sometimes to give you space, you know, in case you get a lady friend, but I want to buy one of those new cottages being built in the village."

"How? De León's bloody dead."

"I realise that. Another firm took on the project. They'll be finished at the end of the spring. I thought we could be roomies. I can put a fair bit down as a deposit, so I'd only have a little mortgage. Your part can be paying the leccy and gas bills, half of the community charge and the water."

He stared out of the windscreen. "I don't see why not."

"I need to get out of my flat. With George getting broken into . . . I want out."

"We'll go over it properly later. We've got someone to see, don't forget."

"Nope, I hadn't forgotten. I was just putting it off, that's all." She started the engine and drove towards Scudderton, lost inside her head, pleased Dave hadn't dismissed her idea of them shacking up together as friends.

Now she'd made the decision to move on, she couldn't wait to get started.

* * *

19 Hiddleston Croft

Carol pulled up at the kerb and paused for a moment. "Do you think she'll be relieved to know what happened?" She jerked her head at the front door.

"It'll solve the riddle, so yes."

They got out of the car and approached the front door. It opened before Carol had a chance to knock, and Chippy June stood in the frame, arms folded, fluffy grey slippers and a pink fleece lounge suit her attire of the day.

"Come on in," she said. "Quickly, the cold's getting in."

They followed her into a warm living room, a real fire raging in the grate behind an ornate brass guard. Old Clem sat in one of the chairs beside the hearth, whiskers aplenty, a pipe in his mouth, smoke puffing upwards. He had slippers on, too, and seemed right at home.

"You don't mind that I asked Clem to sit in on this, do you?" June perched on the edge of the other chair.

"Of course not."

"Sit your bums down, then." June smiled and reached for the cosy-covered teapot on the coffee table. "It won't be stewed. I'd not long made it before you arrived." She poured, handing cups over. "Help yourself to milk and sugar. I'll sort yours, Clem."

Carol and Dave did as they were told then sat on the sofa.

"What's this about, then?" June passed Clem his brew.

The old man grunted and took it.

"It's about your husband," Carol said.

"What the bloody hell are you here about him for?"

"We've found a letter in among Ortun Bevan's possessions. It was addressed to the police in a sealed envelope. The date at the top of the letter corresponds with the time your husband died."

"Right . . ."

"I'm so sorry to have to tell you this, but Ortun killed him."

June gaped, her hand shaking as she placed her cup on the table. "What? Why?"

"He'd been looking for whoever killed his sister."

"Nerys, yes."

"And he'd convinced himself your husband did it. He confessed to killing him the night of the stocktake you told us about. They had an argument on the deck behind your chip shop, which broke out into a fight. Ortun had punched him unconscious, then panicked and threw him over the railing into the sea."

June paled. "That's awful."

"It is. Clearly, he didn't post the letter for whatever reason known only to him. It had a stamp on it, so he'd obviously intended to send it then changed his mind."

June's eyes watered. "I watched the news a while back. De León killed Nerys. How come Ortun never suspected him?"

Clem leaned forward. "Because De León went to bloody Spain, June." He speared Carol with his gaze. "This has got me thinking. If Ortun was going round killing people he suspected, you might want to look into Fred Collerton's brother an' all."

Carol's stomach rolled over. She'd thought this was the final puzzle piece, but it seemed she might be wrong. "Why?"

"He was found dead on Fred's boat. Years ago it was. Fred had gone to Whitby for a wedding, and when he came back, he found Hamish. Your lot never did find out who'd done it."

Fuck it. "Thank you for that information. I'll pass it on to the cold case team." She shifted her gaze. "Are you okay, June?"

The woman nodded. "I am, as it happens. Closure at last. He might have been a bastard, but it's good to know he wasn't killed by some tart's husband."

"I suppose it is." Carol smiled.

* * *

Four Months Later

Carol stood in her new cottage surrounded by boxes. Some contained her belongings from her old place, but others had flat-pack furniture inside. With more room here, she'd splashed out on some new things, and tonight, she and Dave had the onerous task of putting it all together with the help of a takeaway and a couple of bottles of red wine.

She left him opening the box for a TV unit and wandered into the garden. The beautiful Sunday afternoon weather cheered her no end, as did the rattan furniture and the spring flowers bobbing in the breeze. She'd planted them in barrels yesterday while Dave had hung pictures, a way to see barrels as something other than the torture device of her childhood. She had to get past these hang-ups and stop comparing then to now. Her recovery was going well, and while she didn't think she'd ever be completely over her past, she was on the road to better days.

Using her father's money had been easier than she'd thought. She also owned a static caravan and had asked the holiday park manager to deal with bookings. She'd told herself it was just a load of numbers that had enabled her to purchase her own home, her second income with the caravan, and that the man himself had nothing to do with it.

She cast her gaze to the blue sky and smiled, imagining him looking down at her, his dark eyes full of thunder. "Cheers, you fucking bastard." She gave him a wave. "This little rat will be happy here."

She imagined him turning in his grave and laughed until she cried.

Life was on the up.

THE END

THE JOFFE BOOKS STORY

We began in 2014 when Jasper agreed to publish his mum's much-rejected romance novel and it became a bestseller.

Since then we've grown into the largest independent publisher in the UK. We're extremely proud to publish some of the very best writers in the world, including Joy Ellis, Faith Martin, Caro Ramsay, Helen Forrester, Simon Brett and Robert Goddard. Everyone at Joffe Books loves reading and we never forget that it all begins with the magic of an author telling a story.

We are proud to publish talented first-time authors, as well as established writers whose books we love introducing to a new generation of readers.

We have been shortlisted for Independent Publisher of the Year at the British Book Awards three times, in 2020, 2021 and 2022, and for the Diversity and Inclusivity Award at the Independent Publishing Awards in 2022.

We built this company with your help, and we love to hear from you, so please email us about absolutely anything bookish at: feedback@joffebooks.com.

If you want to receive free books every Friday and hear about all our new releases, join our mailing list: www.joffebooks.com/contact

And when you tell your friends about us, just remember: it's pronounced Joffe as in coffee or toffee!

ALSO BY EMMY ELLIS

DETECTIVE CAROL WREN MYSTERIES
Book 1: SPITE YOUR FACE
Book 2: HOLD YOUR BREATH

Printed in Great Britain
by Amazon

46157032R10158